SLO-MO!

By Slo-Mo Finsternick

(as told to Rick Reilly)

DOUBLEDAY   New York London Toronto Sydney Auckland

SLO-MO!

My Untrue Story

PUBLISHED BY DOUBLEDAY
a division of Random House, Inc.
1540 Broadway, New York, New York 10036

DOUBLEDAY and the portrayal of an anchor with a
dolphin are trademarks of Doubleday, a division of
Random House, Inc.

Book design by Dana Leigh Treglia

Library of Congress Cataloging-in-Publication Data
Reilly, Rick.
    Slo-mo!: my untrue story / by Slo-mo Finsternick,
as told to Rick Reilly.
        p. cm.
    I. Title.
    PS3568.E4847 S59 1999
    813'.54—dc21   99-33240
                                                       CIP

10   9   8   7   6   5   4   3   2   1

Author's Note

This book is a work of fiction. References to real people and organizations are used solely to lend the fiction a sense of authenticity and irony. All other characters and all actions, events, motivations, thoughts, and conversations portrayed in this story are entirely the product of the author's imagination. Any resemblance to actual persons or events is entirely coincidental.

SLO-MO!

Coauthor's Note

When I first inked the pact to cowrite Slo-Mo Finsternick's life story, I had no idea that this odd, naive, and, frankly, rather dense teenager would fascinate the nation like no athlete since Michael Jordan. If I had, I would've negotiated more points on the back end.

I think you'll agree, Slo-Mo has handled his end of the assignment with courage, grace, and humor, sometimes even intended. From his roots in a bizarre cave cult to his blossoming as a hero in the NBA, from the death of his mother to the search for his father, from his hoops career that began at a small Catholic high school and ended with America glued to its Sylvanias, this is one wild ride, so hop aboard!

Slo-Mo is a remarkable young man. Someday, I even hope to meet him.

—Rick Reilly, June 1999

JAN. 2, ORLANDO

Dear Kind Reader,

Well, I can't believe I'm writing a book and this is because I've hardly ever even *read* a book much less wrote one before, on account of evil surface trappings like books, TVs, and automobiles weren't allowed in the Spelunkarium where I grew up.

As you probably know, my name is Maurice Finsternick, although the people at the Spelunkarium always called me "Mo" but the sportswriter gentlemen have given me a nickname which is "Slo-Mo" because they say I have the same speed and agility of the Istanbul Hilton.

But it doesn't matter anyway because I'm also tall as a hotel! I'm 7 feet 8 inches tall, and 195 pounds, which is pretty skinny I admit and, in fact, Mr. Charles Barkley, one of my teammates on the team, asked me today if I'll travel with the team or will they just fax me everywhere!

I've been big ever since I was little, but I guess it's a good thing because starting tomorrow I join the long line and great tradition of professional basketball's most wonderful franchise, the New Jerseys! It's real great because, like I told the sportswriter gentlemen this morning, even though our record is only 16–13, I really think we have the chemicals on this team to really go somewhere, a comment that they all seemed to like a lot on account of they wrote it down very fast.

But at the same time I'm very scared and lonely because I really don't have any family and I don't know anybody on the team and they're not going to let me keep taking trains like I did to here to Orlando and I'm a little nervous to fly and I miss the Spelunkarium and miss my high school teammates who I got to know for only one season before my agent accidentally turned me pro, which I never really wanted to do at all but I guess that's another story.

Still, my new teammates on the New Jerseys have been real nice to me. Tonight, for instance, after we were narrowly defeated by the Orlandos, 111–79, Mr. Barkley took me into the hotel bar so that we could talk about the exciting life in the NBA. It's the first bar I've ever been in because I'm only seventeen and because I've hardly been out of the compound most of my life.

Unfortunately, women kept interrupting us and rubbing his bald head and giggling, although Mr. Barkley didn't seem mad at these interruptions and, actually, seemed to kinda like it. I kept asking him questions, but finally he said, right into my ear, "Yo, chill, man, get yourself a freak!" And I said, "No, thanks, I don't drink." And just then Mr. Barkley must have got something caught in his throat because he spit out his beverage.

JAN. 4, NEWARK

Well, I'm just back from my first airplane ride of my life which I liked a lot, except for the well-known policy on all NBA teams that all supplemental rookies, which I'm one of which, have to serve the drinks and the meals onboard and also clean up but that's the rich tradition of the NBA for you. Anyway, I'm all settled in for the season here at my very nice hotel, the Newark Airport Ramada Hotel, which I'm very excited about, as I think it is much better than moving into one of those pandemoniums the other guys live in.

I got a collect call tonight from my best little buddy, Microchip, although his real name is Mustafa Unity Smith, and when I say Microchip is little, I don't mean little compared to me, I mean little compared to a collectible action figure. Microchip stands only 5-4 but he is "faster than rent money" as he always says, kidding.

Microchip played basketball with me at Most Virgin Lady High School in Boulder, Colorado. And I could not have made it to the New Jerseys without him and, really, I wouldn't have made it and didn't really want to come at all but I had no choice and Microchip said he'd call me every night since he didn't have much to do anyway since he got cut the day I turned pro and he'd always wanted to play on the playgrounds of New

York. "You just practicin' till you play Hell's Kitchen, Stumpy," which is what he always calls me, kidding, of course.

Microchip doesn't talk like a professor at all, even though both of his parents are professors at the University of Denver, and both of them do not like one bit his playing basketball, which is fine since they don't even know he plays basketball. He told his parents that Most Virgin Lady High School didn't even have a basketball team, much less that it had won four Class 5A titles in the last seven years, and that its specialty was Black Studies and he told them he was living with a man who studied under the great black leader Dick Gregory and taking evening Black Studies classes through the exchange program at the Naropa Institute but really he was only playing basketball every second and sleeping on an old mattress in the basement of our assistant basketball coach, Scooter Chambers.

And it was funny that we became such good pals because he was the shortest player on the team, Microchip was, and I was the tallest and also because his skin was the blackest and mine was the whitest and he'd done so much in his life and I'd done so little. And I'm glad to have at least one true friend in the world.

Actually, I may have two friends now because today I met Mr. Harley Pearce from the local newspaper although everybody calls him Harley the Stain because his shirt usually has something on it from lunch that day or perhaps the day before, and usually there's also some of it in his teeth, just to the right of the Tootsie Pop stick he's always chewing on.

Mr. Stain was here in my room this morning before

practice, ordering us up a lot of room service and drinks and asking me a lot of questions, which was nice of him, and he asked me if I minded being so tall and large at 7-8. And I replied that people ask me that a lot and also say funny things to me like, "How's the weather up there, stretch?" and "What time you due back at the lab?" which are very funny except maybe I have heard them a few hundred too many times. I really don't mind, as I say that it is truly stupendous that I turned out to be 7 foot 8 inches tall when you have considered that my mother, Phyllis, was only 5-4 and 102 pounds when she was living with me at the Spelunkarium, which was until she died in the cave-in at the King Soopers grocery store.

I guess I should have told Mr. Stain that my dad is very tall, too, except that I don't know his real name. Although I do know that his fake name was Genghis Korn, the 7-foot-tall giant who drives to supermarkets all over America and promotes Krispy Korn imitation-corn frozen food products. Of course, Phyllis told me that "Genghis Korn" is not really even his real name though she didn't know what his real name was.

Unfortunately, after their one night together, he went on to another city to display his imitation-corn frozen food products and Phyllis never got an address or anything for him and, besides, I guess they couldn't really have been together because how would he have liked spelunking, which is, of course, cave exploring, as much as she liked it, being as tall as he is. When you are as tall as he and me are, you can't really spe-lunk very well on account of you're constantly knock-ing down million-year-old stalactites and stalagmites. Which is really sad because you don't get close to the true God, which is what we believe at the Inner Door Spelunkarium where I lived, but what can you do? Life is no better roses.

JAN. 5, NEWARK

Tonight will be my first game with the New Jerseys! I'm a little nervous and everything is so new. Like, I have a secret admirer, I think, because this secret admirer has been doing nice little things for me like leaving little mints on my pillow and newspapers outside my hotel room and I looked through it and there was my picture talking about how I was selected by the New Jerseys in the special midseason supplemental draft, but what I don't get is how they got my picture because I've never in my life been in New Jersey before.

I wanted to look my best because I knew some of the fellas from the TV stations would be there so I wore my best (well, only) suit. And I hate to be a braggart but I must have looked pretty good because everybody stared like crazy when I walked in. And then Mr. Barkley said that Wal-Mart called and said they wanted their suit back but I went to the phone and there wasn't anybody there so I think maybe he was kidding me the way pro athletes are so well known to do.

It did not go all the way good, though. I was late to the morning shootaround but I still don't think it was my fault. Coach Phil Jackson said the shootaround would be ten to eleven. So I showed up and he was mad at me and asked where I'd been.

And I said, "Well, I'm sorry, but I thought you said

the practice was ten to eleven and that's what time it is now."

And he looked at his watch and that's what time it was, ten to eleven, and I guess he felt bad for yelling at me when it was actually him who messed up and so he started laughing and didn't stop for five minutes.

Afterward, Mr. Barkley said it is tradition that any first-round pick of the year has to buy McDonald's for everybody on the team after his first shootaround and I said that there were sure a lot of historic traditions in the NBA. But they began saying things which made no sense, like "Big Mac" and "Double McCheese" and "Supersize my ass" and I had to tell them these things made no sense to me, were they people at this McDonald's or what exactly. And Mr. Death Dedman, who is one of our power forwards, said, "Well, what the (word for intimate sexual relations) do *you* order at Mickey D's?"

And I said, "I'm sorry?"

And he said, very slowly and clearly, "What (pause) the (pause) (intimate sexual relations) (pause) do (pause) you (pause) order (pause) at (pause) Mc (pause) Don (pause) ald's (pause)?"

And I said I had never been to McDonald's in my life and I think that is the quietest I have heard a room since Meditation Month at the Spelunkarium.

I'm writing this part now after the game from my room here at the Newark Airport Ramada Hotel and I think some of the players and administration officers are a little confused why I don't play near the basket at 7 feet 8 inches tall. In fact, in the first quarter, I heard our owner, Mr. Trump, say that he did not pay $4.5 million over three years for a 7-foot-8-inch point guard that cannot dribble a water glass. But, see, I don't like to play under the basket because I only like to shoot the standing hook the way my basketball hero, the fearful NBA scorer Bob "Bobby Hoops" Houbregs, did in the 1940s. Only I can shoot the hook with either hand because I'm amphibious, and also I like to hook my shot from way, way outside, especially from the top of the key about three feet outside the 3-point circle. And I think when I took my first Bobby Hoops hook shot and swished it through to the delight of our home crowd, they were not so worried. Because, as I say, I don't wanna brag, but that *is* my shot.

I guess everybody thought it was kinda of a fluke, even though that's all I shot in high school, because I never got the ball again to shoot it but I'm sure I'll get it plenty very soon or why would they have drafted me?

Anyway, I'm afraid we were narrowly defeated again, 101–82, and I only played seven minutes, but it was still quite a thrill.

JAN. 6, CLEVELAND

Well, we flew to Cleveland tonight and I tried again to talk to our shooting forward, Mr. Justin Dominic from Arizona State, and he is a nice person although Mr. Barkley says he is a person who thinks all the time about sex. Everybody calls him "Woody" but I'm not sure how they get "Woody" out of "Justin."

I have so many questions about this amazing new electronic world I'm suddenly living in and these airplane rides and all these hotel rooms and how am I going to pay for them but Mr. Woody couldn't help me because he was very busy with a young woman named Miss Silver. I think she was an actress, because she kept asking me would I like to engage in a "three-way scene" sometime, and I said no, because how stupid would I look, not knowing any of my lines?

And so I said goodbye and went up to my room, which is where I am now, only I think they ended going into Mr. Woody's room because I can hear them in there, engaging in that scene Ms. Silver talked about because I keep hearing Mr. Woody saying, "Who's the king?" And Ms. Silver keeps going, "You, baby!"

I had no idea NBA players would like Shakespeare so much.

Tonight is my first night with my road roommate and teammate, Mr. Mockmood Rahim-Abdur, our starting point guard and a very serious believer in Muslim, and I mean serious. He doesn't allow us to have on the television or the radio and five times a day he must set down his little cloth and face toward Mecca and pray.

And he doesn't say much besides the praying because I think he's listening for people outside in the hall because he seems very nervous about them coming in to get us. For this reason, I guess, he has a complicated alarm system for when we're in the room, in which he hangs a whole lot of hangers from the chain that locks our doors and stacks about fifteen empty hummus cans in front of the door in case anybody opens it.

"America is a nation of killers, thieves, and pagans," he says. "It was foretold by Mohammed, peace be on him."

It's for that reason that Mr. Mockmood doesn't like me to come and go from the room very much, but that's okay because it gives me more time to stare at the picture of my dad, Genghis Korn, that I bring everywhere with me. Phyllis told me it's the picture he hands out to kids at his promotional stops at grocery stores. It's of him standing up next to his special Kornmobile (which was really only an old 1966 Corvair painted bright yellow in the Krispy Korn label), with the front seat pulled out and the steering wheel with the top half cut off and the whole thing extended so that he could drive it from the backseat.

Sometimes it hurts for me to look at the picture because I want to know him so bad because he looks just like me and is very, very tall like me and he seems to have such a nice smile. But then, just when I wished Phyllis had never shown me that picture, I think that then I wouldn't know what he looks like at all, I decide that I'm glad that she did.

JAN. 7, CLEVELAND

Tonight before the game I had my first conversation with Mr. Big County, our center, and it was very unusual. He and I had lockers next to each other and we were getting ready for the game and I hadn't got up the nerve to say hello to him yet and he turned to me and said, just casually, "Do you mind igwaddes tonight?"

And I didn't quite hear him so I said, "I'm sorry?"

And he said, "What'd you decide on that gwallesore?"

And maybe it was his Texas accent or maybe my hearing isn't very good but again, I said, "I'm sorry. What did you say?"

And he got a little perturbed and he said, "You know! That dee ana fore. Don't you think?"

And he was just looking at me in such a way that I knew I couldn't say "What?" and so I said, "Yes, I guess."

And he said, "Why?"

And I knew that whatever I said yes to had completely made it worse and I was now in a kind of word trap and I was so confused I didn't know what to do and he was looking at me like my answer meant somebody's life or death and then all of a sudden he broke out laughing and so did everybody in the whole locker room and, in fact, they were laughing so hard they were laying on the carpet and beating on their lockers, as it turns out they were listening to the whole thing.

And when they finally stopped laughing I said, "What?" because I had no idea in the world what was going on.

And Mr. Barkley said, through his tears, "You just got double-talked by the only fluent double-talker in the league."

And it turns out it's just a little trick Mr. Big County plays on new players or fans or the sportswriter gentlemen sometimes and I have to say it is a very good trick because the words sound exactly like words and come off in the sentence like they belong there but, in fact, they are not at all words and are only the cause for much hilarity and hijinks among the players.

And Mr. Big County said to me, "You gotta admit, it's just a prubanny when you think about it."

And I said, "I'm sorry?"

And this caused much more beating on lockers.

We were defeated again tonight by the hard-fought Clevelands, 128–90, although I only played four minutes and didn't shoot once. And afterward, Mr. Ahmad Rashad, our colored analyst, stood me up after the game and said, "A hard-fought game tonight, Maurice."

And I nodded in agreement because I was taught never to interrupt someone when they're talking but he held the microphone in front of me as if I should say something, so I leaned down and said, "I agree, Mr. Rashad."

And he said, "This Cleveland team is going to give the East big-time problems down the stretch."

And I said nothing but he put the microphone up to me again as though he'd asked me a question. So I said, "I'm sorry, Mr. Rashad. I don't understand what you mean. The Clevelands are having problems stretching?"

And he said, "What I'm getting at, Maurice, is, this is some impressive Cleveland team."

And he looked at me in such a way that I understood that he felt this was a question which I should answer, so I answered it the best I could, which is to say, "Yes, Mr. Rashad, you just have to take your hat off to them and hand it to them."

Mr. Rashad was not all that friendly after the interview so maybe he hasn't done many of these.

———

I have to tell you about one of the fellows on my team although this is a little embarrassing but my ghostwriter for this book told me on the phone that I should tell you about him, so here goes.

I'm told that Mr. Woody thinks about his general talia all the time and is fond of having sex in very odd places, like coffins, which he says, "Why not? It's all velvet and (s-word)!" and church.

"That's sacrilegious," said Mr. Reggie Black, our very Christian-oriented backup shooting guard. "You'll burn in hell!"

"It's not sacrilegious," he says. "Didn't Jesus say, 'Come in my house'?"

"Damn!" said Mr. Black.

In fact, today on the luxurious bus that takes us to and from the big, beautiful NBA arenas absolutely free of charge, Mr. Woody was explaining to Mr. Barkley about his goal in life which he has pursued his whole life, he says, and that is to "think off."

And Mr. Barkley asked him what this was, to "think off," and he said to "think off" was to achieve orgasm without anybody or anything touching your personal member, which is just so embarrassing that I am only glad Phyllis is not alive to hear me talk like this.

Anyway, Mr. Barkley seemed real interested in this, and I have to admit I was, too, and Mr. Barkley asked him to tell us more.

"Well," said Mr. Woody, "I don't even know if it can be done," but he said the idea is that sex is so much in your mind anyway that he thinks why not try to go all the way in your mind and you-know-what just by thinking your way to it.

I'm ashamed to tell you that although I'm a virgin and would never desecrate a woman's body unless it were as her Life Partner, I have pleasured my "little stalagmite," as Phyllis called it, twice now and know I will suffer many years high from the earth's warm center for it. But I was real interested in what Mr. Woody said because I'm thinking maybe if nobody touched your personal muscle including yourself that there wouldn't really be anything wrong with that and, in fact, might not even be a sin.

"Are you allowed to wiggle?" asked Mr. Barkley.

"No, man!" said Mr. Woody. "It's gotta be totally with your mind! You can't move or gyrate around or touch it anyway, anyhow!"

"Couldn't you at least have some ho blow on it from a few inches away?"

"No!" said Mr. Woody. "No, it has to be entirely in your mind! Don't you have any *ethics?*"

And Mr. Barkley thought for a while and then said it was impossible and could never be done but Mr. Woody said it will be done by him someday and he even said he came close once.

"In college. Remedial reading. I got this beautiful teacher's assistant facing me and she had these huge Bettys and this beautiful blond hair and you could see right through her shirt and I was just buggin', right? So I just closed my eyes and started thinking like a mother(f-word)er. But I had on Tommy Hilfigers, man, and they were way too tight. No way man is ever gonna think off in Tommys."

"A rule to live by," said Mr. Barkley, and so that's why I'm passing it on to you.

We have a very nice guy on our team although he has a little problem and his name is Mr. Flip Lowery, who is a shooting guard with a very blond stand-up haircut even though his eyebrows are dark who would like it very much if he never played again this year. Mr. Lowery says it's on account of something in his contract about incentives that would pay him $1 million at the end of the year if he shoots 45 percent or better from the floor. And it really is a whole bunch of money and he is above 45 percent right now, but not by much and, as he says, "Dude, I'm shooting out of my mind! I can't keep this up!" Mr. Barkley says he only makes the minimum salary and I happen to know that's only $5.50 an hour, so it really would be quite a big jump for him.

He's sure if he plays anymore his percentage will go down and he wouldn't get the very large snaps, as he says. And so he is always asking about ways he could possibly get injured and not have to actually be hurt too much.

"Femur," Mr. Lowery said today on the bus. "You think a broken femur would be painful?"

"Hell, no," said Mr. Woody. "What fool put a stupid idea like that in your head?"

"What the hell's a femur?" asked our center, Mr. Bryant "Big County" Reeves.

"Legbone. Upper legbone," said Mr. Lowery.

"Depend on how you broke it," said Mr. Barkley.

"I'm thinking maybe if I dropped my fridge at home on it."

"Yeah, well, what if it doesn't break it?" said Mr. Barkley. "Or what if it messes up your leg so bad they have to cut it off?"

"And what if it broke your fridge?" said Mr. Big County.

"Shattered kneecap?" said Mr. Lowery.

"How would you break *that?*" said Mr. Woody.

"Well, I was thinkin' of slamming the car door on it."

"I'd be glad to help y'out there, Hoss," said Mr. Big County. "I once cut off the tip of my Uncle Harlan's tall man slammin' my Chevy truck door on it."

"Would you?" asked Mr. Lowery hopefully.

"Sure, glad to help a buddy."

"Well," said Mr. Lowery. "Lemme think about it."

"I'll bust it so bad you'll get a lifetime handicap sticker."

"Thanks. Thanks a lot," said Mr. Lowery, which is what I mean about team spirit.

JAN. 10, NEWARK

A lot of the guys at practice keep asking me why I don't play basketball more by the basket itself and that's okay, because it's something I've had to explain to many, many people since I began shooting the basketball more than a foot ago.

I'm really an excellent shooter when I'm feeling good at my One Point, which is the centermost point of your soul, as I averaged 61 points a game in my only half-year of organized high school basketball, which was my junior year at Most Virgin Lady in Boulder, Colorado, which is just down the mountain from the

Spelunkarium in Nederland, Colorado, which is one of the biggest networks of caves in the entire world and which also almost nobody knows where it is because everybody is usually in the caves except at night when they sleep in their cubicles in the old deserted Nederland High School. And so I only shoot from the outside because this is how I learned the game, which is shoveling the compost heap behind the high school at the Spelunkarium.

This will surprise you maybe, but I didn't even care about basketball until one day when I was about eleven years old when a Roto-Rooter man with bright orange hair and a bright orange mustache named Lenny O'Connor was in our compound. It was very rare to see an outsider anywhere near or above the Inner Door Spelunkarium because Doorians do not like outsiders at all because most outsiders make fun of Inner Doorians and call us Trog Squadders and ask us if we've seen Alfred the Butler and also make fun of our belief that when God comes back for us on the Judgment Day he will come through a door inside of the earth, which is where the true heaven actually is, not above the earth like people falsely think, but this couldn't be helped because our main sewer line was plugged up.

And so this Roto-Rooter man, Mr. O'Connor, was inside the gate and I was not with the others on the Tuesday Spiritual Spelunking Sojourn as usual because I was getting too tall for a lot of the caves and was kinda clumsy and as the Elder always told me I am not the sharpest stalactite in the cave, and, besides, the healer said my spine was starting to curve because of so much bending over and also I already had fifty-seven stitches in my forehead. So I was supposed to be shoveling compost but instead I'll admit that the Roto-

Rooter man saw me reaching up into the eaves of our school looking for larvae—caterpillars and butterflies and bugs—to feed my many snakes, many of which you could see in my tanks right here in my room if you were here.

And the Roto-Rooter man saw that I was very tall for what would be your sixth grade being 6 foot 6 inches tall and being able to reach under the eaves of our school, I guess, and he said he would give me a dollar if I could dunk a basketball. Of course, I didn't know what he was talking about, as sports aren't allowed inside the Spelunkarium, especially since the Elder says testosterone is the most evil chemical on the planet and sports is just testosterone with trophies and besides there isn't enough room, not to mention a whole lot of other stuff that "distracts" us from the inner God. And he went to his truck and threw me a very worn-out old basketball and pointed to the old school's basketball hoop and said, "Go dunk it."

And I said, "Are you pointing to the clothesline attachment?" because that's all I'd ever known a basketball rim was useful for, holding one end of the clothesline at the Spelunkarium and the other end was tied to the roof, which used to be over the Nederland High School until there weren't enough kids in Nederland to actually have a high school and everybody got bussed to Ward High School or stopped going altogether. When he finally stopped laughing, he said yes and said I should jump up and throw the ball through the hole violently. I tried, but I couldn't.

"A big galoot like you can't even dunk?" he roared at me. "What a stiff!"

And so he pulled over one of the compost cans and flipped it over and stood on it and then he jumped off and threw the ball through the clothesline loop very hard and he made a horrible noise, like, "Agghahh!" And I didn't like it one bit because for one thing he killed a perfectly nice wolf spider that I was going to feed to Willard and for the other thing, it made the Elder come out of her office and I had to do an extra evening in the Fluid Room because of him.

The only good thing was he forgot about his basketball and I'm ashamed to say I kicked it behind one of the compost heaps so that he couldn't find it and just left.

That night, I secretly showed it to my Life-Giver, Phyllis, and asked her about basketball and dunking and I think she felt sorry for me having to stay back alone from the spelunking trips and that maybe I could practice that when I was left all alone doing my compost shoveling. And the next night she used her great privilege as one of the only Doorians allowed to go into town to bring me a book from the library on Bob "Bobby Hoops" Houbregs and he was doing a perfect standing hook in the picture and so she took me out and showed me how to shoot it through the clothesline loop like Bobby Hoops and I made my very first shot and it felt so good to finally do something right.

But we heard someone coming so we rushed back to our cave, and she whispered to be sure I was alone when I shot the basketball because if the members caught me playing sports the Elder would practically make me move my cot into the Fluid Room.

Unfortunately, the compost pile was on top of what used to be the basketball blacktop and so I was forced to shoot from where I did my shoveling, over the compost pile, all the way to the loop. Unfortunately for me, the ball would always land in the compost and that is not the most pleasant smell in the world, so I learned to shoot it cleanly through the loop, hit the pole, and have it bounce back over the pile and straight to me. When I missed, it meant wading through the compost to get the ball, and that is a smell you wouldn't wish on a surface rat. But I loved to do it—it was the only fun I ever really had—so I found that since I was doing it hour after hour, day after day, it was best not to miss.

I hope this clears up all that.

JAN. 11, NEWARK

We play in a beautiful basketball arena in a place here known as the Meadowlands and the arena is really nice, but I'm disappointed I haven't yet seen the beautiful meadows my teammates keep telling me about because all our games are at night. We had a lot of nice mountain meadows near the Spelunkarium and once, Phyllis snuck me out to have a picnic in the beautiful sunshine, so I hope to ride my bike out some-day to the Meadowlands and have a picnic there and all the fellas on the team encouraged me to do just that.

"As soon as possible," Mr. Barkley suggested.

"Or even sooner," said Mr. Big County.

Our coach, Coach Phil Jackson, is a great man who won many championships with the Chicagos, and seems very likable although every time he talks about his religious beliefs, which is Zen Buddhism and stuff like that, it seems to get him very excited.

Like today, he was saying, "Fellas, in order for you

and I to achieve perfect peace and harmony, as the Zen masters had, I need you to box out. Okay? Box out? Is that too much to (f-word)ing ask?! That you (f-word)ing BOX OUT ONCE IN A (F-WORD)ING WHILE?!? DON'T I DESERVE A LITTLE PEACE AND HARMONY? ONE TIME?"

Each day before practice starts, we gather in the team locker room and Coach Jackson shuts off all the lights and lights some incense and some candles and we sit on meditation stools that he bought us and we chant. Some of the other players think it's stupid, but I like it very much because it reminds me of the cave meditations at the Spelunkarium only maybe better because I never bump my head. But it seems like every time we do it, he gets mad at somebody for coughing or sneezing or purposely breathing too loud or chanting mantras that really aren't mantras you would probably use like, "hai-ree-crotch-ya-hair-ree-crotch-ya," and I mean he really gets mad and all of a sudden he'll jump up and scream, "Well, if you're not gonna even TRY to understand the meaning of nothingness, then WHAT'S THE (F-WORD)ING POINT!" And he'll go around kicking the candles and throwing the pyramids around.

He takes his religion very seriously.

JAN. 12, NEWARK

I was able to shoot three times last night and I made them all and wound up with 9 points in only four minutes, which they say is crazy, and the New Jerseys finally won a game!

Oh, and this morning, somebody gave me a copy of

the story Mr. Stain reported about me and I liked it a lot, because it contained a picture of me going all up one side of the paper from top to bottom and had the headline over it which read, "The Spelunker Who Won't Dunk 'Er."

Since me and Mr. Stain are sort of friends I asked him if he ever heard of a man named Genghis Korn and he said sure, he saw the movie and I had no idea my dad was in a movie! And I hope to see it someday or at least on the free previews that I get to see for nothing on my TV set at the Newark Airport Ramada Hotel which I now call home.

JAN. 14, NEWARK

I was taught never to say anything mean about anybody, but I'm ashamed to say I don't get a comfortable feeling from the men who follow me around in the very nice suits who represent the tennis shoe companies such as Reebok and Mikey and many others. I think it's because I'm shooting very well right now and had 11 points tonight and only missed one shot out of four and made two free throws besides as tonight we beat the hard-fought Detroits, which seems to be causing quite a fuss and is causing me to sign women's T-shirts very near their bosom, which is very embarrassing for me.

I recognize a few of them, these tennis shoe men, from my single year at Most Virgin Lady High School, which I never really wanted to leave but had to because the Roto-Rooter man, Mr. Lenny O'Connor, became my agent even though I never wanted an agent at all and accidentally turned me professional, which for sure

I never wanted at all. The tennis shoe men always want to ask me the same thing now as they did when I went to Most Virgin Lady, which is why I won't wear their shoes, which I always tell them the same thing, which is, "I have a pair of shoes."

"But we will pay you to wear our shoes," they say.

"But I like my shoes," I say.

"You can wear your shoes when you are *off* the court," they say. "All we want you to do is wear our shoes when you're *on* the court."

"But I only wear these *on* the court because they're special to me and I don't want to wear them out," I say.

"But if you just sign here, we will give you enough money to buy a thousand pair of shoes."

"But I *have* a pair of shoes," I say.

And this is when they begin rubbing their faces.

By the way, we New Jerseys won tonight as Mr. Barkley went nuts with 48 points. "Got to have nights like that once in a while," he explained to me afterward. "I got too many relatives on scholarship at the University of Charles." I think it's great that Mr. Barkley is helping so many of his family get their education.

Our hardworking public relations director, Mr. Dalton, is a very nice man and very well dressed and he came up to me tonight and asked how I was feeling and was I feeling sick or fluish at all and did I think I'd be able to continue shooting like I was? And I said yes, I was fine and yes, very much so about the shooting, and he suddenly had to go make a few phone calls. And I told Mr. Barkley how nice I thought it was that he was checking up on me, and Mr. Barkley said that yes, he nearly makes it his business to see how we're all feeling, "especially when we're big dogs on the road," which, of course, is slang for a very good team like ours.

JAN. 15, NEWARK

Mr. Big County came up to me today and said, "Hoss, how come you don't dunk?" and I explained to him that my hero, Bob "Bobby Hoops" Houbregs, one of the NBA's great immorals, never dunked, at least not in the book my mother, Phyllis, brought back from the library, and also that when the other fellows dunk it seems like they're so angry about it and I'm just not very angry and so when I get up there instead of throwing it down I only drop it gently in.

And Mr. Big County looked at me for a while and said, "Boy, if I didn't know better, I'd say you're just about as gay as a French horn."

I do admit, I *am* a pretty happy guy.

I'm learning so much about professional basketball already and one of the things I'm learning is that you must keep your muscles "supple" and "relaxed" at all times and this I'm learning from our trainer, Mr. Bruce, who seems to like me very much and gives me lots and lots of hamstring and "gluteal" massages and does I'm sure the best groin tape in the league. Sometimes I am not even sore in my hamstrings and gluteals, but Bruce says that an ounce of prevention is worth a pound of cure and always has me come in early so that he can massage my hamstrings and gluteals.

He says I have "wonderful" hamstrings and "very, very supple" gluteals and he is very good at massaging them with oils and music and candles and whale-mating tapes and everything in his "special" room in the back, although today my shoulder was a little sore from so much shooting and he only massaged that for a couple minutes before he went back to my gluteals and hamstrings.

JAN. 16, NEW YORK CITY

Tonight, all four shots from my spot went in and when they fouled me at my spot, all six of my free hooks went in, too, and I had 18 points and also I almost got a rebound in only eight minutes, all in the last minutes of the game, because we were losing so badly to the New Yorks, although my points helped get us to within 30.

I will also say, without bragging, that I can shoot from other spots besides my spot, and every bit as well, because, at the compost heap, there were lots of places that had to be shoveled, but my number one favorite place is my spot. But I don't apologize for this, because, as Mr. Barkley says, it just happens to be one of my pecadildos.

After the game, Coach Jackson, a very wise man, said he'd love to play me more but I have to block some shots and maybe get a rebound once a week and perhaps pretend to play some defense, which I haven't really yet learned to do. "Right now," he said, "you are the sound of one hand clapping."

And when he left, Mr. Barkley pinched his cheek and made a lot of saliva sounds and said it was the sound of one hand slapping but just between you and me I think it's an impression he needs to work on.

Mr. Barkley took me to a club in New York City tonight although I spent the whole night trying to figure
out what kind of club it was and never could because
nobody really seemed to have any special interests or
handshakes, but they all did seem to like to drink and
wear very tight clothing.

I was in there having a nice, big bulgur casserole
which I found at a natural food place two doors down
and brought in with me and also having my Squirt,
which I always have, and I got jinxed!

I'm only kidding, really. It was a woman named
Jinx. Her real name is Jacquanda Silver, but Mr. Barkley told me later all the players in the league call her
"Jinx, 'cause she's ruined more careers than the cover
of *Sports Illustrated.*"

Well, I thought she was very beautiful and smelled
very, very nice and she was very friendly and looked me
right in the eyes the whole time, although I don't think
she liked her friends much because she kept calling
them "my bitches," but maybe they're trying to patch it
up. And the first thing she said to me, which was very
nice, was, "Oh, honey, I love a good Squirt!" and her
bitches laughed.

She said she saw me play tonight.

"You must have wonderful aim!" she said.

Her girlfriends laughed again.

I said thanks.

"I've got a *thing* for really tall men with good aim,"
she said, although she didn't show it to me.

It was a wonderful coincidence when I said I loved
caves and *she* said she loves caves! And I asked her if
she liked them for their peace or because you feel so

much closer to God down there or was it just because she liked bats and insects?

And she said, "No," uncrossing her legs real slowly. "I love caves because of those things that shoot straight up from the cave floor, what are they?"

"Stalagmites?" I said.

And she sort of licked her lips and said, "Yeah, stalagmites, because of the way they just go straight up and are rock hard for millions and millions of years." And her girlfriends laughed very hard this time, so I guess they are used to her being so funny.

Jinx is a private investor who may someday be a marine biologist, too, and lives in New York and sees a lot of NBA games, knows a lot of the players, and loves basketball.

"It's my second favorite indoor sport, baby," she said, but she was too humble to tell me what her first favorite sport was but I hope to get it out of her someday.

I told her all about myself and the Spelunkarium and being too tall for the caves and how my mom died when a roof collapsed on her in a King Soopers grocery store.

"Oh, that's so ironic!" she said, covering her mouth. And I said I knew since she usually went to Safeway.

I liked her very much because she doesn't drink so much like other girls in the bar and only has ice teas although the bar was charging her seven dollars an ice tea which isn't cheap, but I still think she was smart to drink them, since she still had to drive clear back to her hotel, which I know was about fifteen minutes away because she gave me a really good map which even showed her room number.

Finally, we kinda ran out of things to say and she left without really saying goodbye but I think she will be a good friend of mine, but when I told Mr. Barkley I liked her he said I was a straight-up idiot to even be talking to her.

"Why you think they call her 'Jinx'?" he said.

I said I thought it had something to do with magazine covers and Mr. Barkley said, "No, it's because she has such awful luck with birth control."

And I said what does that mean and he said, "It means that you and your beanpole dick oughta stay about two football fields away from her and her supply of the world's worst condoms if you know what's good for you."

And I said what does that mean and he took a long, deep breath and said, "Look, Slo-Mo, she's a body snatcher, man! People call her 'Jinx' because no matter how beautiful she looks or how nice she seems or how great she smells, you *will* end up buyin' her ass a villa. You know what I mean? She's got better lawyers than Clinton, you down? Stay (pause) away!"

And I asked did that mean she was in science fiction movies, but he only just snapped the arm of his chair off instead.

JAN. 18, VANCOUVER

I'm getting very lonely for home and I'm not sure the NBA is the place for me, although I never really wanted to be here in the first place, but at least one of my teammates, Mr. Kinity "Death" Dedman, our power forward, is very supportive of me. Mr. Barkley said he asked him once how he got his first name,

Kinity, and he said, "How you think, dumb(f-word)? President Kinity." But he gets very angry if you call him "Kinity" and instead wants only to be called "Death" or, by his close friends, "the Black Jesus," but mostly "Death." And so Mr. Death asked me after our early-morning practice today if my husband played, too, so I guess he is kidding which professional athletes are so well known to do. At least he is interested in me at least.

He is a very colorful person although we are as different as two birds in a bush and I think I am going to like him. We sat together on the airplane ride to Vancouver, the longest airplane ride of my life—three different services. He does things which I have never seen before, like spell out words on his toenails which are too embarrassing to put in a nice book like this. I'm embarrassed to say that he not only dyes his hair and his armpit hair but also the hair around his stalagmite, which is something I would never do to mine.

I asked Mr. Barkley why Mr. Death did such a crazy thing and he said, "Look, stay the hell away from Death. All he wants is the pub, man, and he'll do anything to get it, including trying to run your skinny cult ass outta town or under an Avis bus, whichever's easiest."

But I'm afraid I have to disagree with Mr. Barkley, because Mr. Death seems like a very sentimental person, as he has a tattoo that says "MUTHA" on one shoulder and how can you not like someone that thinks that much of his mom and another in his right of someone named Marilyn Manson, whom I am sure he loves very much although she is not much to look at.

I'm also getting to know Mr. Mockmood, our fast and very serious little point guard, although he told me today that his name used to be Chris Simpson, "a name born between Slavery and Degradation." He changed it to Mockmood Rahim-Abdur last season and he gets very angry if people still call him "Chris," though you'd be amazed how much it happens.

For instance, Mr. Barkley will see him in the elevator and say, "Whassup, Chris!," forgetting of course.

"Mockmood to you, infidel," he says, his eyebrows making a "V."

And usually, right behind him will be Mr. Big County, who will back him into the elevator, look right down on him, and say cheerily, "Wail, hail, Chris! How's ever' little thing?"

"Mockmood (pause) Rahim (pause) Abdur (pause) Abdullah (pause), swine!"

I've never knew a guy with five names before.

JAN. 19, VANCOUVER

We defeated the gritty Vancouvers tonight and I didn't get to play because there was no "garbage time," as the players all call it, which is the time when, as Mr. Death says, "the NBA puts their garbage out." But that isn't an insult to me because, after all, I've always played basketball around garbage, which is really what the compost heap was. Just as the flowers and vegetables grew up in the Spelunkarium garden thanks to the compost I placed upon it, so did my shot grow from it.

And I was explaining this amusing fact to our assistant coach, Johnny "Tex" Summers, and he said, "Shut the (f-word) up and mix in a rebound once in a while, will ya?"

I told him I'd try.

Actually, I was supposed to play late in the game because Coach Jackson told me to go in for Death and they were about to buzz me in when Death came over to Coach Jackson and said, "I ain't comin' out."

I've noticed that Death and Coach Jackson get along worse than many but still Coach Jackson was very surprised and said, "What?"

And Death said, "I ain't comin' out."

And Coach Jackson said, "Oh, yes, you *are* coming out! Mo, get your ass in there!"

And Death came up real close to him and said, "Maybe you better ask the three dudes behind you if I'm comin' out or not."

And Coach Jackson turned around and there were these three tough-looking black guys sitting behind the bench in these long overcoats and hats and when Coach Jackson looked at them, one of them opened up his coat to show him that he had a gun in his coat.

And Coach Jackson swallowed and then looked at me and said, "Slo-Mo, sit down. I changed my mind." And that's why I didn't play in the fourth quarter.

JAN. 20, SEATTLE

I'm proud to be this tall, as I have told you before, but sometimes being so tall causes problems, even more now here on the surface, and now I'm going to share with you an antidote that happened to me today to illustrate this. See, I was just standing next to a regular-sized guy at the airport gate, waiting to board, when Mr. Barkley and Mr. Big County and Mr. Woody came up to me and started talking to me only they must not have seen this little bald guy with a mustache and a briefcase who was standing next to me. And this little guy was suddenly surrounded by all these big guys, and Mr. Big County and Mr. Woody and Mr. Barkley kept talking to me and somehow didn't realize the little guy was even there. And he kinda started to move away only to bump into Mr. Big County, and then he apologized and started to back away only to bump into Mr. Woody and so forth and the fellas still didn't notice him because they were so busy talking and the poor little guy couldn't get out until finally I made a space for him to leave. And I'm sure it was embarrassing for the little guy but the other fellas didn't mind and, in fact, seemed to be laughing a lot, but not about that, I'm sure.

Tonight, before the game, Coach Jackson seemed a little upset about us making the same mistakes and so he got our attention and said, "In Zen, the master must know that his pupils are understanding their lessons. But I don't get the idea that my pupils are hearing what I'm trying to teach you." Then he asked one of the ball boys to come forward with a Styrofoam cup half full of coffee. "Like the cup, you are full of yourself," Coach Jackson said. Then he took the pot of coffee and started pouring so much so that it poured out of the cup and over the boy's hand and he screamed and dropped the cup and Coach Jackson said, "Your cup must be empty first for me to fill it with the truth. Think about this, my pupils."

And as soon as he went back into his office and slammed the door, the boy sprinted into the bathroom to run his hand under cold water.

And Mr. Big County said, "That'll teach the kid to listen."

I played in garbage time again tonight because the hard-fought Seattles were somehow able to defeat us, 131–98, although I felt we outplayed them. I took three shots and all three went in, the last one right at the final buzzer.

It was a very bad night for Mr. Lowery, our surfer shooter, as he got very sick before the game and couldn't play. He is still above his shooting percentages though, which is a good thing.

"I don't know which made him sicker," Mr. Big County told me on the bench in the first quarter. "Knowin' that Gary Payton was going to be on defense against him or the half a bottle of ipecac he drank before the game."

I said I thought it was probably the ipecac.

JAN. 21, PORTLAND

I really think Mr. Death Dedman and I could become friends. He is already starting to kid me with the jocularity style that many NBA players are so well known for. The other day he came up to me and said, "Hey, you going anywhere right now?"

And I said, "No."

And he said, "Well, then why don't you go (f-word) yourself."

And then, today, he came up to me and said, "How the (f-word) did you ever become a basketball player anyway?" and so I will now try to answer that question and maybe Mr. Death will read it in this book because he said he had to go rotate the tires on his car or he would have loved to hear my story.

About three years after Phyllis died, in what would be around your ninth grade or the Doorian 47th Gate, I was alone as usual and I was, I admit, neglecting my compost shoveling and I was instead looking for mice under the school to feed to my snakes when what should happen but the same Roto-Rooter man, Mr. Lenny O'Connor, the little wiry orange-haired plumber which I spoke about before, should drive up in the same truck. And what do you think he should say to me but "Hey, Donkey Kong, you dunk yet?"

And so I dug my ball out from under the tarp I hid it under each day and I tried again and even though I was 7-6 by then, I failed badly because I'm really not a very good jumper in the least and my feet seem to go sideways instead of up, which is why Mr. Barkley says I have the team record in the horizontal leap. The Roto-Rooter man just laughed and shook his head. And I said nothing except I walked thirty feet away to get the ball which had rolled away, and it had rolled away to my favorite spot! And so I looked around to make sure nobody was watching who would take me to the Fluid Room and I shot my hook and it swooshed right through the clothesline circle and spun back off the pole right back to me, as usual.

And I would say this Roto-Rooter man was more than surprised as he slammed on his brakes and his big bushy orange eyebrows went straight up and he said to me, "Lessee you do that again." And I not only did it again but I did it left-handed and I did it nine more times without a miss—five left and four right—because

I was really feeling my One Point that day and must confess to you without being a big braggart that I probably could've made ninety-nine more if the Elder hadn't suddenly walked out of one of the surface buildings and asked, "What in the hell is going on out here?!?" as she is usually grumpy in daylight anyway. And I had to pretend to have never seen a basketball before and began to try and kick it. And she walked off muttering she had never seen brain removal done with only fifty-seven stitches.

And I whispered to Mr. O'Connor that he should be going now and he left. But a week later, I was shoveling compost and shooting when I was called into the Elder's office for the very first time in my life and I was very, very scared because when someone like me is called into the Elder's office it's "Katy at the door" and maybe a weekend in the Fluid Room besides, but who should I see when I get in there but Mr. O'Connor and another large man, though not as large as me, of course. And what do you think the Elder said to me? She said that she had agreed to let me leave the Spelunkarium each day and attend Most Virgin Lady High School in Boulder, which was down the mountain, and play basketball for the other large man who she said was a priest named Father DeMeret.

And I was very surprised by this and very scared, too, because I'd only been out of the Spelunkarium two or three times and I said to the Elder without actually looking at her, which I was never allowed to do, "I would like to stay here, please."

And she explained that because of my great height I wasn't very good at spelunking at all and was missing the whole point of the Doorian belief and that if I did this she promised God would open a huge hole for me when the time came and take me down to Him and besides, the Roto-Rooter man is a kind of spelunker in himself in a way, and a few of his friends and the coach would be very good influences on me and that even though it was against the Inner Doorian philosophy to mix with the outside world, Mr. O'Connor and his friends had agreed to provide some services free of charge to the Spelunkarium while I was playing for them such as plumbing, painting, and all new roofs on the surface buildings besides. And so they had decided it wouldn't be such a bad thing for me after all.

And I wished Phyllis or my dad, Genghis Korn, could've been there to talk for me but nobody was and I couldn't say a thing so she said go change clothes because practice started in forty-five minutes at the school and the school was a good twenty miles away, depending on traffic, of course. And Mr. Mockmood is starting to grumble about my writing into my pad now, although I don't grumble when he gets up at three in the morning to face toward Mecca, which always seems to be toward the minibar, but I would never tell him that, but I have to go now.

JAN. 22, PORTLAND

The difficult Portlands edged us tonight, 101–71, but I got in during the not-garbage time of the game. In fact, I got in when we were only 15 points behind at the start of the fourth quarter. But the problem is none of the guys would give me the ball and so I never got to shoot and so I never got to score. I did get a rebound, though! It bounced out to me at the top of the free-throw line and I was going to back up and shoot it, but Mr. Mockmood took it from me, but this is the way it is supposed to be on account of he *is* the point guard.

A man named Mr. Barter Soals of the Mikey Corporation introduced himself to me tonight and asked me to wear his shoes, but I will not ever, never wear his shoes or anybody's shoes and maybe I should've told him why and that is because my Life-Giver, Phyllis, got them from my dad, Genghis Korn, himself.

They are size 22EEEEEs, which is exactly what I wear now that I am a man, which tells me again that he is really and truly my dad. You can see spots, like on the right toe, where he must've dragged his right foot. Phyllis says that he actually wore them some before she asked him for them. Since all property belongs to the Elder in the Spelunkarium, I would hide the shoes in the back of my bottom drawer, behind my socks, and pull them out late at night and just hold them and stare at them even though it's pretty dark in our cubicle in the gymnastium on account of lights had to be out at nine.

And though I look for posters and ads that he may be coming somewhere I am to do another Genghis Korn frozen imitation-corn products show I have not seen any. But maybe someday he will see me on the television and notice the shoes and say to himself, "Hey, I had a pair of shoes exactly like that!" and maybe notice how much I look like him, I hope, and understand all of a sudden that I'm his son and that is why I will never, ever give them up until the cows come home to roost.

JAN. 24, SACRAMENTAL

I'm not sure why, but Mr. Rashad and a lot of the other TV and radio and sportswriter people are asking me to tape a lot of interviews, probably because of being so tall at 7 foot 8 and being so very skinny and being a very good shot and only being seventeen years old.

"You're only seventeen, but, really, 'fear' just isn't part of your vocabulary," Mr. Rashad said.

And even though this was not formed as a question, I knew by now that Mr. Rashad wants you to respond as though it is a question, so I said, "No. Fear is a part of my vocabulary."

And Mr. Rashad said, "Exactly. Now, anytime a kid goes from his junior year in high school straight to the pros, it's got to be amazing."

"It's happened before?" I said.

"It has?" he said.

"No, you said it happened before?"

"No! I didn't say that."

"You said, 'anytime a kid goes from his junior year in high school straight to the pros' and so that's kinda what I'm asking, when did it happen before? Is there someone else my age in the NBA because it'd be nice to maybe make friends?"

And Mr. Rashad said what he always says to finish the interview, which is a Hollywood/TV/entertainment kind of thing to signify that everything's fine, which is, "Cut!"

And so, anyway, when I came back to my locker everybody was gone and my uniform and my warm-ups weren't there but only a janitor's overalls were hanging there instead. And I was late to begin shooting with my teammates for the game and so I had no choice but to put on the janitor's outfit. And so I ran down the hallway to go to the court and who do I see there but Mr. Death, who was grinning.

And he said, "Let's see how much America loves your skinny Gomer Pyle ass now," he said, which I appreciated.

And as soon as I got out to the court, where more than eighteen thousand people were watching, I was very, very embarrassed. And my teammates all laughed and so did the other team, but the fans seemed to like it. I heard one kid say, "Swag warm-up!" And I heard a very pretty woman go, "LOVE your retro look, Maurice!" And I heard a radio play-by-play man say, "Maurice Finsternick is making a statement here! He's saying, 'I'm not one of the stars! I'm the people's player! I'm a blue-collar worker! Just putting in a hard night's work for a hard night's pay!' And doesn't America need more people like that?" And as the applause started to build in our arena to a very loud loudness, I looked over at Death Dedman and he looked like he'd eaten a plate of bad oysters.

Anyway, after warm-ups, our trainer, Mr. Bruce, brought me a new uniform and added that he thought it was a good idea that I'd gone out there anyway because he said, "I *love* the idea of you wearing nothing under that overall, Maurice," and patted me on the butt, which, as everybody knows, is what trainers do to check for contusions and adhesions. And the crowd was so good and positive toward me that I felt very peaceful and happy in my One Point and when Coach Jackson finally put me in during garbage time, I had my best game so far, playing six minutes and making six out of eight 3-pointers and scoring 20 points and we beat the rugged Sacramentals. People were hollering, "You're really cleaning up, Slo-Mo!" and "Way to take out the trash, big man!"

And while we were all standing in the locker room afterward, somebody said, "Yo, shut up!" and everybody pointed at the TV and it was ESPN *SportsCenter* and I was there in my overalls and Stuart Scott, this TV sports announcer with crazy eyes and crazy things to say, said, "Boo-ya! I'll broom your ass!" and going on and on about "sweepin' the NBA."

And after everybody'd left my locker, all the writers and TV and radio men, it was pretty much only me and Mr. Death left and he said something very nice to me which was, "Someday, you'll get yours."

And I can only say I sure hope so as I would really like my warm-ups back.

JAN. 25, LOS ANGELES

Microchip got ahold of me today and read me what one of the sportswriter gentlemen said about me in a newspaper in Denver which was . . .

A 7-8 hat rack with spectacles named Maurice "Slo-Mo" Finsternick killed the Kings last night, which, when you consider that he is just slightly slower than erosion, is like saying that gingivitis killed the Huns.

There has been every kind of player in this league—leapers, refrigerators, slugs, geeks, dunkers. sharpshooters, knee-dribblers and pine-sitters—but there has never been a creature like seventeen-year-old Slo-Mo Finsternick, who wanders around the fringes of the game like an orphaned giraffe looking for its mother until somebody throws the ball to him five feet outside the 3-point line. Then he swoops into his lazy faucet-drip standing hook shot, right- or left-handed, like some sort of bad George Mikan training film. You watch him start into it, and you can't help but laugh at the sheer ridiculousness of it. You laugh, that is, until it goes swishing in, time after impossible time. If this kid can keep from sliding down the hole in a shower drain cover someday, he's going to be something.

I thought it was a very nice thing to say, but when I went to Mr. Death to ask him how to write the gentleman a thank-you note, he just batted it out of my hands, grumbled, "I don't read the (f-word)ing papers," and went back to the very long and difficult process of putting his jewelry back on.

Today, on the long bus ride to the airport, the weather was very hot, which is something I've never experienced in January, growing up in Colorado as I have told, and we were all very tired and nobody was saying much of anything, until, finally, Mr. Big County said, "I believe it's too hot to car(f-word)."

"Bro, it ain't *never* too hot to (f-word)," said Mr. Woody. "You ever had a girl take a wintergreen Life Saver and then hum you? That'll cool your boy off."

"What about those lightning sparks?" said Mr. Barkley. "How can you let any sparks come near the King?"

"Ever had a ho put a Alka-Seltzer in her gash just before you did it?" said Mr. Woody. "Man, that's a *rush*, homes. All those bubbles, feels like you're (f-word)in' Lawrence Welk or somethin'."

I secretly like to hear this kind of talk, though Mr. Mockmood very much doesn't. Mr. Mockmood is our point guard and Muslim mosque leader, although nobody ever goes to mosque but him and sometimes me and I only do it because I feel bad for him all alone in there sometimes.

"Your spirit is diseased and rotting," Mr. Mockmood said to Mr. Woody. "What do you think Allah thinks of you when you talk like that?"

"I don't know, Chris," Mr. Woody said. "What do you think Allah thought a your ass when you did half the Providence yell squad one hour before the NIT consolation game?"

This made Mr. Mockmood angry.

"My name is Mockmood, fetid serpent," Mr. Mockmood said. "That was before I turned to the grace and wisdom of Allah and you know it."

"I don't get y'all's religion anyway," Mr. Big County said. "Why y'all cover up your womenfolk's faces like that and cut off their clits and stuff, hoss? I mean, y'all's on Woody's butt all the time about women, but at least he ain't runnin' no spay and neuter clinic. What kinda God all you dotheads runnin' anyhow?"

And Mr. Mockmood leaped across the seat at him and hollered, "You will die for that, unholy boar!"

And I was tryin' to stop them when we all heard this, which was: "Why don't all you whack mother (f-word)ers shut up,man?"

It was Mr. Death, who was doing what he was always doing, which was working on a tattoo with a sewing needle and a fountain pen, which he does himself ever since, as Mr. Barkley told me, he went into a tattoo parlor in Detroit late one night and asked for an "Ozzy" on his right buttocks, thinking of the heavy-metal musician Ozzy Osbourne, and when he woke up realized the man had been thinking Ozzie Nelson, the TV father.

Anyway, everybody shut up very quickly because nobody really likes to bother Mr. Death when he's working on a tattoo.

Tonight, toward the end of our excellent victory over the excellent Los Angeleses, I found myself all alone with the ball under the basket. The whole crowd screamed at me to dunk it but I simply dropped it in. They booed so loud at me you'd think I had shot the president or something.

"Hey, Dolph Schayes!" Mr. Tex screamed. "You're the single biggest pussy I've ever seen!"

I'm glad he wasn't yelling at me.

JAN. 27, NEWARK

We lost to the Clevelands tonight by 2 points and I know I could've helped because I made twenty-three straight hook shots during warm-ups, all 3s, but I never got to play.

I really have to confess that I don't have many friends and I'm starting to feel pretty lonely and I wish my Life-Giver, Phyllis, was around to do what she always used to do which was kiss me on the forehead and stick her chin out and pat the bottom of it with the top of her hand, which was her signal to me which meant: *Chin up. I love you and chin up and everything's going to be fine.* She'd do it whenever she'd see me from a ways away and wasn't allowed to come talk to me or when she had to leave me to go into smaller caverns that I couldn't get into or when I had to shovel compost as her pod filed by. She'd look at me and pat the underside of her chin and I'd feel better because I knew she loved me and everything was going to be all right.

I hope Microchip calls tonight because with my Phyllis dead he is the person in the whole surface world who knows me best and, in fact, he's really the only person who knows me at all. We have so much in common. See, he had to sneak out to shoot the basketball same as I had to. "My parents think it's beneath a black man to play basketball," he would always say. "They think it only furthers the stereotype of black men only being good at running and jumping." He said if they caught him watching ESPN or wearing high-tops he would be locked in the den for the weekend and be forced to read John Edgar Wideman and I told him about having to spend an entire weekend in the Fluid Room, which is probably just as bad although I don't know Mr. Wideman.

Microchip was the first and maybe only person who understood that I shouldn't be put under the basket with the other big fellows, but be allowed to shoot from my favorite spot instead. That first horrible practice day at Most Virgin Lady High School was very painful for me because not only was I scared, but Father DeMeret, our coach, put me in with the big fellows right away and had me start shooting layups, which were very foreign to me. I was pretty awful shooting them. I could dribble very well, of course, because I dribbled up and down the 147 steps leading to the cave when the rest of the pods were way down below, but I made almost none of the layups, and all the other Most Virgin Lady Ascenders laughed a whole lot at me and said to me, "Why don't you just dunk it, (f-word) face?"

And all through practice Father DeMeret yelled at me and called me a girl and said what was he thinking, I wasn't even worth the gas he spent driving up to Nederland to see me. He seemed very disgusted all in all and you could've hung an icicle inside my One Point that day. I don't know why it affected me so bad because he was just as mean to Microchip, even though he was such a good player, making fun of his height, forgetting to mention him after good games by saying, "I'm sorry, Mustafa, you're so small I didn't even see you sitting there."

After that first day and for three straight days after it, I would ride my bike back up the canyon because I wasn't allowed to travel in pollution machines like cars and I'd like to take this opportunity to say that the people of Boulder are not very polite when they pass a bicyclist, screaming and honking and sometimes trying to push me over just because they had to wait their turn to do it. And I told the Elder that I didn't want to go back and how I didn't think this religion was any better for me because I didn't fit in the confessional booths any better than I did in the caves, and that riding my Schwinn up and down the canyon from Nederland to Boulder got a little tiring even though I'm ashamed to admit that many was the time when I would grab onto the back of a truck and get a hitch up. But they said, "Once you make a commitment you have to stick with it" and besides, they were finally getting a new septic tank, so they made me keep going back and I was very miserable.

And after the first week of practice, Father De-Meret said I better start dunking or "I'm sending your ass back to those cave freaks on the first hippie van."

And that night, after all the guys were gone, I was sitting alone on the floor and I really did want to cry and Microchip came up to me and said, "Seriously, why *don't* you just dunk it?" And I stood up and started telling him that I did not like dunking and didn't think there was anything fun or challenging or spiritually rewarding dunking and it seemed like dunking was done with such anger and I really didn't have any anger although I said if I stayed here at Most Virgin Lady High School much more I could learn. And so that's why I so much more liked the arc of a shot from my favorite spot as you watched it spin through the air, drifting so freely and yet so cosmically tied to the basket, on its way to making the hole and the ball complete, and as I was talking to him I kinda lost track of what I was doing and I made a whole mess of them straight from my favorite spot. And Microchip said, "Damn, Mo! Do you realize you just made seventeen straight treys? You gonna Jordanize this dump!" which is how Microchip talked, which was using words in a way you had never heard before, making nouns into verbs all the time, like, for example, saying, "Man, if that guy doesn't stop foulin' me, I'm gonna Tonya his knee."

And then he made me shoot twenty-five more of those with him fouling me and hanging on me and it was so fun I made twenty-one of them and he was so excited about our prospects for winning that he went straight to Father DeMeret, in his office, and said, "If you start me at the point and Mo at the two-guard tomorrow in a fifteen-minute scrimmage and we don't win, we'll *both* quit the team."

And though I don't think Father DeMeret wanted to kick him off, he said it'd be his pleasure to kick both "Elephant Man and Spike Lee" back to whatever episode of the *White Shadow* we crawled out of.

And Microchip was so excited he said, "We gonna mad chow! I'm gonna take you to your favorite place in the whole world. Whachu want? You want Country Buffet? You want Sizzler? Let's go to Country Buffet and eat cobbler till we puke! Wanna?" And I said, well, my favorite place on earth was probably Whey to Go, which, amazingly, he said he'd never heard of. And I told him I'd only been there once before, with Phyllis, my Life-Giver, and it was so much better than Spelunkarium food I almost fainted. And he said, "What about Mac's Lounge, homes?"

And I said, "What?"

And he said, "McDonald's."

And I said I'd never heard of it and he laughed and laughed like it was a joke and so we went to Whey to Go and he said to the girl, "Let my buddy just go completely Roseanne here, baby, cuz it's all on me," and I had not five, but six Wheyburgers, three of them smothered in their sinfully delicious Secret Sorghum Sauce. Plus, I polished off three rice milks. And after the fifth, he said, "Damn, you goin' to the 'lectric chair or what?"

He really is a very funny little guy.

I got 12 points in only three minutes of garbage time tonight and we won over the no-holds-barred Vancouvers again and I didn't miss a shot and no free throws either and afterward I heard Mr. Harley the Stain asking Coach Jackson how come I don't play more, since I've been with the team a month and have missed only two shots. And afterward I asked Mr. Stain what Coach Jackson said.

"He said you're too young, too skinny, too inexperienced, and too gentle," Mr. Stain said. "He said you were one of those guys who were good for fifty points a night."

"Really?"

"Yeah, score twenty and give up thirty."

But I would like to tell him that if he'd let me, I could do much better than that, say 60 or 70, but that would be rude and, besides, anyone who talks back to his coach in the NBA is usually cut immediately and how would that be then?

Besides, I'm not sure all my scoring makes everybody happy and I'm afraid I'm one of those people, only because what good is it to be on the front of the sports page or on the eleven o'clock news and be so popular with the fans when they really don't even want to talk to you except get your autograph with their head down and won't even look you in the eye?

I really get tired of seeing the tops of people's heads and nothing else. Here I am, with no real friends and everybody wants to take pictures with me and have me sign stuff and try to hide in my hotel room when I'm out, but as soon as I sign and try to talk to them, they walk off staring at the signature. I guess they like me, but they don't like me enough to stick around, I guess.

Mr. Soals, the Mikey man, keeps hanging around and he's almost starting to make me angry.

"Nikey," he said to me tonight after the game.

"I'm sorry?" I said.

"Nikey with an 'N' like in Nimrod," he said. "Not 'M' as in Meathead."

I explained that I was very sorry about that.

"Pally," he said, because he seems to call everybody "pally." "We will make you very rich to play in our shoes."

"I already have a pair of shoes," I said.

He buried his face in his hands and then ran them through his perfect hair, which I've never seen him do before, and when he came back up, his hair was sticking up and his face was very red.

"Pally, if it's my last breathing act, I *will* sign you to a contract with us. It's not the quote-unquote money anymore," which is how he talks, putting things in quotes and unquotes. "It's beyond that. It's a quote-unquote challenge to me, personally, and I've never been beaten in a challenge. Never! I will sign you to a contract if you have to sign with my last drop of blood!"

And I told him I was sorry he felt that way and I didn't want him to bleed to death but that I wasn't going to wear anybody's shoes but Mr. Genghis Korn's. I told him again how much my father means to me and in fact that in each city we go into, I check all the ads in the local newspapers, even the supermarket shopping guides, for an appearance by my father at one of the local grocery stores.

This seemed to brighten his face. "What's his name, Maurice?"

"No," I said.

"No?"

"No, it's not Maurice."

"What?"

"My father's name. It isn't Maurice."

"No, no, I understand that. What I mean is, what's his name, pause, Maurice."

I had to think about that for a while.

"Ohhhh. His name is Genghis Korn," and I went on to explain how he is the giant who arrives at grocery stores in a specialized Corvair with no front seat and promotes the use of Krispy Korn imitation-corn frozen food products.

"Really!" said Mr. Soals. "That's very interesting!" and he zipped off.

I was standing there feeling very ashamed at how much anger I was feeling toward Mr. Soals when Mr. Barkley, our power forward, said a very wonderful thing, which was: "Why don't you just call the company, Lurch?"

"I'm sorry?" I said.

"They can probably put you through to him," Mr. Barkley said.

"I don't know their number," I said.

"Just call information, you Jell-O brain," he said.

"Call information what?" I said.

"Didn't you even have *phones* up there in Deliverance?"

"One, but only the Elder got to use it."

So he told me to just dial 411 and ask for the number of the Krispy Korn imitation-corn products frozen food company and then ask for somebody in public relations and then ask them how I can get ahold of my dad as I would like to very much.

I was so happy I kissed Mr. Barkley right on his bald head, which he began rubbing instantly with a towel.

JAN. 29, NEWARK

I was so excited last night I ran right home and hit 411 on the phone but it didn't work. It just was this beeping sound. I tried it over and over, maybe fifty times, because it sounded like it was busy and it was so sad because I finally had some hope of finding my dad and I just laid on my bed and cried like I used to when I was a small boy. Well, a boy at least.

I told Mr. Barkley my sad story this morning and he said, "Did you dial 9 to get out?"

I admitted no.

He looked perturbed.

"When you walked in those caves, did you get lost for, like, months at a time?"

I tried 9 first and then 411 and spoke to a very nice girl who gave me the number, which was in Boston, even though she was in Dallas, which amazed me very much. I called the company, dialing 9 first, who gave me a Mr. Dalrymple, who said, "The company no longer uses the services of Mr. Genghis Korn."

That just about broke my heart in half. I called Mr. Barkley in his room and told him.

"Well, did you ask them what the guy's real name is or where he lives or do they have a number for him?"

I called back. Mr. Dalrymple said they weren't allowed to give out that information. I was crushed again. I called Mr. Barkley in his room again.

"Well, did you tell them you're in the NB-fricking-A and the world seems to love you like damn Benji and the guy might be your dad and you might do a free ad for one of their horrible imitation Colonel Kornholesticks if they'll just find this lanky geek for you?"

I again thanked Mr. Barkley very much.

I called Mr. Dalrymple but he wasn't in all of a sudden and so I spoke to another man and I told him that I was actually Mr. Maurice "Slo-Mo" Finsternick and I was in the NBA and had only missed a few shots and he might have seen my picture on the cover of *Sports Illustrious*—

"Sure, sure you're Slo-Mo," he said. "And I'm Matlock. I'll investigate this fascinating case and get back to you, pal." And he hung up.

I can hardly wait for Mr. Matlock's call.

JAN. 30, TORONTO

Tonight, we were edged by the hardworking Torontos, 121–97, and I got off one shot and made it.

Mr. Lowery hasn't been playing lately because he told the coaches he thinks he might have torn his knee's crucial ligament even though nothing shows up on the X rays. Tonight, though, he said it hurt so much he couldn't even get up out of his chair in the locker room even to test it. He kept calling guys over and whispering in their ear and they kept shrugging, so finally he said to me, "Slo," whisperlike, and

54

motioned me over there and I leaned down and said, "What?"

And he whispered into my ear, "Can you remember which knee I hurt?"

I noticed something tonight but maybe it's nothing but it kinda bothers me and that's the fact that the inside of the arenas seem to be filled with only rich, white guys in suits and their wives sometimes but outside the arenas, it's a lot of kids, black kids and brown kids and poor kids, waiting all that time outside the arena in the freezing cold just hoping we'll stop the bus and come out and meet them but we never do.

In fact, I don't see how they can even see us inside the bus through the black bus windows and I guess that's why none of the fellas wave at them, but I always try to, although they're not really waving at me, they're waving at Mr. Barkley and Mr. Death and Mr. Woody and them.

And tonight, as we were driving by them, Mr. Death said, "Yo, that kid's got my old Filas on! Look at that, man! I ain't been with Fila in five years! Man, they all worn through to the bottom, man! They're about to fall apart right on his feet! Don't that just flip you out?"

And I said, "I feel so bad for him."

And he said, "Bad? You (f-word)in' crazy? Kid like that is why I'm the king, man! The king of sneaks, fool!"

I didn't mean anything by it, as I told Mr. Barkley afterward. But what I don't get is, how come every night Mr. Death throws away his pair of shoes after he uses them only once? That boy might've been able to use them.

And Mr. Barkley said, "What? And flood the market?"

FEB. 1, NEWARK

I'm so excited about Mr. Matlock working on finding my dad that I've never shot better. My One Point is full of joy and the basket and the ball just feel so cosmically drawn to each other, just as the cave light and the cave shadow are drawn inexorably together. I know that if Coach Jackson would just put me in more I could really help our team win, but tonight against the multitalented Minnesotas we lost and I played only four minutes and scored only 11 points.

I told the sportswriter gentlemen that we just aren't capitalizing on our mistakes, but I think it's more than that, if you want to know the truth, and that's why I wanted to ask Coach Jackson why I play so few minutes, but of course he's the coach and I'm only the player. But then, talk to the devil, he came up to me and said, "I want to play you more minutes, Slo." And I was very happy until he said, "But in order to do that, I need you to play more inside with the taller fellows under the basket. Each man must carry water and chop wood."

He said if I did I could help the team with not just points, but rebounds and blocked shots, too. "Maurice, it's very difficult for me to start a seven-foot-eight three-point shooter. Like the Zen masters, I, too, have learned to seal my self-worth off from others' opinions, but our owner, Mr. Trump, would fire me so fast I'd be back coaching AAU cuts in the CBA."

When he asked me this, he stroked his beard and looked at me very centered and said, "You know, Maurice, the strength of the pack is the wolf and the strength of the wolf is the pack."

But I've missed only three shots since I was turned professional, I thought to myself, but of course, I never talk back to the coach, as any professional athlete knows not to do, in case you could get cut, just like that.

Microchip called me collect again tonight which made me very happy.

I guess I never told you what happened when my little friend Microchip tricked Father DeMeret into the bet where he and I started at the one- and two-guards in a scrimmage. Well, what happened is Father De-Meret gave us three guys for our team who were really not so good and, in fact, Microchip said they completely "Lewinskied." So really it was just me and Microchip, and Father DeMeret said, "Good luck getting the ball across half-court, gentlemen," and he stuck this really hard full-court press on us. But Microchip came up with a plan, which was: I would in-bounds the ball to him and then just start setting picks for him all the way up and he'd dribble guys' faces right into my hips and fellas got tired of having their noses bleed and their eyes water so much and stopped trying to chase him and that is how we got the ball across.

And then I would go to my spot and Microchip would get the ball to me up high and I'd hook it in the manner of the feared NBA immoral Bob Houbregs and most of the time it would go right in. And after I'd made about five straight of these, Father DeMeret yelled some things at the other team that you would not normally expect from a father at a place called Most Virgin Lady and assigned two and three guys to guard me at once but unless they were standing on each other's shoulders, it didn't make a difference, as my shot starts about a foot above my head and only goes higher from there.

And so, after I made about five more of those Father DeMeret decided to have these guys grab my arms as soon as I got the ball from Microchip and before I shot and Microchip said, "He gets to shoot the free throws, don't he? I mean, this ain't China or somethin', right?" and Father DeMeret agreed that it wasn't China and I missed about ten in a row of those.

And just before I was about to try the eleventh and the other team kinda catching up to us, Microchip took me aside and said, "Feel free to make one of these mothers, stretch, or our ass is gonna be takin' up skateboarding. Okay?"

And I said to him, as I've explained to you, my reader, "The free-throw line is not one of my spots."

And then Microchip had a funny look on his face like he'd just discovered a wonderful new cave passage and said, "So shoot 'em from your spot!"

"But that's probably illegal," I said, although I did not remember it in the rules Father DeMeret was making me memorize.

"Show me where it says," Microchip said, so I took the ball and went to the 3-point line to shoot a free hook and Father DeMeret screamed, "Whoa, whoa,

whoa!" and insisted in a very loud voice that shooting free throws from the 3-point line was illegal, but Microchip made me go get my rule book from the crocheted bag which I carried each day to school and back and believe it or not, it *wasn't* in there. It said you must not touch the line with your foot but it didn't say anything about how far you can shoot behind it. So I got to keep shooting free throws from my spot and I made all but one and we won the game very easily and maybe more so.

And from then on, Father DeMeret started us at the one- and two-guards in the real games and I think he very much was glad to, saying that day, "Well, *this* is gonna make me look like a genius." And then he did what he did quite often, which was screw open this huge jar of Tums and chew a handful.

FEB. 4, NEWARK

Tonight, Coach Jackson told me before the game, "All water must eventually flow to the pool," and I asked him what did that mean and he kinda lost that real peaceful expression on his face and his eyebrows kinda grew together and he barked, "What it means is I'm the goddamn coach and you're the goddamn Catholic high school stringbean and what I say goes," and then said I have to play center. Before, I'd go inside now and again to get a rebound and get the ball to Mockmood, our point guard, and then hurry down to my spot for my 3-pointer. But Coach Jackson said if I didn't play inside both ways tonight against the Washingtons, something would happen to me that would permanently damage my soul, possibly ruin my life, and affect my being forevermore, which was that he would trade me to the Vancouvers.

So I played inside and I must tell you I would rather be bitten in the eye by an engorged bluehead than ever do that again. Every time they'd throw it into me in the middle, guys would throw elbows into my stomach, punch me in the kidneys, and, worse, say mean things to me. "Listen, pussy," Mr. Steve Smith said to me. "You score on me and I'll burn ya house down." And Mr. Juwan Howard said that if I didn't get out of the lane right away, he'd make me his "bitch." I asked the referee, Mr. Nunez, if this was legal to say these kinds of things and he said, "Lemme call the ACLU and get back to you."

And I asked the other referee, Mr. Crawford, and he spit the whistle out of his mouth and said, "Why don't you just dunk it, you great white dope?" But I didn't dunk it. In fact, I got only 4 points, no offensive rebounds, one chipped tooth, two knees in the groin, three shots blocked and a big loogie on my dad's shoes while waiting for a free throw to be thrown, for which Mr. Howard said he was sorry, he missed. Afterward our owner, Mr. Trump, came at me with a big smile and said that I was to the center position what the *Exxon Valdez* was to flounder, although it didn't make me feel any better.

FEB. 5, NEWARK

Coach Jackson keeps mentioning to me that maybe it's not such a good idea to ride my Schwinn to practice wearing my practice uniform and sweat suit, which has the logos of the New Jerseys on it, because you never know what kind of nuts are out there so I went to the store and bought a pair of bicycle shorts, which make the biking very much fun indeed.

They're very tight and black and I know that they're pretty cool because everybody was staring right at them when I walked in, and going "Damn!" and "Everybody back!" Mr. Woody said I wouldn't have any problem getting dates if I wore them more, which was nice of him to say. And I went in to show Bruce my new shorts but he said he had to go lay down because he was feeling light-headed.

I would also like to mention I'm gaining weight rapidly in the professional ranks as I'm up to 198 from 195, thanks to the New Jerseys' strict policy to try and eat thirty thousand calories a day, which includes a dozen raw eggs, even though I usually throw them up. I think my success in the weight-gaining area is from piling down some serious rice cakes—I'm letting myself have the Quaker Oats cinnamon now—and more than my fair share of beets.

The fellas on the team say I really need to gain some weight if I'm ever going to get a girlfriend and I think it won't be long now because you wouldn't believe the kind of girls you meet in the NBA. Today, for instance, we all met Miss Universe before the game and I just couldn't believe how beautiful she was and, in fact, I couldn't help myself and said, "Are you *really* Miss Universe?"

And she said, "Yes."

And I said, "Of the whole world?"

And Mr. Barkley interrupted and said, "No, Mo, just for this planet."

But I still think it's pretty neato.

FEB. 6, NEWARK

It's a long season, but Mr. Woody said today during free throws he's determined to work hard, stay with it, and "think off" by the play-offs. He said he feels like he's getting close.

"Do you realize how important this could be to the world?" Mr. Woody said. "If I can think off, and teach *others* to think off, I could make *billions!* Do you know what this would mean to married guys alone?"

"Change their lives!" said Mr. Barkley.

"Priests, rabbis, yogis!" said Mr. Big County.

"Colossal!" said Mr. Barkley. "And what about our handsless friends!"

"And really, really, really fat guys!" said Mr. Lowery.

"The rubber underwear industry!" said Mr. Barkley.

"How about just the way it'll change the language?" said Mr. Woody. "You'll be like, 'Hey, bro, heard you had a date last night. How was she?' And your buddy will say, 'How was she? Man, she was a thirty-second think!' "

"Women will be less threatened by men," said Mr. Barkley. "They'll want a guy that can think off for a few nights before they have sex. They'll compare men in a whole new way. One woman will be like, 'Whoa, did you see the size on that guy?' And the other woman will go, 'I know! His hat *had* to be a size 8!' "

"I don't know, though," said Mr. Big County. "Now guys'll have a whole new way to get in trouble."

"Yeah," said Mr. Black. "They'll have, like, a whole week of *Nightlines* trying to decide whether thinkin' is cheatin'. NOW will be all pissed. They'll call it, like, 'brain rape' and they'll try to make it illegal for dudes to do it. And there'll be pro-think-off groups running around saying, 'A mind is a terrible thing to waste.' "

"Yeah," said Mr. Barkley. "Until somebody teaches *women* to think off. Then the whole race will be doing it! Mattress companies will lay off millions! The condom industry will go broke! The porn industry will dry up!"

Mr. Big County took Mr. Woody by the shoulders and shook him wildly. "Goddang, man! These are people's lives you're playing with!"

I don't think he's going to stop.

I played inside again tonight—seventeen minutes— and didn't enjoy it one bit, and maybe not even that much.

I'm sorry, but I don't think I'm the kind of wolf that likes being under the basket one bit and, in fact, if I didn't know better, I would say some of the other wolves are being intentionally unkind under there. The Doorian motto is "Let sweet and pure springwater flow up from every schism" and I do not mean to be unkind but I do not think someone purposely throwing their elbow into your larynx and saying, "Suck on that, Sasquatch," is either sweet or pure.

We lost again to the Philadelphias, 101–92, and I didn't even take one outside shot and missed all three of my close-in ones and I was so sore and grouchy after the game that when I got home, I didn't even say good night to my snakes individually and only sang them one song.

FEB. 8, NEWARK

I went to my first mall today and it was pretty amazing because of all the things I saw, including fantastic stores like the Gap and Banana Republic and the Sharper Image, stores that I'll bet no other mall in the *world* has.

Many people asked me what they always ask me, which is, "How's weather up there?" And I said what I always say which Mr. Bob "Bobby Hoops" Houbregs used to tell people, which is, "Hot at the peaks, cooler in the foothills."

And guess what? I also saw Mr. Barkley and Mr. Lowery and I asked them what they were doing and they said they decided to go see *Doctor Zhivago.* And I asked them what was wrong, but they just stared at me, but that's okay, as I guess people's health is very private.

And not only that but twenty minutes later, I saw Mr. Death, but I guess he wanted not to let on who he was in the mall because he just ignored me when I said hello so's that we both weren't mobbed by autograph seekers, of course.

I know most of the guys don't want anything to do with Mr. Death, but I think once you get beyond the dyed hair, the earrings, the nose rings, the dog-collar crucifixes, the gold tooth caps, the hair braids, he's just like you and me.

And even though he dresses a lot in women's undergarments and wears boas and sometimes comes to the games in pearls and women's fluffy hats and always talks about "experimenting" with homosexuality, I don't think he's homosexual because whenever I see him, like today, he's usually got two or three real pretty women hanging off him although he's not much to look at and, as we used to say in the Spelunkarium, has a face that would scare a bat.

I asked Mr. Barkley why Mr. Death wants to come off as so homosexual and so weird and Mr. Barkley said, "Are you serious? Look at how many ads he gets out of it! Kodak, Domino's, Nike. He's found the role of his life. He's got this image of a freak who is, like, one step from going off the ledge and all these companies want that dark-side image and so he makes millions out of it. The weirder he gets, the more salable he is. Until you showed up, he had the whole weirdo circus sideshow thing to himself."

I still felt a little sorry for Mr. Death, having to be something he's really not, and so I went into a bookstore and saw many books like the one I'm writing and I know one thing which is I hope mine has an exclamation point in the title. They all looked very exciting and informative, but I could only afford to buy one, so I bought *Death!: My Life as the Satan of Hoops!* (*As Told to Mitch Albom*) and found out all about him, and how he grew up in West Virginia without a mother, just like me, and never went to college, just like me, and is kind of an outcast, just like me. And so I went to find him and I did find him and I asked him if he'd sign my book for me, just as a show of friendship, I thought, and he knocked it out of my hand and said, "If I ain't ever *read* that piece of (s-word), why would I sign it, bitch?"

And I can only say I hope Mr. Reilly lets me read mine.

Mr. Soals called me in my room today and said, "Listen, pally, make you a deal. You sign with us and you don't have to wear our shoes. You can wear *your* wonderful old quote-unquote sentimental Keds. But you have to wear our shirts and warm-ups and hats and sunglasses, everything, all the time. Marketing says they can make this bullshit loyalty-to-the-dad thing play. It wouldn't be near the jing, but it won't suck."

"Would I have to tell other people to wear your shoes?"

"No, duh."

"Well, that's good, because how can I tell other people to wear your shoes when *I* don't even wear them?"

He buried his face in his hands. "Yes, it'd just be a little white lie. You never told a little white lie?"

"Yes, and I know I will suffer many years in the freezing Hades away from the center of the earth for it."

"What's a few more years when you're talking about all eternity?"

I told him sorry but no. And I'll tell you something else: The day I wear his shoes will be the day hell melts.

FEB. 10, NEWARK

Mr. Reggie Black, our very devout Christian leader, asked me to pray with him before the game tonight against the never-say-die San Antonios.

66

He took both my hands and we knelt, right there in the locker room. "Almighty Father," he began, "ruler of all You see, make our bodies strong tonight. Give us the courage to slay our enemies in Thine name. Let our aim be true and our will great. Father, grant me the chance to glorify You extra-special tonight with a whole grip a threes and show the peoples my mad hops, and please let Slo-Mo see how open I am on the spot-up and kick it back out so I can smoke that little bastard Avery Johnson. Provide for us and our families, Father. Let us do Your work in the kind of style and class which does You honor. Let our financial representatives be wise and clever in their dealings with the tricky Israelites. Let Mr. Epstein at 3M and Mr. Davidson at Chrysler understand how much help I could be to their current ad campaign. Heavenly Father, grant us a strong and sure victory tonight over athletes who do not love You anywhere near like we do, especially considering this is a TNT game. We praise You, Lord Jesus, and thank You for showing us Your neon light, constantly flashing 'salvation!' Help us win tonight and see what You can do about getting that paternity lawyer off my jock, okay? In Your power, honor, and glory we pray, amen!"

Mr. Reggie says he and God "got each other's backs, you know what I'm sayin'?" and that sounds like a very nice thing for both of them, I guess.

I was put in the game tonight underneath the basket at center, and I played seven minutes, and it didn't go all that well, or, as Mr. Death said, "You are now the single biggest pussy in this league, including Madonna."

It's just that I don't enjoy all the mean-spirited intentions and violence that go on under there. I scored only 2 points and that was when everybody fell down trying to knock me over and the ball fell into my hands and I simply dropped it in the hoop. And even that made people so, so angry!

"Dunk it, you (f-word)ing geek!" I heard someone yell.

"Why don't you jam it, you giant monkey?" another man said.

And even a mother with two small kids in the front row screamed at me that "a (f-word)ing moron can just drop it in." I'm surprised a mother could get that angry.

Plus, I got only one rebound, no fouls, no assists, a black eye, a split lip, and my left bicuspid knocked out.

Afterward Coach Jackson almost broke a vein in his forehead yelling at me. I was on the trainer's table and he lifted the bag of ice off my face and started talking to me, very, very quietly at first. He said, "Slo-Mo, I have meditated on this many mornings and I realize now what your problem is. You see, great athletes are about anger—*sports* is about anger—and you are not at all comfortable with your anger. To dunk, you must find some anger inside you and I'm going to help you find it, so help me God! To achieve greatness in sports, you must have an anger that needs to come exploding out of you every game! Michael Jordan, the greatest athlete sports has ever seen, is all about anger. Jordan was the most viciously angry athlete in history! I saw him reduce guys to blubbering messes with his viciousness— and that was in practice! There's no room for compassion in sports! There's no room for peace and centeredness in greatness! You need to find your inner Tyson, boy! You need to find the anger boiling inside you and

USE it! And if you don't have it, then trick yourself into it! Pretend the man guarding you just raped your wife and tortured your kids! Pretend he's doing it right in front of you! THEN GET OUT THERE AND DUNK THE (S-WORD) OUT OF IT! YOU EITHER START FINDING SOME (F-WORD)ING JORDAN INSIDE YOU OR I'LL SHIP YOUR HAPPY, SAPPY SEQUOIA ASS OUTTA HERE! IS THAT CLEAR, YOU PATHETIC SEVEN-FOOT-EIGHT MAHATMA GANDHI?"

I nodded yes. And when he walked out, slamming the door, Bruce whispered, "Insensitive brute."

FEB. 12, NEWARK

I got in more trouble with Coach Jackson today because I missed practice and he asked me why and I said the truth, which was, "You said it was a closed practice," and I only hope that he didn't hurt his knee when he broke his clipboard in half.

I'm sorry to be a big sourpuss, but it's been two weeks now since Mr. Matlock said he would look into where my dad Genghis Korn is, except I've heard nothing at all, but I suppose he's undercover and doing dangerous work and everything, so I know I have to be patient.

Besides, I think I'm starting to make some real friends here on the New Jerseys because for the first time, one of the fellas came by my room tonight. It was Mr. Flip Lowery, our surfing shooting guard.

He walked in with a half-finished bottle of Everclear in one hand and he was looking at my many cages of snakes and mice and he said, "Dude, it's like *Willard* in here!"

"Thanks," I said.

"Slo-Mo, I need, like, a favor."

"Sure, Mr. Lowery."

"Dude: Flip."

"Sure, Dude Flip."

"I want you to break my pinky."

He pulled a crowbar out from behind his back.

"Oh, well, that is very nice of you, Mr. Lowery, but I don't think that would be so right."

"Pleeeease, Slo," Mr. Lowery said. His eyes were very wide and also very bloodshot. "I'm losing it, man! My numbers are going down! I don't have much more room. If I get below 45 percent, I'm gonna lose almost a million dollars! Man, you gotta help me, Dude!"

I asked him why his pinky.

"Well, see, I've given it a lot of, like, thought, right, and I think the pinky on my shooting hand is one bone I have that I could break that won't really affect my daily life too much. I'll still be able to pick up things, eat, brush my teeth, sleep, surf, skateboard, screw, that kind of thing. But it'll still keep me out of, like, games! Perfect, right?"

"I can't, Mr. Flip."

"Pleeeeeease, Slo! Please!"

"Why don't you do it yourself?" I asked, because as much as I liked Mr. Flip, I really didn't want to break his pinky.

"I tried!" he said. "I keep flinching! I can't keep my pinky down long enough for me to hit it. See, as much as I try to trick myself, I know when it's gonna happen and I pull away at the last second. I've busted half the stuff in my house. I've tried it half-awake, I've tried it on 'shrooms, I've tried it high, I've tried it on Ecstacy, and now I've tried it drunk. Nothin' works."

"Well, you'd know when I'm gonna hit your pinky, too, wouldn't you?" I said.

"No, I'd sit here at the table and keep my eyes shut and you and I would just be talking and then, *wham*, you'd do it. Sweet, right?"

"I can't, Mr. Flip."

"Slo, there's a lot riding on this, dude. I know I'm not gonna last in this league. The more I play, the more these guys are learning my moves. I signed for next to nothing, Slo. A white shooter? Please. The NBA is the most racist organization in the world, Slo. Check the numbers. Check what white guys and black guys sign for with the exact same numbers, exact same conferences, Slo! White guys got no shot in this league. I got one million riding on this. Slo, listen to me, I got two kids and my wife's dork brother lives with us. If this doesn't work out, I gotta go into hole life with him! You wouldn't wish that on me, wouldya, Slo? Dude! Stuck in an office somewhere? Nine to five? That's ultra whack, dontcha think? Me?"

It did sound kinda bad, living in a hole all your life, so I sat and thought while Mr. Flip took a big guzzle from his bottle and I finally said I'd do it.

"Great!" he said.

He handed me the crowbar and sat down at the little table in my little room at the Newark Airport Ramada Hotel. I stood on the other side of it. He put his right hand under the edge of the table, but set his pinky on top. He sat a ways away from the table and took one last big gulp of his bottle and said, "Okay."

"Okay," I said. I was very nervous.

"Okay."

71

Mr. Lowery clenched his eyes.

"Okay, here goes," I said.

"No, dude!" he said, jumping up from the table. "You can't say, 'Okay, here goes!' If you say, 'Okay, here goes,' then I know it's coming!"

"Oh, sorry."

"You got to just, like, stand here and talk to me and then in the middle of a sentence, just WHAM! Got it?"

I asked him what I should talk about.

"Just whatever's goin' on in your mind. Anything. Just what you been doin' today, stuff like that."

"Okay," I said.

"Just talk to me," he said, closing his eyes.

"Well, I've got this really heavy crowbar in my hand and I'm about to smash your pinky with it and . . ."

"No, dude!" he said, jumping up again. But just as he jumped up, I was coming down with the crowbar and I guess because his eyes were closed he didn't realize I'd moved a foot to the left to get a better angle and he scared me and I lurched a little and he jumped forward and the crowbar caught him square in the nose, kinda hard. And that sent him spinning around the room, which isn't a good idea in my room, especially, and he landed on Zeke's cage—that's my bull snake—and Zeke bit him in the right gluteus, kinda hard. And that made him jump about three feet in the air with blood going everywhere and Zeke still stuck to his right gluteus and he jumped up on the bed he was so scared and jumped again and he gashed his head open on the fire sprinkler in the ceiling, kinda hard. And the water come on, soaking everything, including Mr. Flip's very nice leather jacket and, also, all my stuff.

And after I finally convinced Zeke to let go of his right gluteus, I had to put all my other snakes out in the hall to keep from getting soaked but that meant the guys from the ambulance wouldn't come any farther than fifty feet because of my pets, so I had to carry Mr. Flip on my shoulder because the blood dripping down into his eyes made it impossible for him to see and I accidentally caught his ear kinda hard on a picture frame.

After the ambulance left, I felt so bad the rest of the night, and I think Zeke did, too, until our trainer, Bruce, called from the hospital and said the doctors fixed up his broken nose, and stitched the gashed forehead and stitched the ear and iced his sore right gluteus and said he was in a whole lot of pain and he'd be out at least two weeks.

And that made me feel much better.

FEB. 13, NEWARK

I didn't play very good tonight, in fact, I actually didn't even play at all, and next to my name the score sheet after the game said only "DNP" and I asked Mr. Death what that meant and he said, "Dickless, Nutless, Pussy," and I can only say I'm sure glad they abbreviate it.

Mr. Mockmood wore a black headband tonight to protest the NBA's refusal to allow him to recognize the Muslims' holiday after the national anthem. Apparently he wants to read a passage out loud from the Qur'an after the national anthem, but the league won't let him. During the month of the Ramada, which is right now, he won't eat between sunup and sundown and is not allowed to have sex, either, and I'm wondering if I'm supposed to be doing this, too, as I live in a Ramada as well.

Anyway, this not eating must be very difficult for him, I'm sure, since, just by coincidence, Mr. Big County and Mr. Barkley have been ordering in steak sandwiches and pizza and eating them just after the morning practices and usually Mr. Big County will let out a big burp and say, "Well, I reckon that'll push a turd."

Mr. Mockmood has a little man bring him food after the game, but sometimes Mr. Barkley and Mr. Big County will find him and sit down and say, "Bless this food in the name of the Lord Jesus Christ" and Mr. Mockmood will yell in some foreign language and stand up and toss it in the trash and have his little man bring him some more because he cannot, by Muslim law, eat any food that has been offered up to anybody except Ali. And every time, Mr. Barkley will go, "Damn, Chris, we're sorry. We forgot about that rule."

This is not unusual, though, because Mr. Mockmood protests a lot as he is basically just always angry, which is why Coach Jackson likes him so much, I think. He wears black suits and a black knit cap at all times, even in the summer, to protest the USA—which he kiddingly calls "United Slaveship America"—and his knuckles have tattoos which spell out his "Slave 40862," although I don't think they're real. And he does not stand for the national anthem, calling the flag a false god, and he does not shake any player's hand after or before a game in protest against "this tyrannical Christian society" and he won't sign autographs for anybody because "only Ali shall be deified" and he has the television removed from our room in every hotel we go into because "it is the devil's instrument," and he refuses to come to Fan Photo Day as protest against "the evil capitalistic regime."

He explained all this to me one day at his mansion and I understood it much better then, especially when his servants gave me all the nice literature.

FEB. 14, NEWARK

Sometimes, dear reader, I feel like you are the only friend I have in the whole world.

See, I've waited a full sixteen and one-half days and I couldn't wait any more and I took the phone number of Mr. Matlock down from where it was taped up on my headboard, right above my pillow, and called him and they said there was no Mr. Matlock there but I recognized Mr. Matlock's voice and I am ashamed to say I raised my voice a little and I said, "No pun intended, but I *know* you are the man I spoke to the other day!"

And he said, "What?"

And I said, "Mr. Matlock, why aren't you telling the truth? You said you'd find my dad for me and that you'd get back to me and now you're pretending not to be yourself."

And Mr. Matlock said, "You mean you were serious? You really wanted to know where this Genghis Korn freak is, this schmo that only worked for us for, like, a cup of coffee? You really are this dope's kid?"

And I said proudly, "Yes!"

"Well, hell, why didn't you say so?"

And I almost cried with joy until he said . . .

"We'd have told you to (f-word) off right from the start!"

And he hung up.

And I stayed in bed the rest of the day and Lassie, my little bush snake, crawled up my pajama pants leg just for laughs but it still didn't cheer me up.

FEB. 16, NEWARK

Mr. Dalton, our very well dressed publicist, came into the locker room before the game and asked me how my One Point was and I said my One Point was shattered into a million pieces and he said, "Whoa!" and he ran out of the room so I guess he didn't want to bother me.

But that's how I felt. I was at the game but I wasn't really there. I was so down I couldn't even make a shot in warm-ups much less the game. I only took two shots and passed it the rest of the time and I actually wanted guys to elbow me in the gut and take my skin in the back and pinch and twist it when the ref wasn't looking and slam me in the back of the head going for a rebound, which they were only too happy to do, and we lost to the Miamis by 41 and I know Coach Jackson was unhappy with me because he said, "Mo, I believe in the reincarnation of souls. So I'm sure that in your next life, you will come back as something completely different and new from what you are now, which is a (F-WORD)ING PROFESSIONAL BASKETBALL PLAYER!"

And I thought to myself, "I hope not because I'm not all that excited about it in this life."

Coach Summers, our fine assistant coach, came up

to me and said, "Congratulations," and I said why and he said, "You got exactly one more rebound than a dead man," but that isn't much to brag about in my mind.

I saw Jinx in the hotel bar after the game and bought her the special ice teas that she likes, but I'm afraid I wasn't very good company. "What's wrong, sugar?" she said, rubbing my back.

And I told her and she gave me a hug. "You want me to come up to your room and make it better?"

And I asked how she could make it better. And she said, "Honey, believe me, Jacquanda can make it *better.*"

And I said okay, although I really didn't see how, and as we were leaving, Mr. Barkley grabbed my arm and whispered into my ear: "Lurch, just remember. This woman is the best in the league. She's won every suit she's tried."

And I thought this wouldn't be so bad, since I could use some nice clothes.

When we got to my room, me bicycling and her following in her car, I was so sad I just collapsed on the bed and I guess Ms. Jinx wanted to go to sleep, too, because she came out of the bathroom in just her undies and I wanted to look but I didn't think that'd be very polite. Still, she laid down next to me and started to rub my back again and I told her how much her friendship meant to me.

And she said, "What?"

And I said, "Well, it's just been very hard for me since I left the Spelunkarium and then to leave my only friends at Most Virgin Lady when I didn't really want to even though I don't really blame Mr. Lenny O'Connor for turning me pro and then to come to the

NBA where I have to move around so much and not see my snakes as much as I'd like and so many of the other fellas are mean to me, especially under the basket, and I miss Phyllis and I miss my dad even though I never met my dad and you're really the first person who has listened to me or really seems to care about me at all except for Mr. Lenny O'Connor, my agent, but he's usually at a meeting in the Bahamas. So I just want to thank you for being so kind to me."

And I'm ashamed to say that tears came to my eyes and it was not a manly thing to do in front of a woman and I know this because Ms. Jinx said she had to go to the bathroom to get some Kleenex and when she came back she was dressed again and I guess that meant she wasn't going to sleep over.

But she laid back down again and rubbed my hair until I fell asleep and then I guess she let herself out. I found out something else interesting about her, too. She's Jewish. I know it because when she was in my bathroom she accidentally dropped her rubber yarmulke in my trash can.

FEB. 17, WASHINGTON

In the bus today, Mr. Woody got us up to date on his goal, which is to "think off" as he says, which, unfortunately, he hasn't been able to do but then nobody else in history has, either, so he shouldn't feel bad.

Mr. Barkley asked him what he had tried so far.

"Oh, man, you name it," he said. "Porno movies. Porno mags. Phone sex. Man, this is *tough*."

"A man's gotta have a dream, bro," said Mr. Barkley.

"Yeah, so then I met some girls who *pose* for the porno mags and I got one of them to come back and just pose. But that didn't work. So then I got one of my phone sex girls to come to my *house* and talk in person. But that didn't work. And I even met a girl who'd been in one of the *movies*. Kitty Kanyon."

"I'm a huge fan of her work," said Mr. Barkley.

"And . . . ?" said Mr. Big County.

"Nothin'. Close a few times, but nothin'."

"And so what do you do with the fillies after a while when it don't work?" asked Mr. Big County.

"Whaddya mean?"

"When you've decided it's not gonna work, what do you and the girls do then?"

"Whaddya think we do? Needlepoint? We just knock like hell, man, whatchu think?"

"Bummer," said Mr. Flip.

"Well," said Mr. Barkley, "nothing great is ever easy."

"That's not true," said Mr. Woody. "Carmen Electra."

"Point made."

I took the bus over to the Ritz-Carlton tonight to see my agent, Mr. Lenny O'Connor, and he looked different to me somehow since I'd seen him last, which was quite a while ago, really, and it wasn't just that he kept pulling a new beeper off his belt and holding it to his ear to see if it was working and punching all the buttons to see if the sounds were still coming out all right.

And I said, "You look different."

And he said, "I ought to. I got a new nose, had my eyes done, and took my neck up. Do you like the suit? Zegna, baby! Only the best!"

We had a nice dinner and he said he's working on some big endorsement deals for me and did I need anything.

And I didn't want to be greedy, but I said I could use some money because the $200 I get a week he gives me doesn't really cover everything, plus I've got these huge hotel and plane bills coming from the New Jerseys.

"You big dope!" he said, still looking down at his new beeper. "You don't have to pay for any of those flights. The team covers everything. All your food, hotel, travel, and incidentals."

And that was a big load off my mind and he said it was good, because all my money is tied up still with the lawyers and investments and in accountants and, besides, he said he needed to borrow some of it against his future commissions for his nose, on account of he'd gone top-shelf, the Harrison Ford, although I'm not sure I'd trust an operation like that to a car dealership.

FEB. 18, WASHINGTON

Tonight, there was a man in a white shirt and black tie and thick black glasses and not a lot of hair who sat in a chair right behind our bench and constantly yelled very loudly so everybody could hear about the fact that I don't dunk.

I don't know what his name is, but the players call him "Mr. Limpet" because his voice sounds like a foghorn, but he does it nearly every night and he brings things to the game to make fun of me with, such as trumpets and kazoos, and he sings songs about me which aren't very nice at all. Tonight, he sang this song, which sounded exactly like "Row, Row, Row Your Boat," but had different words:

> Why, why, why won't Mo
> Dunk the stupid ball?
> Possibly, possibly, possibly cuz
> He doesn't know he's tall.

I don't think our owner, Mr. Trump, is all that fond of me, either. He's losing patience with me more each night. Coach Jackson has decided that there's no fighting it so he started me and played me most of the game at shooting guard, but my shooting is kinda bad right now and, actually, not even that good. Tonight, I made only five of twenty-one shots and we lost our eighth in a row and afterward Mr. Barkley asked me if I wanted some ice for my right arm but I said no thanks.

Some people think I'm in a slump, but I'm not, I'm just shooting badly. Mr. Stain kept asking me if there was anything about my shot that was different that was keeping it from going in the basket and I'm afraid I got a little short with him when I said, "I don't know the technicalities of it. I'm not a gynecologist or something."

But personally, I don't think I'm shooting so poorly because the defenses have figured out my favorite spots. Because I can hit my shot with two men and a class of kindergartners hanging off me. It's because I'm not happy without my friends or my dad and being so far above ground all the time and I'm not peaceful inside at my One Point which is the only way I can shoot with perfection.

"Forget your One Point!" Mr. Trump screamed at me, tonight, right in front of one of his beautiful nieces. "I'll tell you what point I'm worried about. Four *point* five million, that's the *point* I'm worried about."

One of the sportswriter gentlemen from New York wrote that I'm the "single biggest stiff in New Jersey since Jimmy Hoffa" and another one said I was "the only ninety-three-inch waste this side of Nell Carter's pants" but I don't think it's fair to compare me to other players when I'm just a rookie.

On the bench tonight, I was talking to Mr. Woody about my dad and he said, "Why you so messed up about not knowing who your dad is? Hell, I don't know who my dad is. I don't wanna know."

Then he looked down the bench and asked the guys, "How many of you know who your dad is?"

And only one out of the six sitting there knew and that was Mr. Flip.

"My dad tries to call me through my agent," Mr. Reggie Black said. "He keeps wanting to come to my Jesus Knows Best family meetings. Tryin' to cash in on my fame. The thing's only grossing 11 percent as it is!"

FEB. 19, MIAMI

A man from the players' union met with us today and it was very interesting to me although maybe not to the others because most of them were on their sell phones and answering their beepers most of the time.

The man was there to talk about safe sex and wearing condiments but none of the players wanted to talk about that, because, as Mr. Woody says, "Can't get no AIDS from screwing a girl 'less you doin' her on the bus station toilet!" And everybody said, "Really?" And Mr. Woody said, "Yeah, you don't have to be no Alvin Einstein to know that!"

And that was good to know, although the man said it wasn't true, but most of the guys believed Mr. Woody and not the man because, as Mr. Reggie Black says, "Woody talkin' about sex is like Oprah talkin' about hamsteaks."

But mostly what the fellas wanted to talk about, or "discuss," was the new deal the players made with the owners which, Woody said, "got stuck right up our shooters," which I can only say I'm glad I wasn't around then, as I'm a shooter myself.

"Look, now," said Mr. Reggie. "You guys hosed us on that deal. I been prayin' on this thing and it looks like I'm gonna have to get seriously tight over this thing. I may have to sell my red Benzo, man!"

"So what?" said Mr. Mockmood. "You got *eight* cars, gluttonous swine!"

"Yeah, but my Benzo is *fine!*" said Mr. Reggie.

Mr. Death complained that every time he leaves the arena, there's so many kids who want his autograph that it takes him an extra two or three minutes to drive out.

"What are you talking about, Death?" said Mr. Barkley. "You hardly ever sign."

"Yeah, but the (f-word)in' peeps get fingerprints on the windows, man!"

Before he left, the man handed out the timetable for discussing the next contract, plus the major issues involved, but as everybody was walking out reading it, Mr. Death crumpled it up without even looking at it. "All bull(s-word), man," he said.

I don't think Mr. Death is a big reader.

Guess what? Mr. Stain came up to me after practice and said that Mr. Barkley was telling him about my dad and how I can't find him and said he could help.

And I said how could he help.

And Mr. Stain said, "Duh?"

And I said, more slowly, "How—can—you—help—me?"

And Mr. Stain took his rumpled old Yankees hat off and then put it back on and said, "Well, I'm a sportswriter and I could write a sports story about how you're looking for your father. Then the newspaper would *print* my story in the newspaper and people would *read* the story *in* the newspaper and perhaps the Associated Press would pick it up and run it in other *newspapers* around the country and maybe, somewhere out there, your *father* would read it *in* a newspaper and contact you on the *telephone* and then you would, therefore, have *found* your father, get it?"

I was so excited I picked up Mr. Stain and held him over my head and started spinning him and he nearly swallowed his Tootsie Pop stick.

FEB. 20, MIAMI

I called Mr. Stain in his room this morning and asked him if he wrote the story in the *Newark Star-Ledger* newspaper and had it come out yet and had the

A & P picked it up and delivered it all over the country and had he heard anything from my father.

"I don't think so," Mr. Stain said.

"Why not?"

"BECAUSE IT'S FIVE-THIRTY IN THE MORN-ING!" he mentioned, before hanging up.

I guess I'll ask him about it later in the day.

Mr. Flip is very worried about his health.

It's getting better.

Coach Jackson told him if he keeps improving, he'll have him back on the court very soon.

When Mr. Lowery came out of the meeting, he looked like Coach Jackson had just cut him.

And Mr. Barkley came up and put his arm around his shoulder and said, "Cheer up, dude. Maybe you'll get hepatitis D."

The Nikey man, Mr. Barter Soals, does not leave me alone which doesn't make me very comfortable because not to be unkind, but I'm not sure I'm all that crazy about him. For one thing, he's always trying to talk to me and for another thing, when anybody else wants to talk to him, he always goes, "Hey, pally, can't you see we're talkin' here?" He's divorced to his ex-wife in Los Angeles and as part of the divorce settlement, they couldn't decide who got to keep their little dog, Pepe, and so every week, they fly poor Pepe all the way across the country and that is cruel and inhuman especially as, Mr. Barkley says, "He doesn't even get miles."

Mr. Soals came into the locker room before our loss to the Miamis tonight.

"Pally, you're making a giant sucking noise every time you go on the court lately and yet we *still* want you. Doesn't that mean anything to you?"

"I have a pair of shoes," I said.

"Fine, we'll just tape the swoosh on," he says.

"The swoosh?" I ask. "What is the swoosh?"

"Our *logo*," he said, getting kinda mad at me "The big quote-unquote check mark? You see everywhere? On shoes and shirts and buildings and jogging bras and *the NBA basketball?*"

I told him I was sorry but I hadn't noticed a swoosh.

And then his allergies must have affected him because he began rubbing his face again and finally he pounded his hands angrily on the shelf in my locker and said, "You know what? Talkin' to you is a complete exercise in futility!"

And I appreciated it, although I've never been to Futility.

Even though I'm the youngest player in the history of the NBA, I think I'm becoming a spokesman for the team because tonight the sportswriter gentlemen asked me what was wrong with the team lately because we've lost so many lately and I said that we'll improve soon. "We just have to maintain our consistency," and they all of them, every one, wrote it down.

FEB. 22, NEWARK

I don't mean to be such a complainer, but I have to tell you that I am so lonely and sad and now I know why cave crickets don't chirp because they just don't see any end to the darkness.

For one thing, though the people and accommodations are very nice in my room here at the Newark Airport Ramada Hotel, and I can watch previews of almost any movie I want for free, there are a few problems. For one thing, my feet hang off the bed and so I put Zeke's cage at the end of it and put a pillow on that and rest them on that, but I must've broken the screentop with my big feet and Zeke got out and when I woke up, he was wrapped around the ceiling sprinkler and very upset.

And I still haven't heard from Mr. Stain to know if he wrote that story about me and my father because he's never home and his wife always just says, "I think he went out to look for his liver," but I guess I should be more patient because everybody has their own searches in life.

And I think because I feel an emptiness in my One Point, my shot continues to be a little off. Last night, against the bitterly fought Orlandos, I made only two shots out of seventeen and I am down to an average of only 7.2 points per game now and, of course, 0.1 rebounds, although Death told me that I shouldn't worry because even if I get kicked out of the NBA any day soon, I would still dominate the Seven-Foot-Seven-and-Over YMCA leagues.

Today, two of Mr. Mockmood's representatives were waiting for him to get out of the shower when Mr. Big County turned to them a little and said, "Hand me the dee ana fore, will ya?"

And they said politely, "I'm sorry?"

"Well, at least let the prubanny before you guys go."

And the one said, again politely, "Sorry, sorry, I just didn't quite get that. What did you say?"

And Mr. Big County became very angry.

"Ohhh, I get it!" he said. "It's because I'm southern, right? The big stupid redneck doesn't speak clearly enough for you sophisticated northerners, right? I don't speak your cool city talk so I'm just a big country cracker, right? Not *worthy* to speak to you suave black guys!"

And the two men began apologizing and stammering and saying they were so sorry and no, they didn't think he was dumb at all.

But Mr. Big County wouldn't listen and just went into the accent of a big dumb dopey guy and said, "Duh, hyuck, yeah, George, we'll get a faaarm and we'll have raaaabits and—"

And they were terribly embarrassed and they said they didn't mean anything by it and whatever it was he wanted they would gladly get.

And he said, "When?"

I thought I was going to pee my pants.

FEB. 23, NEWARK

The Orlandos' bus was outside the Meadowlands arena today when we got out of practice and Mr. Lowery asked the driver how much the bus weighed.

"About forty thousand pounds," said the driver.

Mr. Barkley was standing there at the time and when he turned around, he said to Mr. Lowery, "I like your thinking. True, you'd pretty much have to amputate all your toes, but we could fit you with a special shoe and you could kick field goals for the New Orleans Saints."

And I thought that was a very good idea and, besides, maybe Mr. Lowery would like that career better.

FEB. 24, NEWARK

Tonight, I missed all seventeen of my shots I took in the first half and when I went to the locker room, somebody must've accidentally locked the door, so I could not go in with my teammates like I usually do. I thought the mood in there would be kinda grouchy, since we were behind by 29 points but I heard lots of laughing, so I felt a little better.

So then I walked back toward the court and stood in the tunnel and saw something that made my heart swell up like the Indonesian moccasin at mating time.

What I saw was the Spinning Stankowskis, a family of four members who do the most amazing spinning and twirling and throwing of each other that you've ever seen. The announcer said it was their thirteenth straight year appearing at halftimes around the league, but the audience still seemed very excited at their performance. What happens is, Mr. Stankowski sits in a kind of vinyl chair tipped backward and spins his kids crazily around on his feet, round and round and round, like a merry-go-round that is getting way too much electricity. And then, after that, the whole family joins hands in a line and they all start spinning and pretty soon the two kids' feet are completely off the ground and are going around like a whirlybird. Sometimes Mr.

Stankowski gets on the cushion and sends each of his family members flipping off his feet for double and triple and quadruple flips and landing them back on his feet, all of which is pretty amazing because Mrs. Stankowski does not look all that light to me and the son, who looks to be about fourteen, is not that small either and looks like he's not helping very much. But the girl is very slender and beautiful with a blond ponytail and blue eyes and skin the color of a fresh new tulip and she seems to be about my age and this is what has given me a funny feeling in the places Bruce works so hard on.

And when they were done the crowd seemed very moved by them and gave them a huge ovation but as they came off the floor I could see the Stankowski family were unhappy with each other and I could hear it, too, because Mr. Stankowski said to Mrs. Stankowski out of the side of his mouth, "You think you could mix in a cottage cheese plate once in a while? Christ, it's like spinning an Amana."

But I don't think Mrs. Stankowski could hear him, because she was growling at the boy, "Maybe if you cut back to a pack a day, you'd be able to finish that trick, you little hood." And he replied to his mother, "Bite me, bitch." And behind them walked the lovely daughter who seemed to have a very sad expression on her face. And I was standing off to the side so she didn't see me, but I wanted to say something to her because I felt we were both people who had to put on a happy face for all the cameras and the people but underneath we're very sad people actually, but she slipped by and I was about to say something when Coach Jackson threw a basketball off the back of my head although I'm sure it just slipped.

The paper this morning said that my 0-for-17 the other night made me the first-ever New Jersey Nyet. I don't get it, but I don't think it's good.

Mr. Death gave me very much help today in explaining what is needed in the NBA in terms of "lifestyle," as he said. "What you need is an entourage."

And I said, "Well, I don't even have a driver's license," because I was thinking why buy a new car when you can't even drive?

And he looked at me for a long time and finally said, "No, no. What I'm sayin' is, someone in your position, a future star of this league, you need people *around* you, man, you need people who got your back. You need a driver, and a bodyguard, and assistants. All the big superstars have them. Iverson has two. Shaq has four. Michael had six!"

"Oh, but Doorians aren't allowed to drive," I said.

"Exactly. But they can ride."

"No."

"You can't even ride in a car?"

"You're not supposed to."

"Well, how come you're always on the team bus? And the team plane?"

"The Elder gave me a special permission for anything that involves the team. Otherwise, I'm on my Schwinn. I really don't mind it. A lot of people talk to me on the New Jersey Turn Pike."

He rubbed his forehead some more. "Man, you a trip."

This afternoon, Coach Jackson and Mr. Barkley and Mr. Trump, and another of Mr. Trump's really very beautiful nieces, and our assistant coaches all joined me in my room at the Newark Airport Ramada Hotel, although it was difficult to find a place to sit because of my extensive collection of snakes in their glass tanks everywhere so everybody just stood, except for the niece who screamed and waited in the limousine.

And Coach Jackson said to me, "Maurice, we're very concerned about you. I can see your aura and it is very weak right now. I'd say your aura is about the weakest aura in the whole goddamn league if you want to know the truth of it."

And Mr. Barkley said to him, "Coach, that's not exactly true. Maurice only sucks in games where they've played the national anthem beforehand."

And Coach Jackson said, "We're all here this morning to ask if there's *anything* we can do to help you play the kind of basketball we know you can play."

"Like," added Mr. Barkley, "for instance, send your Herman Munster ass to Rockford in the CBA for a month."

"Charles only kids because he loves," said Coach Jackson, stroking his beard. "But know this: One finger alone cannot lift a single pebble. We must all be in this together. Is there something we can do or say or discuss with you that would help?"

And since they asked I told them how lonely I was and how I really didn't have any family and I really didn't have many friends yet and would it be at all possible for them to send for Microchip?

And they all said, "Who?"

And so after a long explanation about my very good friend, Microchip, they still didn't seem very excited about it and they said where could they find him and I said he was just a senior at Most Virgin Lady, and had been cut from the team when I left because of Coach DeMeret being so mad at him not watching out for me better and could probably get away for a while if he could think of something to tell his parents and turn pro which has always been his wide-awake dream, although not his parents', and come and be a New Jersey with me and not be very expensive on top of it.

And Mr. Trump said, "Four point five million and I gotta buy the valet, too?"

FEB. 26, INDIANAPOLIS

I tried something today I've never tried before—room service! I've never tried it before today because before today I was always the roommate of Mr. Mockmood and if you were to try to order room service it would take you fifteen minutes to get his security system untangled from the doorknob and the room service waiter would've just left it outside the door, which is what they do when Mr. Mockmood orders it, and every time, either one of the other fellas comes out and either steals it because they dislike Mr. Mockmood so much or sprays it with shaving cream or substitutes the ice tea for urine, although they could just *take* the ice tea if they were that thirsty.

But with Mr. Mockmood back home in New Jersey serving a one-game suspension for holding up the flag of the nation of Serious during the national anthem, I got to order apple pie à la mode and, since it was such a special occasion, I asked them to put ice cream on top and they had to ask their manager but they finally agreed.

And guess who knocked on my door while I was waiting for it but Jinx! When she walked in, though, I didn't say anything because I didn't want to embarrass her but she must be very forgetful sometimes because she was only wearing a slip and not the dress, but maybe she was in a terrible hurry to come over from her hotel room but I don't see how since her room was in the same hotel!

Still, she smelled so good and looked very good, too, and it was lucky that Mr. Mockmood was not there and she said she knew that he wouldn't be on the trip and, in fact, "that's one of the reasons I came, sugar," she said. And that made me realize what a great fan she is of our team to know that we would need extra rooters without our excellent point guard, Mr. Mockmood.

And so we talked for a while and watched TV as she was giving me a very good leg rub and how I knew it was a good leg rub was because it's the same kind of leg rub that Bruce, our trainer, gives me at the arena. Jinx said rubs were her specialty, and something about her started making me think of Lisa Stankowski of the Spinning Stankowskis. And so I told her that she was making me think of Lisa Stankowski of the Spinning Stankowskis and she dropped my leg immediately, which meant she wanted to listen to more, so I told her all about Lisa and my love for her.

And she said, "Well, this whole day was a complete waste of makeup," and she was getting her purse and getting ready to go as apparently she really was in a hurry to go to the next place or maybe go find her dress and she kinda sighed and turned back around and said, "Why don't you just ask her out?"

And I explained that I was too scared for one thing and that her dad glared at me the one time I saw them for another thing and also that I wasn't sure she liked me back for a last thing.

"How will I be able to know when someone is interested in me?" I asked.

And as she was walking out the door, she took a look at herself in the mirror in the slip and the bright, red lipstick and the hair all done up and she sighed and said, "Honey, I got *no* clue."

By the way, I didn't play at all tonight, so I wonder if Coach Jackson has given up on me. I don't blame him really. I wouldn't play me either when I'm this unhappy because I can't shoot when I'm unhappy. And I really don't know why anybody would like this NBA life, always traveling and being away from your loved ones, if you have any, and everybody criticizing each other in the back all the time and so I asked Mr. Barkley why guys want to be part of the NBA so badly and he said, "Because as soon as you leave, you're JAG."

And I said, "What's JAG?"

And he said, "Just Another Guy."

I keep trying to make friends with Mr. Death because I know he's not as mean and nasty as he looks and tonight I made a little progress. After the game, he snuck up to me with a letter and asked if I'd read it to him because he said he forgot his reading glasses although I've never actually seen his reading glasses. I was surprised he cares about a letter because he gets a lot of mail in his locker and usually just holds them up to the light to check for dirty photos and then throws it straight into the trash can. Most of the players do that, throw away most of their mail without even looking at it, unless somebody sends them a birthday cake. When that happens, they do what is a time-honored tradition even if it doesn't sound very nice and that is to set it in the middle of the shower and all pee on it and one time, while they were doing it, Mr. Big County said, "Dear fans, thanks so much for your thoughtful gift. The whole team really carved into it."

But this letter was just some legal mumbo jumbo about a charity that didn't make sense to me, but I read it to him anyway.

"Dear Mr. Dedman,
    Pursuant to California civil code C645090, child support malfeasance and neglect, we have no choice but to . . ."

"—all right, all right," he said, ripping the letter out of my hand. "Mind your own (f-word)in' business."

FEB. 27, NEWARK

I can't wait to tell you the news and here it is! Microchip will be here soon! The management of the New Jerseys has agreed to sign him to a ten-day contract! And that is all I can write tonight because I have to clean my room and I've arranged for Microchip to have the room next to me and I even made a huge banner besides which reads, "Welcome, Microchip!"

And I hung it out under the Newark Airport Ramada Hotel sign, which many of the employees were amazed that I could reach. And the employees seemed very excited, too, that Microchip is coming, although one of them, Angel, said, "I can't believe it! Bill Gates! Here!"

Many of my teammates are very interested as to why I don't eat at the fast-food chain restaurant McDonald's and never have in my whole life. I told them because I only eat what comes up from the center of the earth, nearest to God, such as vegetables and minerals and stuff.

"But McDonald's is the dadgum *center* of America, hoss," said Mr. Big County.

"Right," said Mr. Barkley, "in every American town, there is at least one McDonald's. In fact, do you realize there's almost twenty-five thousand McDonald's in over one hundred countries? It's the one thing that holds all of God's people together."

And Mr. Death looked at me and said, "What are you, a (f-word)in' Communist?"

"McDonald's represents all that is evil with the American way of life," said Mr. Mockmood angrily. "Grease-laden corpulent gluttony, nutritionless garbage served up with plastic pollutants by exploited minority workers forced to live below the poverty line."

"And?" said Mr. Woody.

"Ah, Chris, you just got the red-ass cuz they ain't come out with the McYak yet," said Mr. Big County.

"I would only step on the grounds of a McDonald's to tear down the American flag hanging there and burn it," said Mr. Mockmood.

"You touch our flag, diaperhead, and I'll bury you in it," said Mr. Big County.

"I will gladly die a hero if it meant slaying a rotund Satan such as you!"

"What are you gonna do, hoss, smoke a goat and throw it at me?" said Mr. Big County.

Right then, a fight broke out. I turned away from it because I didn't want them to crush my tofu sticks, but what happened is Mr. Mockmood snapped the silver crescent moon off the necklace he bought in the nation of Serious and heaved it at Mr. Big County, who ducked, and it hit Mr. Lowery right in the neck. It was still stuck there when I looked up, kinda sitting there, wiggling and bleeding like crazy.

And Mr. Lowery was in serious pain and bleeding more than somewhat and Mr. Barkley said, "Some guys get all the breaks."

Today, Mr. Woody came in all excited, saying, "Yo, my new issue of *Cavern* just came," and everybody ran to his side to see it, especially me, but it was not at *all* the kind of caverns I was hoping it was going to be about.

"Hey, Wood," Mr. Barkley said to Mr. Woody, "haven't I seen you out with that girl?"

"That's Turquoise!" Mr. Woody said. "I played bag and shaft with her!"

"Bag and shaft?" Mr. Barkley asked.

"Yeah, you get a party goin' with a buncha couples and get a little loose, you know, and one of the women chooses one of the guys and makes him expose one square inch of skin at his fly and she has to guess whether it's the bag or the shaft."

This seemed to impress a whole lot of the players

because there was a whole lot of hooting, except for Mr. Big County, who said, "Hell, where I come from, that's a damn family reunion."

FEB. 28, NEWARK

Today, a very terrible thing happened, which is that as I was riding my Schwinn with the knobby tires along the New Jersey State Turn Pike, two men in a red and black Range Rover ran me off the side of the road into a cement culvert ditch and then robbed me of everything in my wallet, which included twenty-seven dollars plus my WheyStation bonus card from Whey to Go, which was very bad because it had nine punches on it and all I needed was one more for a free bulgurburger. Plus, they cut the tires, which were brand-new knobbies, and kicked in my spokes besides.

It was a very horrible thing and also humiliating because they laughed as they were going through my wallet because there really wasn't much in it as Mr. Lenny O'Connor, or, as he's asked me to call him lately, Y. Leonard O'Connor, has not sent me much money lately, and one of them even said, "Bitch, you oughta be muggin' us!" and they drove off laughing.

I will never forget how meanly they treated me and I'm only sorry they were wearing brightly colored hockey masks as I would've liked to remember their faces for all time. But I don't think it will be hard to find them because I'll just have Mr. Stain check through all the NHL programs until I recognize them.

Anyway, I tried to flag someone down on the New Jersey Turn Pike but apparently visibility must be very poor there because nobody picked me up and so I had to walk to the game and didn't arrive until the first quarter and I was fined $5,000, which I don't have and will have to ask Mr. Y. Leonard O'Connor for a loan if I can reach him by either of his new sell phone numbers.

After the game, Mr. Death was asking me why I was late and I told him and he said, "See, I told you! You need a bodyguard, fool! You need a driver to at least drive alongside you as you ride! You need a posse to watch your back, boy. You're not going to last long in this league without them. You're too big a name!"

And I had to finally agree with him, but as I told him, where do you find these kind of people and he said, "I can hook you up, bro." And I agreed to meet him at the wonderful Newark Airport Ramada Hotel coffee shop the next morning, although they serve much more than just coffee.

The doctors informed Mr. Lowery that the silver crescent moon was rusty and unclean, too, and Mr. Lowery will have to get lots of shots and miss at least two weeks of the season.

We all called with our congratulations.

MAR. 1, NEWARK

I'm very excited and I'll tell you why and it's because this morning I met my new entourages!

Mr. Death introduced me to them and they seem like wonderful guys although it's kinda hard to understand them because they use words which I don't really understand like "fly" when they don't mean fly and "down" when they don't mean down and "you know what I'm sayin' " when I really *don't* know what they're sayin', but that is okay as Mr. Death says it's important for security people to have their own secret code.

They are Mr. T-Bone Crip, who is my head entourage, and Mr. Li'l T-Bone Crip, his brother, who will be my driver, and Mr. Doggy $tyle Crip, which is actually, legally spelled like that, he said, with a "$" instead of an "S," who will be my bodyguard, and, of course, Doc Star Crip, my scheduler. I think I got a good deal, too, as I will pay them only $50,000 each for the season, although Mr. T-Bone, as my head entourage, gets $100,000, but that is still much less than the $3 million I understand Mr. Shaq pays. I didn't think I could pay all that but they explained to me that my agent, Mr. Y. Leonard O'Connor, *has* to give me whatever money I need and that it doesn't all *have* to go into the Christmas Club account he manages for me now at his bank in Las Vegas. And so I felt good about that because the Newark Airport Ramada Hotel is starting to ask when I'm going to pay the bill.

Another reason I feel good is that my entourages are all members of Mr. Death's "family," as he says— "We all Crips," Mr. Li'l T-Bone Crip said—and I think that is so nice when families stay close, because I don't really have any family and that's the thing I miss the most. We will be a real family together! They gave me all their sell phone numbers, and times when I can't call them, and so, as Death said, "We all really in bizness now."

And they said they need to begin getting some office supplies and begin setting things up and I will begin paying them immediately even though they won't start for two weeks.

"Because you have to get me all set up, right?"

And Mr. Doggy $tyle said, "Oh, you set up already."

And that's a good feeling.

Just now, my old friend Microchip arrived! He looked almost the same except his glasses were real big and black and thick now but he had on what he always has on which is the warm-up of the Los Angeleses' Magic Johnson that he stole out of the baggage compartment of a bus outside McNichols Arena and which is miles too big for him but Mr. Magic is Microchip's favorite player by far and so he honored him by stealing his stuff.

I picked him—Microchip, not Mr. Magic—up on my new Schwinn with the knobby wheels and put him in a cab and I pedaled in front of it and soon we were at the Newark Airport Ramada Hotel and we even have a connecting door!

Microchip seemed really excited. "Yo, Stumpy, are you buggin'? Cuz I'm buggin'!" But he didn't really mean "buggin' " in the way I mean it, because, in a way, I'm always "buggin' " because my snakes do enjoy bugs so much. He always calls me "Stumpy." "The N-damn-BA, you big crazy two-iron!!" And he repeated this over and jumped around and knocked Phoebe, my rattler, onto the floor and then jumped up into my arms so high that he almost knocked me over into the butterfly tank and screamed, "What the HELL?!?" and "It's goddamn Mutual of Omaha in here!"

Which is too bad because I was hoping to put a few cages in his room.

And after we got all the guys put back in their cages

safely, he looked around and then he said, "Man, this team is seriously Wal-Martin' your butt, stickin' you in this toxic cracker box no-tell hotel, huh? I mean, what, all the youth hostels booked?"

But I explained to him that I stay in the Ramada because I like it and it's the first hotel I've ever stayed in and the people who work in the bright red Ramada uniform are so nice for the most part, although maybe it's because I clean my own room when I'm not on the road because I don't want them kicking over any cages. And I also explained that the New Jerseys don't pay for anything.

And Microchip looked very depressed and said, "You are, without a doubt, the biggest Gomer in the history of Gomers."

And then his frown turned into a huge grin. "And I love ya!" and he jumped up and kissed me on the cheek and started bouncing from bed to bed in his room again and screaming about the NBA.

I forgot what a lively little guy he is.

MAR. 2, NEWARK

At the shootaround today, I introduced Microchip to all the fellas and they seemed to like him okay although many of them mentioned his height, which is only 5-4, and Death said, "Man, I crap bigger than you."

Mr. Woody took the opportunity to inform us that his mission is continuing to come up dry.

We all comforted him.

"I been through everything," Mr. Woody sighed. "I've had girls do each other in front of me. I've had couples do it front of me. I've had triplets do it front of me. I've had girls give me phantom blow jobs. Nothin' works."

"And what do you do with all these freaks when it doesn't work?" asked Mr. Barkley.

"We quilt, whaddya think?" said Mr. Woody glumly. "I got to just (f-word) 'em. That's it."

"Bummer," said Mr. Lowery.

"Well, I ain't tryin' to come off more Catholic than the pope here, but maybe that's your problem," said Mr. Big County. "Maybe you got to lay off the filly for a while, hoss, and then you'll be horny enough to screw the crack a dawn."

Mr. Woody considered that proposal for a long time and finally his face brightened.

"Okay," he said, "I'll try it. From now on, I'm going cold turkey. I'm gonna get no pussy! I'm gonna make Slo-Mo here look like (f-word)in' Alberto Tomba."

I said thanks.

Unfortunately, neither Microchip nor I got into the game, but Microchip still seemed very excited, although most of the time he watched with a towel sort of hanging over his face or he'd use the towel to wipe his face, especially whenever the camera took shots of the bench, and when anybody asked him why, he said, "Allergies."

I have noticed this before because New Jersey is a very bad place for allergies on account of it's the Garden State.

———

I don't know what my entourages' old jobs were but they must not have been very hard ones because even though they're down to their last two weeks, I've seen them hanging around ever since with Mr. Death. They were very well treated, too, because they talked about having Crystal Meth and Coke and that's nice that their boss let them have all the pop they wanted.

"Do you work nights?" I asked Mr. Doggy $tyle.

"Oh, most definitely," he said.

MAR. 3, NEWARK

I now understand why Microchip hides his face and that's because Microchip's parents don't know he's here.

He told them he was in Boulder studying political science and working on a thesis: "America's Systematic Rape and Branding of the Black Cowboy." He figured out a way to have all his calls sent to a mailbox he bought at a Mailboxes, Etc., and I would like to see a mailbox like that, but he's afraid his parents might somehow find out he's in the league. "I probably got nothin' to freak about," he says. "My parents think Ahmad Rashad is the national day of atonement."

But I think Microchip will be a big star now that he has joined me and my teammates with the New Jerseys. Microchip is one of the best passers of the basketball I've ever seen. In our single half-season at Most Virgin Lady, he averaged over twenty assists per game. Father DeMeret said, "Yeah, but a trained ferret could pass the ball to you and get twenty assists per night," but that is not true. As Microchip always says about himself,

"I could get the rock to a Pygmy in a phone booth from across the street with the Shriners parade going through."

I agree wholeheartedly and, in fact, I expect Microchip to begin leading the NBA in assists. But if he does this, then his parents will find out although Microchip only says, "Screw they iambic-pentameter-countin', butterfly-mountin', Fulbright-fellowship-winnin', sorority-pinnin', library-ass, Günter-Grass, tall-fat-granday, think-how-I-say selves. I got my own life."

And he said this with a big gulp and a look at his shoes, so I am quite sure he believes it.

Today, Mr. Barkley said I was becoming such a cult figure in New York that I should come out with my own rap CD. He said I should call it "Slo-Mo' Money" or "Mo' Betta." "And you're so skinny they could put your picture on the side," he said, but I think he was merely kidding.

MAR. 4, NEWARK

It's so good to have Microchip back I am already feeling better, although he isn't really getting to practice much or play at all. In fact, today before our game with the Charlottes, Coach Jackson had a special practice walk-through, except he had Microchip and I do nothing but fold towels off to the side, and Microchip asked Coach Jackson, privately, how this is helping our basketball and he said it was a Zen exercise. "It's like wax on, wax off," he said. "Only towel on, towel off."

I'm worried that if Microchip never gets a chance, he can't show them what a wonderful little player he is and his ten days will expire and he will have left Most Virgin Lady for nothing and that would be a real shame although it's not like he was really studying.

After practice, we went to McDonald's and he did what he has done many times before, which is try to get me to eat a Large Mac and I said no, I had packed a dozen or so wheat germ cakes, and he said what he usually said, which was, "Only two people in the world eat that crap—you and Richard Simmons—and neither of you never gonna get any pussy."

I played a little tonight in our loss to the rigorous Charlottes, 105–89, but I couldn't shoot very well because I felt so bad for Microchip, who sat the bench again. In fact, I made only one shot out of thirteen and missed all three of my free throws and was booed pretty loudly by the crowd, although I notice their hating me doesn't keep them from asking me for my autograph, jersey, wristbands, socks, and shoes when I come off the court.

After the game, Mr. Harley the Stain asked Coach Jackson what was up with his new player, David "Microchip" Lawrence, and Coach Jackson said, "He was supposed to come here and make Slo-Mo happy. I guess it's working. The big stiff actually made a shot tonight, didn't he?"

And I'd make more where that came from if only he'd let me and Microchip play *together*.

And then Mr. Trump, our owner, approached me and asked me if I was trying to ruin his life and I said no and he said well I am doing a wonderful imitation of it.

Today, Microchip asked if he and I could talk to the coaching staff after shootaround and they agreed and we went in there and Microchip explained to them how things work best with us. "See," he told Coach Jackson today, "I got the owner's manual on Mo on account of I invented his Eiffel Tower ass."

He explained to them that I do much better if I never have to go underneath because "all that wresslin' under there just shakes Bambi up. He ain't no killa, he's pure vanilla! You gotta think of him as like a really tall Gandhi. Don't think Mr. T, think Mr. Rogers."

He explained that I have four or five spots that I can shoot from, though I like my favorite from the top of the key and he explained that they should just let me shoot from there because I'll make most of them and that will mean the centers in the league will have to come out top to try and stop it and when that happens, I can just pass the ball underneath to Mr. Barkley, who will be able to score underneath like he's locked alone in a gym. In fact, Mr. Barkley, who was standing there, said, "Yo, if I can play every night without centers in the middle, my next contract will have to include South Carolina and parts of Georgia."

And Microchip also explained to them that they need to start Microchip himself at the point guard instead of Mr. Mockmood on account of (a) "Helen damn Keller can see that not one guy on the team can stand Mockmood's camel-eatin' ass" and (b) "All these players are takin' an extra dribble or two just so Mockmood doesn't get an assist from the official scorer and that gives the defender time to put the glove on him again" and (c) "This team doesn't need a shooting point guard, they need someone who understands how to get the ball to Stumpy here or fake like he's getting the ball to Stumpy and drive the lane for a pass or a little bust-out 'J.' Lemme loose and I'll be servin' up mo' dishes than Martha Stewart," he said.

He also mentioned that Microchip and I work very well together, on account of all those days and nights practicing just the two of us, on pick and rolls and backcourt screens and backdoor layups and, of course, "our famous Civ'lization-Endin', Mind-Bendin', Poster-Makin', Backboard-Breakin', One-Hand Scoop, Alley-Palley-Oooop Master Slam Jam," as Microchip named it, which really is exciting because you wouldn't believe how high Microchip can jump for a little guy when he's dunking. "They ain't never ready for it," says Microchip. "The big guy oopin' to the little guy! Rivers flowin' uphill! Sun settin' in the east! Yo, the whole place buggin'!"

Coach Jackson stroked his beard the whole time and when it was time to talk, he said, "Take a hike, grasshopper."

Coach didn't play either of us tonight in our loss to the always-ready Washingtons, 120–103. Also, Mr. Limpet was there and he was really on my face the whole night.

In fact, at one point, he started a chant that must've gone on for two minutes. It went:

"Geek! Wimp!
Dork and Punk!

Fin-ster-nick

Cannot Dunk!"

That was very embarrassing, but what he did after that was worse. He read passages from the Door'an, the gospel of all Inner Doorians, and the way he read them is not really the way you're supposed to read them and people laughed at things which are not supposed to be funny at all and in fact are very holy. Like he read from our Commandments of the Cave, which were sent up from God Himself many, many fissures ago:

"Thou shalt not covet the surface nor the dwellers of the surface!" he yelled at the top of his lungs during a time-out. "For remember the sun is the eye of the devil!" And then he started coating himself with sun-block and holding up a forty-watt lightbulb and making like it was burning his skin off.

He went on. "Thou shalt not eat the flesh of the surface beasts, such as the cow and the pig, who do not grow up from the heavenly dirt and are evil!" And then he took out a hamburger and started pretending like the hamburger was trying to tear at his throat. "In the name of Mayor McCheese, I beseech you!"

And, "Thou shalt not kill the winged bat, for it is holy and pure and God's eyes in the sacred darkness!" And then he put on a Batman mask and started flapping his arms and screaming, "To the batcave for the ten o'clock service!"

And then he yelled, "But does it say, 'Thou Shalt Not Dunk'? No, it does not! So, why, why, why won't you dunk? Do you think you're still in a cave? Are you afraid of bumping your little head? This ceiling is four hundred feet high, Slo-Mo! I promise you, you won't hurt your eraser head! If you do, we'll rub bat guano on it and make it all better!"

And everybody laughed at that, even guys on my bench and all three refs.

If this man doesn't stop it, I'm going to start thinking about getting angry.

MAR. 6, NEWARK

I think Coach Jackson is very wise and centered and everything and I've enjoyed his optional chakra alignments very much, but I'm afraid he's making a big mistake here, because my little friend Microchip can be a great help to any team or any person, really.

I know because it wasn't just basketball that Microchip helped me with, it was suddenly going to a gigantic high school of two thousand kids with a whole new religion where they hung kids without excused absences by their belt loops from the cloak racks for an hour at a time and beat them with big paddles with holes drilled in them for extra speed and said "Peace be with you" a lot.

But at least I had Microchip, which was nice for me because at the Spelunkarium, I was usually by myself. He and me were always together, which was probably because we didn't have anybody else. People called me "Bigfoot" or "Donkey Kong" and they'd see us walking together, me so tall and him so short, and they'd come up and ask me, "How much to see the monkey dance?" They made fun of my uniform because I guess how badly the shirt and pants and blazer fit, stopping about six inches short of where everybody else's did, asking if I'd fallen in a shrink-wrap machine.

And Microchip did not have so many friends there either because he was the only Afro-American kid in the whole school and, in fact, as one of the Most Virgin Lady football players told him, he was the only black they'd had at Most Virgin Lady since one of the seniors left a grease spot in the parking lot.

I would not go so far as to say my classmates were very nice to me, either, at first. Father DeMeret insisted every player serve as an altar boy on Fridays—he said it helps with parishioner donations to the team—and they would laugh at me, especially the time my head banged into the chandelier during the Liturgy. Or they'd think it was hilarious that I'd hit so many people in the chin with the host-catcher during Communion, but it was only because they were so far down there. And then there was the time somebody put marijuana in the incense canister during a funeral and Father DeMeret and I started feeling funny up there and got the giggles during the Mass, especially when Father DeMeret pretended to make a tie out of the sacred Communion cloth, but the next day Father DeMeret blamed it on me and I had to clean above all the armoires in the vestibule for two weeks.

During that time, Microchip was my only friend. Well, except, of course, Sister Mary John Agnes, our very large six-foot biology-teaching nun, who was always very, very nice to me, probably because she came to all our practices and saw how I shoot my terrific either-handed hook in the manner of NBA superstar Bobby Hoops Houbregs. I loved biology, especially the study of anything tiny, like spiders and organisms and amoebas, maybe because I'm so big. And I was really looking forward to taking my first test in her class but imagine my surprise when Sister Mary John Agnes handed me my test and winked at me and I noticed in the right-hand corner it said "A+, 100%" before I had even written a word!

I guess that was very nice of her to be so confident of my science abilities, but I kinda wanted to do the test anyway, as we never studied science in the Spelunkarium, only geology, always geology. But I was only halfway done when she came to my desk and snapped it up and said, "Done already? Wonderful!" and then suggested I go work on my "reverse pivot in the paint."

And I whispered, "But, Sister, I *really* studied hard for this test."

And she pushed me out the door, saying, "Work on your power spin. You're gonna need it against Immaculate Conception. They got a big colored boy."

MAR. 7, NEWARK

Mr. Stain still hasn't written the story about me searching for my father and I didn't know what to do about it I was so upset and so I asked Mr. Barkley.

"So give it to another fishhack," he said.

I stared at him.

"Give it to another sportswriter," he said.

"I couldn't do that. I promised Mr. Stain he's the only writer I'd talk to about it."

"Well, tell the Stain if he doesn't write the story tomorrow, you're going to give it to Johnny St. Rogers at Channel 13. He'd love it. You didn't say anything about Mousses, did you?"

I nearly kissed him right on the lips.

Because me and Microchip haven't been playing very much, in fact, not at all—tonight we were edged by the always-difficult Miamis, 99–68, and neither of us got in—we've had a lot of time to talk and it's great to have an old friend like Microchip around, even though he is much older, eighteen, and I'm only seventeen, but I never made many other friends and I owe him so much that no wonder I think of him as such a good friend.

We were remembering the day we played our first game in front of the kids of Most Virgin Lady and I scored 53 points and Microchip had twenty-three assists, almost all of them to me, and we won very easily although I felt bad for some of the other kids who didn't score that much and, of course, kinda bad for the other team.

And after the game, when Microchip and me came out of the locker room, imagine how surprised I was to see the very same kids who'd been so mean to us waiting for us and asking us to go get some pizza!

In fact, it seemed like I had misjudged lots of people because after the game people seemed to be much more courteous to me and to Microchip, who didn't like it one bit. "Oh, yeah, they all Superglue on our jocks now," he said. "Before, they wouldn't have pissed on us if we was on fire."

But I told him that maybe it was just that it took some breaking-in time for them to get to know us before they arrived at our jocks, and he said, "Oh, Stump, where you been livin'—a freakin' cave?" and then he said he was sorry he didn't mean it.

I could never get mad at Microchip because without him convincing Father DeMeret the way he did, I would've never averaged 61 points per game in high school and Most Virgin Lady would've never gone undefeated at 19–0 (until I left and Microchip got cut) even though every school in the state tried to change the free-throw rule, which they couldn't. We practiced for hours every night in the gym, because Microchip stole the key off Jimmy Ng, the janitor, not to mention the man's wallet, and made a copy. And when Mr. Ng would tell us to get out of the gym, Microchip would mention the freshman girl's phone number he found in that wallet but it never seems like the conversation ever went farther than that on account of Mr. Ng would always seem to remember that he had to go mop some other room.

We would shoot and practice our plays for hours at night. Microchip told me to tell the Spelunkarium I was studying microchip technology in the library and he would tell his parents he was taking a workshop called "The NBA: The New Slave Traders" and that's how we got good together.

And Microchip is now yelling at me from the other room that if I don't turn off the light he'll come in here and turn me into eight feet of lumps, which he doesn't really mean but is only being the funny little guy that he is.

MAR. 8, NEWARK

I make very good money now although to tell you the truth, I still only get $200 a week from Mr. Y. Leonard O'Connor, on account of what his new personal assistant calls contractual complications. But still,

$200 is more than I got at Most Virgin Lady High School, although I admit I was surprised to even get that much.

What happened was Brother DeFrippi, who runs the rectum for Father DeMeret, handed me twenty dollars and I said, "What's this for, Brother DeFrippi?" and he said, "That's your week's pay."

And I said, "What job did I do for you?"

And he said, "Very funny," and he smiled.

And I smiled because ever since I left the Spelunkarium I smile a lot at all the jokes I don't get but I couldn't help say again, "I'm sorry, Brother DeFrippi, I don't know."

And he laughed and said, "Didn't Father DeMeret tell you?"

And I said, "No."

And he said, "Well, that's your week's pay for, uh, for keeping the seashells off the convent walk."

And I said, "But there's no seashells on the convent walk."

And he said, "See? You're doing a terrific job!" and then walked away, but it was very nice anyway, although I wasn't sure I deserved it really making twenty dollars a week for such an easy, easy job.

I felt not quite right about some things like that, for instance dating girls, which I had never done in my life. All year long I'd been working up my nerve to ask out this very tall girl from the volleyball team named Brie, and Microchip and I were at Whey to Go when who should walk in but Brie!

And Microchip kept whispering kind of loudly, "Ask her, Mo! Ask her!" And I thought now is the time to go up and ask her to the Blood of St. Christopher Social and I was just about to when this really quite beautiful girl stepped right between us.

She was a girl who I'd never seen before, but wow, she was really pretty and seemed kinda older than us, with long, red curly hair and real pretty lips and green eyes and smelling like nothing I'd ever smelt before and wearing this sweater that said "North Carolina Tech" across the front and I mean you could read every letter real easily if you know what I mean without being too embarrassing.

And she said, "Maurice?"

And I said, "Yes?"

And she introduced herself as Kimberly from North Carolina Tech, and that she was a "recruiting hostess." And I guess I kind of just blinked a few times at her because, like I say, she just smelled like the winning rose at a contest, and she said, "We want you to come to North Carolina Tech and play basketball and I would be your special friend there!"

And I wanted to say something, but the way she was rubbing my back the words seemed to be kind of stuck on the way out of my mouth.

By then Brie had walked out, mad, I guess, and Microchip said, "Damn, Mo! You gonna be a playa or what?"

And I whispered to him, "Maybe later, Microchip. I think I'll stay and talk to this girl."

And she took me away from Microchip and we talked awhile over in the corner and then she just stomped out by herself and Microchip ran over and said, "What happened!?!"

And I said that I didn't know, that she'd whispered would I want to go back with her to the Hotel Boulderado where she was staying and she could show me some of her brochures of the school in her room and I said very much so yes and she said she would maybe give me an "oral exam" and I said unless it's biology I really don't like exams and she said it's not that kinda exam and I said well, I would do better with my friend with me and she said she wasn't that kind of hostess and I said I was sorry but I don't do anything at all without my friend and she got mad and drove away very fast in her little red sports car.

And Microchip slapped his forehead so hard people looked up from their bulgurburgers.

I just knocked on Mr. Stain's room and I told him that I hated to do it, but if he didn't print the story about my search for my dad, I was going to give it to one of the Mousses on Channel 13.

"All right, don't have a cesarean," he said, wiping the grease from his room-service chicken wings on the wallpaper and reaching for his notepad. "Now, tell me again what you said about this deadbeat dad of yours again?"

MAR. 9, HOUSTON

Sometimes I feel so stupid, especially about things that the other players know about things in the NBA, and here I'm talking about my entourages that Mr. Death was so nice to arrange for me. They are very good at showing up and chaperoning me on my bike to practice and home from practice and Mr. Li'l T-Bone seems like a very good driver, though it isn't easy to talk to him with his music up so very, very loud like that. It is so loud that people in other cars look over in horror at us as we are going along but Mr. Li'l T-Bone says, "It ain't no thing," and I agree, I guess.

My problem is I'm not exactly clear on what each one of my entourages does and why and in fact sometimes I have no idea at all but luckily, they always take time out of their busy days to explain it to me. Like, I was unsure what Mr. T-Bone, my head entourage does, and he says he handles my schedule.

And so I said, "Oh, because I thought Mr. Li'l T-Bone handles my schedule," because Mr. Li'l T-Bone hands me my schedule every day, which is not much if you want to know the truth except for going to practice and coming home from practice and going to the airport and coming home from the airport and doing interviews. But Mr. T-Bone explained to me that Mr. Li'l T-Bone needs somebody to schedule the times when he hands me the schedule, and that made it much more clearer.

My schedule, by the way, should be getting much more busier now because Y. Leonard O'Connor, my agent, called from Fiji to tell me about his new palmtop computer and his new personal walkie-talkie phone but also that he's really been humping the candle at both ends for me. He says he signed for me the best tube sock deal in the league—Groove Tube socks, they're called—and so I will be making numerous appearances at local sporting-good clothing stores and malls in behalf of Groove Tube socks much in the same way my famous dad, Genghis Korn, did in the name of Krispy Korn imitation frozen food products. Not only that, but

I now have a personal representative of Groove Tube socks—the very cool-looking Mr. Quentin LaTroy, or "Q" as he says he wants to be called—to handle any "emergency" I might have with the tube sock.

"What the hell kinda *emergency* is gonna come up with a tube sock?" Microchip asked me today. "What, like, 'My God! This tube sock has lost its tube!' Or, like, what, 'The tube sock is crawling up my leg!' I mean, what the hell?"

And so we asked Mr. Q about it and he said that since this is the first sock contract the company has and because the shoe companies assign "overseers" on their deals, the sock company thought they should do it, too, since they don't want anything to go wrong with the sock or with me although, as my agent explained to me, it is not all that much after his fees, taxes, interest, lawyer's fees, contract fees, license fee, and title.

"Damn," said Microchip. "They didn't charge you for underbody coating."

And, besides, something has gone wrong already, which is that their sign "One Size Fits All" on the sock does not fit for me and my size 22EEEEE foot, but they said that is the idea of the campaign, that their tube sock fits all kinds of people and lifestyles except mine and that's the joke and, really, sometimes it feels like I get that joke too often in the NBA.

We lost to the gritty Houstons tonight, 129–89, for our fourth straight loss and seventh in eight games and on the bench, Microchip almost got us in trouble by saying out loud, "Hell, yeah! I wouldn't put us in either! Not when you got this juggernaut goin'!"

Luckily, Coach Jackson didn't hear us, but Coach Summers did and gave us a dirty look.

And Microchip said to him, "So how was it coachin' against Naismith?"

From the things Coach Summers said back to him, I'm guessing it wasn't all that great.

After the game tonight, we were walking to the bus and a little kid and his very pretty mother stopped Mr. Death and handed him a piece of paper and a pen and Mr. Death had his headphones on, as usual, so he couldn't hear what they were saying, which is one of the reasons why he always has his headphones on out in public, so he just signed his autograph on the paper without looking at them and started to walk off.

But then all of a sudden the woman screamed and hit him over the head with her purse. Turns out it was an old girlfriend of his and his seven-year-old son. He didn't even recognize his own son, which I guess isn't that hard to believe since Mr. Barkley told me Mr. Death has eleven kids in six different cities. But it made me wonder if my father might've seen me sometime already and just not known it was me.

And it made me so sad that I went up to her after Mr. Death got on the bus and told her I was sorry for her and her son that they were missing their father.

And she said, "Sad? I've never been happier in my life. He just signed the court papers giving us another $20,000 child support a month and the fool doesn't even know it!"

We lost again tonight and I had only 3 points because I only shot the ball once and that's because Mr. Mockmood and I don't work very well together and he can't seem to get me the ball anywhere that I like to have it and, in fact, Mr. Stain wrote that Mr. Mockmood "wouldn't give up the ball under order of *fatwa*" and though I have never heard of Coach Fatwa, I believe it.

And so after we'd showered, Microchip went up to Coach Jackson and said, "Yo, Coach. I got a wager for you."

"I don't like to bet on materialistic things," said Coach Jackson. "It's negative psychic karma. And the IRS will (f-word) with you."

Microchip just stared at him for a moment and then said, "Look, it's not a money bet. It's a deal. If you let me and Mo start tomorrow night against the Lakers and if we each play more than twenty-five minutes and we're on the floor together for all twenty-five, and we don't win, I'll quit the team and write you a personal check for everything I've made, the full value of the contract."

"Your ten-day contract expires tomorrow night," Coach Jackson said.

"True, but what kinda karma would you be havin' to deal with the rest of your life knowin' you didn't give another human spirit a chance to flower into his full destiny?"

Coach Jackson thought about that and just then Mr. Trump, our owner, came in the locker room with one of his many nieces and said, "Look, Zen Master, if you don't start winning some games, you're gonna be teaching poetry at the Naropa Institute by April Fool's Day."

And he stormed out and so did his niece but not before giving us all a very good looking-over in our towels and not in our towels, and Coach Jackson looked at Microchip and sighed a deep sigh and finally said, "Well, the masters say that the greatest river begins with the tiniest raindrop. You have your one chance, raindrop. BUT DON'T (F-WORD) IT UP!" And he stomped out.

And Microchip said, "Hare Krishna, bro."

More good news! Mr. Stain finally ran that story about me looking for my dad and he even put a phone number in there about it if my dad's out there, but so far, nothing, but when I found Mr. Stain in the hotel bar he explained that he hadn't time to check if there were any calls yet on account of he had to get to a very important meeting with a fellow named Johnnie Walker, which I can understand, now being a business-man myself.

MAR. 11, LOS ANGELES

I'm in the back of the bus right now on the way to the airport and yelling into my little tape recorder. I'm yelling because it's so loud because of all the music and whooping and beer-drinking and guys screaming into their sell phones on the bus because of the wonderful game we played tonight, which was very, very wonderful and maybe more wonderful than that even.

My little friend Microchip finally got to play tonight and, in fact, started at point guard. Mr. Mockmood was very angry about it and turned his chair
around on the bench and sat with his back to the floor
all night in protest.

I guess it was quite surprising to the sportswriter
gentlemen who follow us to all our games that Microchip was starting considering he hadn't played a single
minute in the NBA, but I was very happy that he was.
It was great once again to let Microchip run his man
straight into one of our "Sternumator" picks as Microchip calls them, which is when Microchip is bringing
the ball up, I sneak up from behind, and he runs his
man's face straight into my chestbone, which is very
bony, I can tell you.

Once his man is down, we both sprint up toward
the basket and we either run a pick and roll to get him
a free ten-footer or we fake the pick and roll and I roll
out to my spot, where he hits me for my hook. I made
my first shot when we did this and then nine more in a
row besides until the Los Angeleses called a time-out.
And when I was going back to the sideline, a man in
the front row stopped me and said with a kind of lopsided grin, "Yo, Slo-Mo, hows about mixin' in a layup
once in a while, huh?"

And when I got back to the bench, Mr. Barkley
said, "Do you know who that was?"

And I said, "No."

And he said, "Jack Nicholson!"

And I said, "Wow! *That's* Jack Nicholson? I
thought he'd be much more tan."

Mr. Barkley just stared at me, like, what do you
mean?

"I just thought he'd be tan," I said, "the greatest golfer in the world, didn't you?"

And Mr. Barkley started banging his head against my chest, over and over.

When we came back out from the time-out, the Los Angeleses decided not to press my friend Microchip at all and just wait for him and also to stand a man right in my favorite spot, in which case, I just spun around the man and set up at the free-throw line, which I can make nine times out of ten. Many times, I would fake like I was going to shoot and instead hit Microchip with our famous "Civ'lization-Endin', Mind-Bendin', Poster-Makin', Backboard-Breakin', One-Hand Scoop, Alley-Palley-Oooop Master Slam Jam," which we successfully worked twice, much to the amazement of the crowd. As I bring the ball up to shoot, Microchip backdoors his guy and I throw it one foot to the right of the hoop and little 5-4 Microchip gets high enough to catch it and dunk it in one amazing move.

Naturally, this caused the crowd to whoop and holler and say things to me like, "Why don't you do that, you stupid ape?" and Microchip hollered over, "Why should he when he's got me, bitch?"

Anyway, everything worked better with Microchip running things. He is more fun to play with, dribbling between guys' legs and spinning and landing on his knees and dribbling on one side of a guy and running around the other and finding the dribble and keeping on going down the court.

When their big center, Mr. Campbell, came out to double me at my spot in the third quarter, Microchip kept tossing it into Mr. Barkley, who had no points at the half but ended up with 26 by the end of the game and said, "I could get used to this."

I had 42 points and only missed one shot and that was when I couldn't decide to shoot or pass and Microchip had 18 points and twenty-one assists and we beat the Los Angeleses by 25 and with a minute to go, the Lakers' other big center, Mr. O'Neal, came up to me and said, "Yo, Godzilla. How much would you take to play for me? I can move some people and have a deal by tomorrow noon." And I laughed because I thought that was very funny, a player pretending to have that much power.

After the game, Coach Jackson said some very nice things about Microchip, but Microchip wasn't around to hear it. He took his clothes and ran to the bus so none of the TV cameramen could get close-ups of him and none of the sportswriter gentlemen could ask about him. And so I had to apologize for him and tell them that he doesn't mean anything by it, but that he's just terribly, terribly shy, although I know if I were at the Spelunkarium, I would spend time in the Fluid Room for lying like that.

MAR. 12, LOS ANGELES

Double great news! Mr. Stain said the paper has received over a dozen calls from people about my dad! I asked him why all of a sudden and he said he thinks it was just a coincidence that all these calls came after my huge game last night. So he's going to call them one at a time and see if they have anything to help us. As Microchip says, I'm just so greeked about it!

Mr. Y. Leonard O'Connor and I had breakfast today and it was good to see him since I haven't hardly seen him at all what with him being so busy working full-time for me around the world.

He was having a little trouble with his new sell phone headset, which is like a pair of stereo headphones that go over his ears and are connected to the tiny sell phone on his belt, although it makes it kind of hard to talk to him as he's usually punching the buttons on the phone to see if it's still working and taking calls on it, usually from his personal assistant, and even when he's not taking calls on it, he talks very loudly though I'm sure he doesn't know it because of the headphones, as I say.

Mr. O'Connor said he's here trying to sign a few college recruits—"You don't even need a license to be an agent!" he said—and we met at his hotel, the "BH" which is the Beverly Hills Hotel to those of you who don't know that, and Mr. Barkley said that it's a very well known place for people to come and sit at tables with each other but talk to other people on their sell phones who are at some other restaurant with other people they're not talking to because everybody's talking on *their* sell phones to somebody else and then hang up and air kiss and say how important it was to keep in touch.

Mr. Y. Leonard O'Connor has changed a lot since I met him, which was when he used to wear the brown uniform of the Roto-Rooter man with the hat but now he wears fancy suits and spat shoes like bandleaders wear and big fedora hats like in old gangster movies on

TV which is how agents are supposed to dress. He didn't use to smoke, but now he chain-smokes these long, thin cigarettes and what with checking his beeper and his walkie-talkie and his sell phone headset, it's kinda hard to get his attention, but when he leaves you, he's still the sincere wiry little guy I met a long time ago and he says, "Peace," and shakes your hand with both his hands, although that usually makes him drop his long, thin cigarette or the beeper or both.

Great news! Because of our recent glorious victory, the New Jerseys have given Microchip a thirty-day contract!

So, to celebrate, we went to Venice Beach and had ice cream cones and looked at all the crazy people and we had a lot of fun until I let him ride around on my shoulders and he caught his neck on an electrical cable, but I think it just scared him more than shocked him.

"Damn, Stumpy!" he said when he came to. "You tryin' to Gary Gilmore my ass?"

MAR. 13, SAN FRANCISCO

The doctors are worried about Mr. Lowery because his infection isn't healing at a normal pace. They sent him back to New Jersey for tests.

"I hope it's nothing serious," I said.

"I doubt it," said Mr. Barkley. "I don't think you can die from steel-wool poisoning."

"What do you mean?" Mr. Woody said.

"He takes a Brillo pad to the infection every night before he goes to bed."

Well, I saw Mr. Stain having a Bloody Mary at breakfast and he said the first two people who called and said they were my dad were total phonies.

"These guys were all liars," Mr. Stain said.

"How do you know?" I asked.

"One was a 5-4 Mexican from Tijuana who said that he was your father but you were adopted and they never got around to telling you."

I told him I didn't think that was true.

"Gee, me neither," he said, eating off my plate. "The other said he was pretty tall and very weird and he had really long wavy hair like Howard Stern and a tie-dye T-shirt, so I figured he could've possibly been your father, until he said that he wasn't sure he was your father in this life, but possibly three lives ago, in Peru."

I guess Mr. Stain could see I was disappointed, although his eyes were so bloodshot, I don't know for sure.

"Look," he said, "there are ten more calls to return, so you never know. Maybe he'll be in one of those."

And I started to pick him up again but he yelled and stabbed me with the little plastic sword in his drink.

We won our second straight game tonight and I personally think it's because Microchip and I are out there, not to be braggarts or anything. I had 38 points and I didn't foul anyone and Microchip had seventeen assists and Mr. Barkley had twenty-eight and we won again. This is getting to be more fun than shedding season.

Microchip slipped into the trainer's room afterward so I had to answer a lot of questions, which I don't really mind. All the other guys talk about how much they hate the press and call them "pond scum" and "vultures" and just before Bruce, our trainer, lets them in, he holds the door and usually somebody says, "Get ready, boys, here come the leeches." But I don't see what's so bad. They ask me questions and I answer them.

Like tonight, they asked, "What's it like to be in the zone?"

"What zone?" I said.

"The zone, you know, to know everything you put up is going in."

"Shots, you mean?"

"No, manned space capsules."

"Manned space capsules?"

"Yes, shots! Basketball shots!"

"Oh! It's wonderful. I have such a good feeling in my One Point right now because my friend Microchip and I are back playing together."

"Where's he from anyway? The p.r. department says they're still trying to get info."

"Den—" and then it hit me I shouldn't tell that so I said "—mark."

"He's from Denmark?"

"Yeah, Denmark. Crazy, huh?"

"Does he speak English?"

"A little."

"What's he speak then?"

"A, well, fluent, uh, salmon."

And they all laughed and wrote that down.

"What one point?"

"Inside here." (I pointed three inches below my belly button.)

"What's that?"

"The very center of yourself, the perfect balance of yourself, where your soul is. All things have a One Point. The earth has a One Point and that is why the closer you get to it, the more centered and whole you become and the closer to the inner God."

"If it helps you shoot," said one of the sportswriter gentlemen, "why don't you call it your Three Points?"

Everybody got that but me.

"Wait a minute," Mr. Stain said. "You're saying God is at the center of the earth?"

"Of course."

"But isn't it like nine million degrees in there?"

"Of course. God is warmth."

"But none of us can live at that temperature."

"Of course. And none of us can completely know God."

"How long can you keep this up?"

"As long as you fellas want to talk about it."

"No, how long can you keep shooting like this?"

"Well, as long as I'm happy in my One Point, I can shoot like this forever."

"Forever?"

"Or longer."

"Do you think it's possible this team can make the play-offs?"

"Oh, yes. We're going to turn this thing around 360 degrees."

And they all laughed at that and wrote it down.

See how easy it is?

After all the reporters left, I had to be very stern with Mr. Soals about the shoes thing. I hadn't seen him in a while, especially when I wasn't playing, and I was glad, but here he was again and I'm ashamed to say I got a little short with him. I said, "No, Mr. Soals. No, thank you."

I felt a little bad about it, especially after he left, when Mr. Big County said, "I don't mean nothin' personal by this, hoss, but you're just dumber 'n a box of tits."

I didn't get it.

"Son, everybody in this league used to have a shoe contract. This league used to be nothin' *but* shoe contracts. This league used to be *run* by shoe contracts! Now the money's all dried up except but for a few guys who can still haul in more cash 'n you can get with two pickups and you could be one of them guys! Look, hoss, I know most of them shoe guys are so dadgum crooked they could stand in the shadder of a corkscrew, but you gotta jump on that bull!"

I didn't get it.

"Look, hoss, when I was in eighth grade, I became a Converse guy. They gave me Converse shoes and Converse sweatshirts and Converse hats and made sure I went to all the Converse camps and played on the Converse summer teams. Then they made sure I went to a Converse high school, where they gave my coach $15,000 to make sure I was always wearing Converse stuff in the newspapers and was going to Converse camps and played on the Converse AAU teams, which is really just a way to funnel guys Converse money, like,

Hey, here's his per diem for the Lubbock tournament, $500 a day! You know how much these good ol' high school boys eat! Then, if I wanted to keep gettin' all that scratch, I had to choose a Converse college where the team was already signed to Converse and my coach got $100,000 to make sure we all wore Converse stuff, especially on television and in the magazines and stuff, and I got Converse money like they was fixin' to make a bonfar with it otherwise and Converse managed to see clear to where my aunt got a *really* good job as a receptionist at the earl refinery which allowed her to *lease* me my custom-built $46,000 Tahoe, as a family present, a course."

"Really?" I said.

"You ever noticed how all them Nike guys ended up in Portland? Look, Nike has the swoosh on the *ball,* man. Is that enough for you, hoss? I mean, Alonzo Mourning came out of college and held out his first year and you know why? 'Cause he signed a $2-million shoe contract right away. Allen Iverson. This guy got *$50 million* from Reebok. He only gets $6 million from the 76ers. You know where he was the other day when his coach fined him for missing a practice? Shootin' his Reebok ad! And if you were him, you'd take care of Reebok before you took care of the Sixers, too, right? Because with free agency, the Sixers are gonna deal him in two years anyway, but Reebok, they'll be with him forever. The shoe companies are your *real* team, boy!"

So I told him the story of my dad and the shoes and how much they meant to me. As always, my eyes kinda teared up and he let me go on for a while and then slapped me hard on the back and said, "Sign the deal, hoss, and get 'em bronzed."

MAR. 15, NEWARK

As great as we played on the road, I'm afraid
Mr. Woody didn't play so good. In fact, Mr. Woody is
acting very strange lately. He can't seem to concentrate
on anything and his shooting has been not all that
wonderful and he says he thinks he pulled a neck muscle trying to think off the other night. Sometimes it
takes him twenty seconds to shoot his free throw and
he hardly makes them ever anymore. Plus, he says he
can't sleep.

"I gotta get me some gash," he said today. "Before I
drown in my own jizz."

"Still holdin' out for the right voice?" Mr. Barkley
asked.

"(F-word) you," replied Mr. Woody. "This is gonna
work. I'm gettin' close. But it's costin' me."

We asked him why.

" 'Cause none of my usual hos wanna come around
anymore. They're sicka pretendin'. Turquoise told me
last night if she'da wanted to mime (f-word) she'da
joined the circus."

"So you gotta get real hos?" Mr. Death asked.

"Yeah. It's kind of a bitch."

And Mr. Barkley said, "You know, you oughta ap-
ply for a research grant."

Mr. Woody looked at him like he thought Mr.
Barkley was pulling his leg. "(F-word) you," he said
sincerely.

"I'm serious! People in this country getting millions
just to find out if the Borneo tree snake takes a dump
with one eye closed or two—"

"Two," I said quietly.

"—and here you are, tryin' to make some serious inroads into the science of human sexuality and possibly save mankind from sexually transmitted diseases that are raging through our society, and you're having to do it *out of pocket!* That's criminal!"

But Mr. Woody had already slammed the door.

MAR. 17, NEWARK

I had my career best game ever in my entire professional career history tonight, 46 points, including thirteen of thirteen free hooks, and eleven of twelve 3-point shots from all kinds of places, the corner andup top and left-handed and right-handed, and, like they say, I was hotter 'n blue blazes.

When they'd send a huge center to come out and guard me, I'd just throw the ball to Mr. Big County or Mr. Barkley and they'd get to play down under the basket against some pretty small guys and as Mr. Big County says, "It's like shootin' Mexkins in a phone booth."

And after the game, Mr. Big County celebrated by putting Microchip on his shoulders and throwing him into the stands as we exited through the tunnel. "Rodman throws jerseys," Mr. Big County said. "I throw jerseys. Mine just happen to have somebody in 'em."

The fans were very glad to have my little buddy and kept passing him around like he was some kind of beach ball, batting him from fan to fan, until finally some of the ushers stole him and brought him back to us.

But it is very strange. It seems the better I do the more unhappy it seems to make people.

"Hey, cave boy, feel free to give up the rock once in a while," Mr. Death said to me after tonight's game.

"I'm sorry?"

"Yeah, you sorry all right," Mr. Death said.

"Excuse me?"

And then Mr. Barkley stepped in and said, "Hold on, I speak fluent Slo-Mo," and he explained to me that Death thinks I don't pass the ball enough, "which is bull(s-word)," said Mr. Barkley, "since even if you did pass the ball you wouldn't pass it to Death anyway because Death is on the bench whenever you're in and that's what really pisses Death off and even if he were in, the dude is just a freak dunker and couldn't bust a 'J' if they locked him alone in a gym all night with two midgets and a stepladder."

And Mr. Barkley also said, "No, what really pisses Death off is that he pretends to be this badass who wants people to leave him alone but what he really is is a badass who wants desperately for people to notice him, only the guy can't get arrested lately on account of everybody's interested in you and all your weird-ass shit that you don't even *realize* is weird-ass shit and not payin' any attention to his weird-ass shit which he pays marketing guys to think up for him."

And Mr. Death reached down into his big, black boots with the schwasticas on the side and yanked out a switchblade and waved it at Mr. Barkley and said, "If you ever talk to me like that again, nigger, I'll cut you a view of your gallbladder."

I'm going to try to pass the ball more next game.

MAR. 18, NEWARK

Jinx knocked on the door of my room at the Newark Airport Ramada Hotel late tonight and I think she must not make as much money in the suit business as Mr. Barkley said because she was wearing a shirt that was so threadbare you could see right through it and I had to look away so as not to embarrass her for being so poor.

"I sure have missed you, sweetie," she said. And she had a bottle of champagne and I'd never had champagne before and so I tried it and I liked it very much and after a while she asked me to hold her and so I did and then finally she said I could let go and so I did.

And we were both feeling very good and I think I might have even been drunk for the first time in my life and there was something I knew I wanted and I tried to give her a signal of what I wanted and she looked right in my eyes and said, "What do you want me to do?"

And I looked her right back in the eyes and I said, "Tell me a story."

And she sat up straight and said, "What?"

See, Phyllis always told me a story in our cubicle each night and no one else had in so long and I liked Jinx very much and trusted her and I know it seems babyish, but I asked her anyway. "Tell me a story. Tell me everything that's ever happened to you."

And she must've liked the idea because she flopped back on the bed all the way and put a pillow over her face, which must be how she gets comfortable. And she told me her story, which was not a very happy story but at least it was a story.

Turns out Jinx comes from the East—East Oakland—and she was very poor, just like I guessed. She said she always wanted to get out of East Oakland because she didn't like it there one bit because her father did all kinds of mean things to her, including stuff no father should ever do to his daughter, no way. Of course, he wasn't really her father, anyway, she said, but her mom's boyfriend who only came by on Mother's Day, which, she said, in her neighborhood, was the first of every month when the welfare checks came out and I said that sounds like a very nice thing for the mothers there.

But she did get out. She got on a bus for as far away as seventy-three dollars could get her and she was sixteen and the farthest she could go was Chicago and when she got there, she didn't have any money but it all worked out because she found a lot of guys who wanted to "date" her and she said she also went exotic dancing a lot, which she was very good at and even got a job exotic dancing in Newark and I said I didn't know how to exotic dance but that maybe she could teach me and we could go together.

The more champagne she drank the more stories she told, most of them about men, but all of them seemed to end sort of sadly, like in divorce or a straining order or one or the other of them "getting over on Springer." And the way she talked about men she seemed awfully angry at them and a lot of the stories were so sad that she cried a little and I even started to tear up and I said, "I'm sorry men are not very nice people that they always have to hurt you. I hope I don't become a man if that's what men do," and she just stared at me for a long time, crying, and I guess maybe I hurt her feelings, I don't know, but she kept looking at me like she wanted to say something but she never did and just left.

If I ask her to tell stories again, I won't do it late at night because they were not at all helpful for getting to sleep.

MAR. 19, BOSTON

It seems the better I shoot, the nicer people are to me, and the worse I shoot, the meaner they are to me and yet I'm the same person. That doesn't seem right, but what can you do? You can't cut off your nose in spite of your face.

I'm getting a lot of wonderful calls and letters and baskets of fruit and flowers, even at my hotel here in Boston, so much so that I can hardly sleep, talking to people who want to congratulate me all night long.

I know they mean well, but I would like to have some sleep, but that is hardly a complaint, I guess. I'm getting a lot of attention from the sportswriter men and on the radio from the "sports talk" shows with a lot of guys who seem to call themselves "Coach" and they always mention my room at the Newark Airport Ramada Hotel or the name of the hotel we're staying at and since the desk has my room number, they just call right up. People are sending me a lot of articles about me and some sportswriter gentlemen are calling me "the Bear from Up There" and "the Splendid Spelunker" and "the Boulder Bomber."

And it's all very nice but I've only had a couple hours' sleep the past few nights and so I'm kinda tired. And Mr. Barkley said I should use an alien which is another word for a fake name. And I said, where would I think of a fake name and he said that he thinks of funny ones like A. Blackman or Mike Hunt, stuff like that, which I didn't get but that's not real unusual. He said an easy way is to think of your first dog and the first street you lived on and you have a name. "Like, mine, for instance, was Pugs Linden, or you could be Fido Grape or Shadow Roosevelt, stuff like that. That way people can still get you but talk show idiots can't."

And I told him that for one thing, I didn't have a dog and never lived on a street until the Newark Airport Ramada Hotel and two, I can't have an alien because I want my father to reach me and any suffering I have to go through will be worth it. Besides, as soon as Microchip and I get out on the floor it doesn't seem to matter.

Tonight, for instance, against the Bostons, they tried something different against me. They fouled me every time I shot and sometimes as soon as I touched the ball in backcourt, figuring it's only two free sky-hooks as opposed to a 3-pointer. They fouled me pretty hard, too. Microchip got in three fights about it—once with Mr. Death, who didn't seem to be one bit bothered by how they were playing me—and he finally got thrown out of the game by the ref for saying to one of their players, a big guy named Matt Geiger, "You so ugly, you make my cat bark."

But it didn't matter by then anyway, as we were ahead by 14 points with only a minute to go and I made a whole, whole lot of free-throw hooks, thirty-one out of thirty-three, which somebody said is a record, and two 3-pointers besides that even while they were fouling me, which, as Microchip says, is no problem, 'cause I can get my shot with a carnival ride on my back. It's funny how Microchip and I think so much alike and, in fact, sometimes it's like we have ESPN.

I did try to pass the ball more to Mr. Death tonight, but after I did it three times and we were behind by 6, Coach Jackson called time out and pulled me aside and Microchip stood on the press table and they both asked me at the same time what "the (f-word) exactly" I was doing.

"Passing the ball to Mr. Death," I said.

"Why?"

"Because he asked me to."

Coach Summers just about had a fit, but I didn't understand.

Coach Jackson said to me, "Mo, there are some parts of life that don't make sense but are nonetheless true. In Zen thought, for instance, there is the idea of the gateless gate. On this team, there is the idea that you must be somewhat selfish in order to be unselfish for the team. You have to shoot, not pass, and you have to especially not pass to Death."

And Mr. Big County said, "Passing the ball to him is like lendin' a bone to a Saint Bernard. You ain't gettin' it back and he'll prolly piss on you besides. He's a rebounder and a shotblocker and a dunker. DO NOT (F-WORD)ING PASS THE BALL TO HIM! Okay? You do not need to understand it. You only need to trust me."

I said okay but on the way back on the floor I asked Microchip if he knew what a gateless gate was.

"It leads to the passless pass," he said.

My friend Microchip knows a little about everything.

Since Microchip always sneaks out after the games, I'm practically the only one in the locker room talking to the cameras and the men with the fancy haircuts and the sportswriter gentlemen. I feel bad for the other players, especially Mr. Death, who was so upset and in his own world I don't think he realized how hard he bumped a few of the press people as he left the locker room tonight.

And I kept trying to tell the press people how important Mr. Death is to the team and, in fact, I said, "Mr. Death is a big clog in our machine," and I think they finally got it because they all wrote it down very fast.

But I still felt bad until, on the bus, Mr. Big County said, "Hoss, ain't no way to be the lead dog without showin' *somebody* your butt."

And I was touched by that.

Bad news: Mr. Stain came to my room tonight and asked if he could borrow a few things out of the nice little fridges the hotels are so nice to stock with stuff, and I asked him how it was going with the search and he said the first six men he's called were phonies, too, and also not my father. "Unless your dad is black, Chinese, or formerly a woman. Or in one case, all three."

"Why are these people lying?" I asked him.

"Oh, I'm sure they just want a son. I don't think it has *anything* to do with you just signing a $4.5-million contract and rippin' the damn league in half lately."

But I told him I disagreed. I think these people are like the cave glowworm. We'd see them all the time at the Spelunkarium. The hungrier they got, the more they would glow, until, when they were really hungry, they would glow a bright green. Insects and flies would be attracted to the glow and then the worm would eat them. I think these people must be, in their own way, very, very hungry to do something so wrong as this.

And he agreed and left, closing the door with his foot.

MAR. 20, ATLANTA

Before the game tonight I was so happy because who did I see but the Spinning Stankowskis. I thought they only performed in Newark, but it turns out they perform all over America, especially at NBA halftimes.

They were going to perform at halftime and they passed me in the hallway near the locker room in their bright and colorful spangly costumes. They didn't really notice me because they were arguing again.

"Hey, this is a family act!" said the father. "You don't get a tattoo without talkin' to me! You're supposed to be a kid? How's a AC/DC tattoo look to people? What are you going for, the drifter look?"

"Oh, get off his back, Jack," said the wife. "It's so small. Why, it's no bigger than your wiener."

The boy cackled.

"Sure, sure," said the father. "This from a woman who wants new tits!"

"(F-word) you, Jack!" she whispered loudly, embarrassed.

"You know what those'll do to my vectors?"

Then the son jumped back into the argument and Lisa finally turned the other direction and came toward me, crying. I wanted to say something to her but I couldn't get my nerve up and she was going to walk right past me but at that very moment, the giant remote-controlled cartoon-man-shaped balloon that flies above the Atlanta crowd and drops gift certificates on the fans was being pulled through and we were both stuck.

And I didn't know what to say, but I really was dying to say something, so I said, "You can wipe your nose on my shorts if you want."

And she kinda choked out, "No, no, thanks."

And I stammered, "Because you don't really have much room to hide a Kleenex." Which was true, since her costume was very, very small and wouldn't have contained enough fabric to cover my snake Lassie's cage, not that I was really complaining.

"No, I guess I don't."

"Or I could get you some Kleenex."

"Oh, that's sweet of you, but I'm fine."

And there was a real awkward pause as the guy was trying to get the balloon out of our way and she said, "I like your hook shot."

And I said, "Well, I just have the one kind of shot."

And she said, "But you can do it with either hand."

And there was another awkward pause and I said, "I like the way you spin."

And she said, "Oh, thanks."

"And you can go either direction."

And she laughed.

I told her I had a dryophis nashwhip she reminded me of.

And she said, "I'm sorry?"

"Well, not *remind* me of, but he can get into some very funny positions, too."

"African or Asian?" she said.

I was very surprised that she knew this.

"Asian," I said.

"With the bright orange spot on their foreheads?" she said. "The one that can mate with both sexes?"

"Yeah," I said.

"Kinda like Dennis Rodman," she said.

We both laughed and she had the most beautiful smile. She must've had twice the amount of teeth most girls have. And her lipstick was so red and her eyes were so blue. Her face was prettier than a wall full of calcite crystals. And she looked right up at me, even though she was maybe three feet shorter than me.

You know, when you spend most of your daylight hours in a cave lit only by lanterns and you often go into the cave before the sun comes up and come out after it's gone and the rest of your time you spend alone in a compost heap, you forget how beautiful a girl can look in good light. So I just couldn't help myself. I stared at her. And she just kinda looked at me, and then we both realized the giant cartoon-man-shaped balloon was gone and her father was on the other side of it, going, "Lisa, you coming to rehearsal or should we pull someone out of the stands?"

The smile left her face and she whispered, "Bye," and she left.

And I was so happy that at halftime, I told Coach Jackson I forgot something I needed on the bench and snuck out and watched her from one of the tunnels and I just think she's the most beautiful thing I ever saw go in circles at sixty miles an hour.

We won again tonight, this time over the rugged Atlantas, even though I had an off night, 30 points and

I missed five shots, too, although I made the one at the end that seemed to get everybody excited. I like to shoot my shot at the end as much as I like to shoot it in the middle or at the beginning. It just feels good to see it spinning in the air and going through the net so sweetly and it really doesn't matter to me whether it is for the win or the loss or the tie.

Afterward I did something fun which was I appeared on a radio sports talk show after the game—*The Coach and the Mad Man*—in which all the fellas do is talk about sports, even though the show is over four hours long! And the conversation went very nicely, I thought, until this happened:

MAD MAN: Look, we know you can shoot the piss out of it, but—
COACH: Don't go there, Mad Man!
MAD MAN: Well!
COACH: Ladies and gentlemen, ignore the Mad Man!
MAD MAN: Well, hell's bells! This is radio, ain't it?
COACH: All right, so ask your question!
MAD MAN: What?
COACH: What, what? Ask.
MAD MAN: Okay, Slo-Mo, we know you can shoot the piss out of it, but do you have any idea how good you'd be if you'd just go and dunk the frickin' thing? I mean, you're drivin' us frickin' crazy with this deal! Just go dunk it, you big dope!
COACH: Mad Man, you're too much!
MAD MAN: What?
COACH: What, what?
MAD MAN: What?

COACH: Slo-Mo. Ignore this cretin and answer the question, if you dare.

ME: Well, I really don't think I'd get any joy out of dunking the basketball. I like to shoot from far away. Dunking the basketball seems to be so easy and simple, anybody my height can do it. I like to prove to people that I'm not just someone who can dunk the basketball all the time. What kinda person would I be if I wasn't trying to do something that challenges me and makes me happy?

MAD MAN: Get the freak out of here!

COACH: Mad Man!

MAD MAN: I mean it! Get outta here with that crapola! "What kind of person would I be?" You'd be the greatest scorer in NBA history is what you'd be, you big ol' Frankenstein!

COACH: Mad Man, if he had enough games played to qualify, he'd be among the league leaders in scoring right now!

MAD MAN: Awwww, Jesus, Mary, and Joseph!

And I guess that was their religious sign-off signal because they played a commercial then and basically I thought it went very well because they gave me a video camera for being their guest on the show! Its list price is $399 and it's the first electronic thing I've ever owned, on account of the ban on those kind of things at the Spelunkarium wherever possible, and I know it's forbidden but I secretly like it very much.

In fact, I like it so much I came into the bar tonight to see Mr. Barkley and the fellas after the game and I was shooting video and the fellas saw me and had a little fun with me because most of them hid under the tables or put their menus up in front of their faces, and so did the girls they were with, making me get down low under the tables and shoot them. A great bunch of kidders.

And when Mr. Barkley told me to shut that thing off before it gets a really good shot of my pancreas, Jinx turned on her barstool and said to me, "Whatcha got, Mo?"

And I showed her and she said, "Ooooh, I love home movies!"

And all her girlfriends laughed. And she said, "Wanna go shoot some?"

And I thought that was a great idea of hers and so I quick ran home and filmed a little comedy starring my water moccasin, Warren, and Juan, my Mexican gardener, sharing an apartment, which is funny because they both come from completely different subbranch phylums.

MAR. 21, NEWARK

This is all so much fun for Microchip except for one thing—his parents.

They're beginning to get suspicious as to why he's never there when they call and also why they're not getting his report cards from school anymore or any of his papers and this is, of course, as you know, that he is not at Most Virgin Lady High School but instead he's on the New Jerseys with me now but we don't want them to know that or they will make him come home immediately and, as Microchip says, "lock me in a room with Dick Gregory."

He is playing so many minutes and doing so well that a lot of people want to know about him, especially the sportswriter gentlemen and women, but he won't speak to them because he's scared they'll find out that his real name is not David "Microchip" Lawrence—Microchip says that David Lawrence is the name of the guy who made the high school varsity the year Michael Jordan didn't—but is really Mustafa Unity Smith.

He's worried but not that worried since his parents don't allow ESPN in the house and they throw away the sports section immediately each morning and, as Microchip once said, "all their friends are people with a *New Yorker* stuck up their butts." And that is one New Yorker I *don't* want to meet.

But you never know what could happen and so today, Microchip said, "I gotta plan. And I need your help."

Microchip's idea is a very clever one. He is going to start taking e-mail courses from Howard University and then forwarding his parents the work through a friend in Boulder, so it will look like he is there and not here.

And I said I had no idea what he was talking about and he said, "It's all on this Web site here."

Naturally, I got very excited as I love web sites and consider myself an expert on web sites but I guess Microchip and I were talking about two different things because he was pointing to his computer.

Anyway, he's going to take Black Issues, Black History, and Black Issues in History, and also Herpetology, which is the study of snakes, and which he wants me to do all the work. Can you believe the guy?

"Will you?" he asked.

I picked him up and hugged him until he pulled

my hair to let me know he was done being hugged and a maid knocked to see if there was some kinda problem.

I can't wait for the first workbook to arrive.

More bad news: Mr. Stain only has two possibilities left. Everyone else hasn't checked out.

"How do you know?" I asked.

"One would've been thirteen when you were born and the other thought spelunking involved the first Russian spacecraft."

One more to go, though. I told him I'm keeping my hopes up.

"You're seven-eight," he said. "Where else you gonna keep your hopes?"

Oh, I almost forgot! Tonight, I appeared on the Lettermen TV show. I got to ride my Schwinn behind my first limo! Mr. O'Connor, my agent, didn't come in with me because, as he said to somebody on his headset sell phone while working his new portable belt fax, "We get the limo for four hours and if you think I'm sitting in some greenroom instead, you got another think coming."

So I went in by myself. I'm not much of a TV watcher as Mr. Mockmood won't let us and I like to read besides and I had never seen the Lettermen show but I told one of the Lettermen before the show that I remember my Life-Giver, Phyllis, had a lot of his albums and though we weren't allowed she kept her albums anyway, just to look at, and I thought he and the other Lettermen looked like they'd have been very good singers. I must've been the first to mention this to him in a long time because he didn't quite know what to say and, actually, was so overcome that he just left the room without saying anything so I'm glad I mentioned it.

During the show, I only got to meet the one Lettermen I'd met before, but he was nice enough and I didn't touch his neck or try to talk to him during the breaks like they told me not to. But I really had to just pretend to get his jokes and really didn't get many of them, although he did seem interested in me when he asked, "I bet you took the short bus back and forth to school every day, didn't you?" but I told him no, I had to ride my bike.

He did something pretty funny though and very unusual, which was he read a list of top ten things that his home office had come up with, although it probably wasn't a real list, but it was kinda funny, I guess. And the name of the list was "The Top 10 Reasons Slo-Mo Finsternick Won't Dunk" and all I remember was:

No. 6: Saving twelve-inch Verticle for Honeymoon.

A man named Biff explained that one to me during a commercial and I thought it was funny once I understood it and blushed about three sheets to the wind. And after the commercial they brought out a basketball hoop and wanted me to dunk, and the orchestra leader sang a whole song about me dunking and the audience chanted "Dunk! Dunk! Dunk!" and I had a little fun with them and started from about twenty-five feet out like I was going to go dribbling up really fast and dunk and instead I ran right past it and then about twenty-five feet away hooked it and it swished right through. And everybody booed, but they kept throwing me basketballs and I kept swishing them and I was having so much fun I actually swished twenty-two in a row, and the people stopped booing and started going "Yeeeeeeeeee-*owww!*" with every shot as it arced through the lights and swished through the net.

And after the show was over I followed the Lettermen to his office just next to the stage to say thank you and see if he couldn't tell the country about my problems finding my dad but he closed the door and his assistant said he doesn't see anyone ever after a show and I asked her what he does in there and she said, "Mostly he just goes inside the room and makes a Prozac shake" and I asked how you do that to a Prozac and she just looked at me funny.

But I missed watching myself on TV tonight as Natasha, my Balkan whip, has a head cold.

MAR. 22, NEWARK

All the sportswriter gentlemen were asking me about money today.

"Are you going to renegotiate?" they asked.

"What's that?"

"Are you going to ask them to redo your contract?"

"No! I like my contract! Why?"

"Because you're playing so much better than people thought."

"Guys do that?"

"Of course!"

"If they're playing worse than people thought, do they renegotiate?"

And they all nodded and scribbled things down like crazy but I never did get my answer.

And then, during free-throw practice, Mr. Barkley

asked me why don't I get a new agent because I'm doing so well and yet all I have is this sock deal for socks that don't even fit, even though Q is a nice enough person, although there are only so many times you can answer the question "Any problems with the socks?" and that's about it.

He asked me who my agent was and I said it was Y. Leonard O'Connor and he said, "Sounds like a good question."

I told him that he was the Roto-Rooter man who discovered me but now he was a big agent with already six clients besides me.

And he said, "You mean you've got an agent that *literally* slithered out of the sewers?"

He asked me why I don't just leave him and I said I couldn't leave because even though he is not really friendly and hardly ever calls, he was my agent and I agreed to let him be my agent and also you never know when you're going to need a plumber.

And he said, "How'd you get hooked up with a damn Roto-Rooter man as your agent anyway?"

And I told him that how it happened is that when I started playing at Most Virgin Lady High School in Boulder so many people came around asking me if I would come to their colleges to play basketball. In fact, every day when I would come down the mountain from the Spelunkarium on my Schwinn there would be five or ten men, well, college coaches, really, waiting for me where I parked my bike, all of them wanting to give me things about their college and asking me for my number, which I told them was "1" which it was, and they'd laugh and say, "I completely understand. You deserve your privacy."

They were very polite men like that and very well

dressed. They were impressive and rich. One man came up to me one day and said, "Larry Foster, Iona College," and that alone was very impressive that a man as young as he was would have that much money to purchase an entire school.

But a lot of them were kinda forgetful for being as well dressed as they were. One time, this balding coach from Fresno State with a very raspy voice and eyes that looked a hundred years old accidentally left a FedEx envelope inside my biology binder with lots and lots of money in it! I was halfway to class when I noticed it. I knew it was his because a little bumper-sticker mascot from his school was paper-clipped to it, which was lucky for him because I quickly figured out the money was his.

I sprinted down the hall and outside the school and caught him in the parking lot and handed it to him and said, "You almost forgot this!" I know he was so, so, so grateful because he had this expression on his face like *complete shock* and his mouth fell open and he just stared at me without saying a thing and so did a lot of the other coaches, who just stared at him. And I said, "You don't have to say another word. I know how you feel."

But anyway, there were so many of these college coaches around—forgetting not only their keys to brand-new trucks but also the trucks *themselves!* Can you believe that! Plus, they kept forgetting to tell me that they were sending around their nieces to meet me after class—that the archbishop heard about it and told Father DeMeret to get somebody to handle all my problems and organize these college coaches so I could do my homework, which I really did love to do even though I never told the other kids, and Father DeMeret picked Mr. O'Connor, even though he had no experience with agent stuff but apparently Father DeMeret owed Mr. O'Connor a few big favors from some of the very aggressive recruiting Mr. O'Connor did for him for the basketball team.

He was a nice enough man and he did discover me and everything, but he was not much help really to me and, in fact, was usually about as much help as adding a rattlesnake to a baby rattler convention, which is my colorful way of saying that he usually just made things worse. I'm sure he was trying his best, but it seemed like he got rid of the college coaches, who I kinda liked, and kept forgetting to keep the pro scouts away.

Every day I'd come out of religion or math and there'd be somebody standing there from the Vancouvers or the Torontos. But I didn't want to go to the pros. I wanted to go to college and study snakes and bugs, which are my true love, as I told you. But Mr. O'Connor didn't seem to care very much for that idea of going to college and said that I was good enough to go straight to the pros out of high school, like Mr. Death had, and that way I wouldn't have to take a terrible job in life like he had done which was Roto-Rootering around in people's toilets.

But I had my heart set on going to college and maybe someday achieving my goal which was to open my own zoo just for snakes, who really don't get any attention at real zoos.

One night, after my best game that year, my junior year, against Blessed Sacrilege, in which I was really feeling my spot, I scored 73 points with no rebounds and no fouls. And after the game, it got even better because Mr. O'Connor and Microchip and me went to Whey to Go and had some Wheyburgers and Mr. O'Connor went in the back and when he came out, he said, "How would you like to eat all the Wheyburgers you want for free?"

And I said it would be like heaven under earth for me and he said would I just sign this piece of paper which said that I, Maurice Finsternick of the Most Virgin Lady basketball team, really, really liked Wheyburgers and more people should go to Whey to Go. And I signed it, no problem, because that is truly what I believe. And so they started bringing out tons of Wheyburgers for me for free and they even went next door and got some McDonald's for Microchip, and then I got lucky hitching onto the back of a bakery truck heading back up to the Spelunkarium and I only had to pedal maybe five miles, tops, which is a very big no-no, accepting a ride from polluting devices, but I did it anyway. And not only that, but the Elder was not there to make fun of me and ask me if I'd accidentally petted the girls to death down there and there was a full moon so Juan was in a great mood and had me scratch his belly.

But the next day, when I got to school, Mr. O'Connor was standing there in front of the school in a nice new suit, waiting for me.

And sitting on the base of the statue of the Most Virgin Mary was Father DeMeret and the Elder and the monsignor from the archdiocese and two men in shirts and ties. And I knew I was in trouble, so I decided I should step right up and take my medicine, as Phyllis always told me to do and I'm sure my own father, Genghis Korn, would've done. And so I parked my bike and walked up and said, "I know what I've done and

I'm very sorry and I will do whatever you say for me to do to make up for it."

And they all looked at each other and they seemed sort of relieved.

And Mr. O'Connor said, "Maurice, takes a big man to face the music."

And the monsignor said, "You will be doing the Savior's work, my son."

And the Elder smiled and let out a big sigh.

And Father DeMeret just stomped off. And the two men in ties came up and said, "Okay, just sign here then and it'll all be copacetic," and I definitely wanted things to be copacetic, so I signed where they said to sign because I figured I definitely wanted everything to be highly copacetic. And they all said stuff like, "You're only seventeen but you're taking this like a real man, Maurice," and "In the end, I think you'll be happier," and stuff like that, which I was glad to hear because I was so ashamed of what I had done.

I immediately went and found Microchip. He was in the library, pretending to read Malcolm X but actually reading *Basketball's Unforgettables* tucked in between the pages.

"They found out," I said.

"They found out what?" he said.

"They found out what we did before Mass last Friday."

"What'd we do?"

"In the vestibule, remember?"

"No, what'd we do in the vestibule?"

"We ate the Blessed Hosts! Remember? We were hungry and you said, 'Let's just eat these!' And I said, 'No!' but you said it was no problem! We were in our cassocks! That's a mortal sin!"

"That's whack, Slo! We ate a handful of Hosts! Technically, since they weren't even blessed yet, they were just very flat little pieces of wallpaper paste!"

"Then why did I have to sign a confession?" I said, and I threw him the copy of the papers they gave me.

"Confession?"

Microchip was reading it and his eyebrows started dancing and he said, "Stumpy! You chump! You just—"

And just then Father DeMeret came in, his face red as a firecracker, and he threw my uniform at me and my warm-ups and he said, "(F-word) you, cave boy! They'll eat your geek ass alive in the NBA!" And everybody in the library was looking at us and he turned to them and screamed, "What are you lookin' at? Do you really think any of that (s-word) you're reading will have any bearing whatsoever in your later life, you buncha (f-word)in' eggheads?" And he stormed out and Microchip had his head in his hands and I had a very sick feeling in my stomach.

As I'm sure you know by now, I should have never signed Mr. O'Connor's piece of copacetic paper about the free Wheyburgers. Turns out you can't get free Wheyburgers in high school, or in college, for that matter, or they won't let you play high school or college anymore, as I didn't know and Mr. O'Connor said he didn't know either although he didn't really seem all that sorry for what he'd done.

"That dumb ass could screw up an anvil," Microchip said.

The piece of paper I signed made me available to the supplemental NBA draft in two weeks. It seemed like me and Microchip were much more upset about it than Mr. O'Connor was, as he kept saying, "Maurice, look on the bright side! You don't ever have to worry about grades again," and saying things like, "That representative from Whey to Go was such a good guy, too," and whistling a lot.

But he would not say much more than that as he said he had to start making business trips to New York, Los Angeles, and Honolulu to speak to the professional NBA teams in those cities, although there was one right there in Denver that I would've liked to play for as it would've been a very easy bike ride for me but he would always say, "Maurice, I said *professional.*"

And that is how I got accidentally turned pro and became the first high school junior to join the NBA in NBA history although nobody asked me if I really wanted to become the first high school junior to join the NBA but I guess when you're 7-8, you don't have a lot of choice about what you get to do with life, especially your own.

MAR. 23, NEWARK

I've been sleeping better ever since Microchip ripped the phone out of my wall although it makes it hard to call people, although the only person I really ever call is Microchip next door and I do that a lot because it's so fun to have my own phone just like the Elder and that may be one of the reasons Microchip ripped the phone out of the wall in the first place.

And I think I'm playing even better than before, and Microchip and myself are working real well together and I got 45 tonight against the always-prepared Philadelphias, including a layup that seemed to make a few people unhappy.

"Seriously, why didn't you dunk that, Mo?" Mr.

Barkley said afterward. "Don't you ever wanna get laid your whole life?"

Afterward there were so many press and media types and sportswriter gentlemen that they set up a table in another room and they asked me their questions in there. They must've had me in there for an hour and a half, so I can't remember all of them, but here are a few:

"Do you realize you haven't scored less than thirty points since March 10?"

"No."

"Do you realize you're shooting 78 percent from the three-point line in your last six games?"

"No."

"Do you realize you're shooting 61 percent for threes on the year and that would break the all-time NBA record?"

"No. Really?"

"Do you think this team can make the play-offs?"

"Oh, well, you know, we have our backs to the driver's seat now."

Scribble.

"Will you visit the Spelunkarium next week when you go to Denver?"

"We go to Denver?"

"Yes."

"Oh, well, of course! If the church will let me."

"Do you think the altitude will be hard to adjust to again?"

"No, because Mr. Barkley explained to me that the altitude will not affect us because we're playing indoors."

Scribble, scribble.

"Do you consider yourself a role model?"

"What do you mean?"

"Do you consider yourself somebody young kids watch and follow?"

"Do I have a choice?"

And they all nodded their heads and said, "Well put" and "I never thought about it that way," and scribbled it down but they never did answer my question.

Mr. Barkley and me and Microchip went to Mr. Barkley's favorite bar tonight—Step Away from the Car—and I brought in a two-liter of guava juice because the owner doesn't seem to mind and who was in there but my good friend Jinx and some of her friends.

As we were leaving, Jinx asked if she could sleep over and I said sure, that would be fun, except when we got back to my room and I put on my pajamas and brushed my teeth and got the cage at the bottom with the pillow on it and got into bed and was just about to turn off the lights to go to bed, she seemed mad and I said what's wrong, which was probably a mistake.

And she said, "Maurice, did it ever occur to you that the bed is good for more than just sleeping?"

"All the time," I said.

"No, seriously!"

"Are you kidding? Beds are good for a whole lot more than sleeping! I mean, under most beds is a whole *world* of insect life. There's usually some really nice dust mites, silverfish, all kinds of smaller-celled organisms. It's like a food court for my snakes."

But I don't think she heard me as she was screaming and slamming the door on me.

Mr. Stain said the last man might be my dad! "Hey, Alfalfa, I wouldn't start buying Father's Day cards yet," he said. "We've only talked to him by e-mail, but you and I will meet the guy in person and talk to him and see if he checks out."

I think the man's name is Jake, because Mr. Stain said, "So far everything about him is jake," but Mr. Stain said to make sure I don't get too excited because this Jake might just be a sheep in wool clothing.

The other big problem is Jake, my possible dad, works full-time in hole life and can't get away, even though Mr. Stain's newspaper is willing to fly him in for it, but Mr. Stain says they don't know when that would be, maybe a week or more.

Still, I'm so excited I doubt if I'll even sleep until then. I could finally meet my dad! I have to go now because I think I'm going to cry and I don't want you to see that.

I'm afraid my friendship with Mr. Death is going pretty lousily, especially since I've been shooting so well and not coming out of the game at all—I usually play forty-eight minutes because I think I'm in very good shape 'cause I don't eat surface-animal flesh and I'm on my bike so often even on days of practices and games and all that mountain climbing last year just to get back to my Spelunkarium—and that means he's been sitting the bench and also especially since that means a lot more of the sportswriter gentlemen come around a lot more and stand in front of his locker and stand on his stool, which tends to make him more than kinda mad.

"Get the (f-word) off my stool, bitch," he said to a woman from Channel 4 before the game tonight. "Do I come to your house and stand on the end of the bed while you're workin'?"

And somebody else asked him a question and he said, "I got nothin' to say and I ain't sayin' it to you, fool!"

I had 51 points tonight and poor Mr. Death only got in for two minutes and made no shots and got only three fouls and so he was not in a very good mood and I guess I can't blame him. And what seemed to make it worse for him was that I was playing with my favorite pet boa, Simone, after the game and I forgot she was around my neck when the reporters came in as I'm so used to having Simone hang out with me—get it? *ha-ha!*—and, anyway, the reporters and the TV cameramen all jumped back, even though Simone would never bite or choke anybody unless something weird happened, I guess. And I told them that, but it didn't seem to make any difference.

So, anyway, I answered their questions, even though it wasn't all that easy to hear them from across the room.

Every night when I go to sleep I wonder if I'll ever have a family or find my dad. Mostly, lately, I can't stop thinking about Lisa Stankowski of the Spinning Stankowskis and wondering if we'll ever be together and get married and have kids and would I have to be in the spinning show with her, which I would if it was the only way we could be together, and will we get old together but Microchip reminded me that we've only spoken once and that I might be getting ahead of myself but I don't think so because I think every person God put on earth above is in charge of his own destination.

MAR. 26, NEWARK

This morning, Microchip was watching *Sports-Center* and he yelled at me to come into his room and the broadcaster, Stuart Scott, was on again and he was showing something I'd said the night before with Simone wrapped around me and Mr. Scott said, "Boa-Ya!"

And then tonight at the game, a lot of fans showed up with stuffed snakes around their necks. There were all kinds of colors and sizes and some women just wore long ropes of feathers around their neck, although it didn't look much like a snake to me. There were all kinds of signs in the stands, too, like, "Fangs a Lot!" And every time one of the challenging Detroits tried a free throw, the fans would all go *s-s-s-s-s-s-s!*

We won again—our eighth straight—and a lot of the guys wanted to know where Simone was and I told 'em I was worry but I couldn't bring her for a while because I gave her a mouse this morning and she just looked at it. She's getting such a big head from all this.

I would not say Microchip is a big fan of my agent, Y. Leonard O'Connor, as Microchip often calls him Agent Orange, because of his very orange hair, I guess, and every time he walks away, Microchip says, "Why you keep him around? Guy couldn't get Michael Jordan a jock itch ad!"

"Well—" I tell him.

"You never have any money! What is this *stipend* deal he puts you on? Why you staying at the Newark Airport Ramada? How come you got no endorsement deals except for those sorry-ass socks?"

"See—" I explain.

"You're pretty much leading the National Basketball Association in scoring, three-point shooting, and field-goal percentage! As a rookie! You high-schooled for a half a year! You grew up in a cave with bats! You're playing with your high school teammate! You think I could David Falk that setup?"

"Yes, but . . ."

"Ah, forget it," he usually says, disgusted, and walks away.

Well, I will tell you, reader. I agree with my friend Microchip in that Mr. O'Connor is not a wonderful agent, but Father DeMeret appointed him for me and it would be sacreligious to go against what Father De-Meret says and, besides, Mr. O'Connor *really* hated his career in Roto-Rootering and maybe he'd have to go there if I dropped him and, besides, he just bought a new belt-hanging portable global positioning system that he likes very much that tells him exactly what his attitude is at any moment.

And, okay, it's true that I don't often have a lot of money, but I don't need a lot of money, I guess, and, besides, Mr. O'Connor says there are many, many expenses and, of course, he is investing it for me mostly in Penney stocks. He says to me, "Some people think penny stocks are risky, but you gotta stick your ass out a little if you ever want to get a tan, am I right, Maurice?" And to tell you the truth, I don't see how Penney stocks can be that risky as JCPenney has been around, what, a hundred years, and was where Phyllis bought my underwear.

And it's true that I don't do a lot of ads or appearances but it isn't because Mr. O'Connor doesn't try. It's just that he brings me these products that I don't use, such as soft drinks and cars, and I just can't bring myself to tell people what wonderful products these are when I don't use them myself. And Mr. O'Connor gets frustrated at me and wants to yell at me but just then usually something goes wrong with his calculator watch and I even got a call from the monsignor yelling at me to do it although I do not know why he should care so much.

Actually, the only product I would like to speak up for is King Korn imitation-corn frozen food products, not because I eat them very much but because of my father traveling the country in his cleaned-out Corvair in their honor. I don't have to eat them because I know if they're good enough for him to eat they're good enough for anyone as he would never put something in his body that's bad for him.

And besides, I do have one ad I do in the greater Newark tristate area, which is for Hu Lin's House of Ginseng—three locations!—and for this Hu Lin pays a very tidy sum of $500 per ad plus all the ginseng I can use and half off the pickled roots.

So there.

Still no word from my possible dad. I've been begging Mr. Stain to let me just call him on the phone but he says the paper wants to make a big deal out of it, maybe fly him in and everything, so I can't call him. But maybe Mr. Stain is right and it's just that I can't see the forest or the trees.

MAR. 28, MILWAUKEE

Mr. Lowery got some very bad news today from the team doctor, which is that his infection is 95 percent healed and he's been cleared to play again.

He took it so badly that we couldn't cheer him up the whole flight here, even when the stewardess served the special Hassidic meal for Mr. Mockmood which Mr. Big County had ordered two days ahead of time. It didn't look very appetizing and, in fact, it did not look like any kind of food I'd ever seen.

"Yummmm, Chris!" said Mr. Big County. "Dried yak! Hope it warn't one a yer pets."

The Hassidic meal didn't seem to look good to Mr. Mockmood, either, because he stared at it for a long time while everyone was laughing hysterically and then announced, "Whosoever has done this deed to me shall be whipped to death by a camel's petrified pudenda!"

And he accused each person on the team of ordering it for him except me and none of them would confess and Mr. Mockmood vowed that a terrible disease would infest each of their sisters. And later, when he fell asleep, the guys filled all his pockets, pants cuffs, and carry-on bag with peanuts.

He did not find that very funny, either, which didn't surprise anybody, but Mr. Lowery didn't find it funny, either, which surprised *everybody*, which meant he really *is* down in the dumps and all we can hope is that he's lucky enough to maybe catch his foot in an escalator or something.

Maybe I could get Simone to help.

Too bad for me, Mr. Soals was waiting for me in my room when I hit Milwaukee. When I asked him how he was in my room before even I was in my room, he said he'd arrived the day before, bribed a maid to find out what room I was going to have when I checked in the next day, pretended to check out, and then hid in the closet while they cleaned the room. The man half scared me to death.

"And do you know why I went through all this trouble, pally?" he said.

"To see me?" I asked.

"No. To *sign* you. And I'm not leaving here until I do sign you. I don't care what it takes. I don't care if you say no a thousand times. You'll say yes on the thousand and first. I'm not leaving. No how, no way, Jose."

And I said okay because I knew who was coming in next. And Mr. Soals went into the bathroom for a minute and right then Mr. Mockmood walked in and he was in a bad mood from the yak and he grabbed the TV and pitched it out into the hall as usual and then locked and bolted the door and took all his cans and hangers out of his bag and hung them off the doorknob and laid down on the bed and Mr. Soals came out of the bathroom and must've seen the very sophisticated alarm system and pretty soon there was a huge racket and that scared Mr. Mockmood to death and maybe more so.

And Mr. Mockmood ran to the door and screamed a very high-pitched scream and Mr. Soals screamed and

Mr. Mockmood snapped off his crescent moon and heaved it at him and it nearly hit him in the forehead and Mr. Mockmood called him an "infidel" and a "trespasser" and a "sin peddler" and was kicking Mr. Soals but Mr. Soals couldn't get through the cans and hangers to get out for the longest time and Mr. Mockmood was beating on him and he finally got out. And it was the first time I can remember being glad to have a roommate like Mr. Mockmood.

MAR. 29, MILWAUKEE

I got a call from Jinx this afternoon in my room, which I was glad to get because (a) I was glad to talk to her and (b) it was free. Do you know most hotels charge you a dollar per local call? I haven't got my bill from the team yet—Mr. Woody says I'll get the bill for all the plane trips and hotel rooms and meals at the end of the year—but I'm sure it's going to be a woozy. And that's why whenever I want to make a local call I get dressed and go down to the lobby phones to make it because down there it's only a quarter, even though it takes me at least ten minutes to untangle Mr. Mockmood's system.

Anyway, we had to whisper because Mr. Mockmood was asleep, but she wanted to play a game, which was What's Your Favorite Body Part, and she said hers was her you-know-what and I said, "What is your you-know-what?"

"My, you know, my special place."

And I said, "What's that?"

And she said, "Where I like to be kissed."

And I said, "Trenton?"

And the phone was silent for a long time and then she said what's mine and I told her my belly button.

"'Cause that's where you like to be kissed?"

"No," I said, "because it's the one thing that connected me to my mom and reminds me that I'm not just all alone in the world, you know? That she was with me once and she'll be with me again someday."

And then Jinx said she had something in her eye and she had to go.

Mr. Death came to the shootaround today with a whole new look—the word "DEATH" spelled out in gold caps across his front teeth and a chain with very small silver skulls that went from his right eyelid to his left ear. I thought it looked very nice and I told him so and I videotaped him but he said. "Get bent, snake boy."

The other players noticed, too, and they had a lot of questions for him, especially Mr. Big County, who asked if he gets depressed brushing his teeth now, and Mr. Barkley, who wondered if he would no longer need ID at liquor stores.

I know Mr. Death wanted to show off his new teeth to the crowds and the media, but unfortunately I scored 63 tonight, making all but three shots, despite the very unfunny thing the Milwaukee fans did which was hang a man upside down off the mezzanine deck and holding up a big sign which said, "Slo-Mo! We Have Your Father!"

But after the game, poor Mr. Death didn't get asked even one question by the reporters and nobody even took one camera shot of his new teeth which he was so proud of.

I tried to tell them. "You fellas need to look at—"

"Say, Slo, you ever have a night like this in high school?" they'd ask.

"Well, once I did. But I'm sure Mr. Death could—"

"Do you realize you broke the Nets' single-game scoring record tonight?"

"Well, no."

"Today, the president of the United States brought you up in a speech. He said you were just the kind of straightforward plain-speaking hard worker this country was built on—"

" . . . well, that's really nice, but Mr. Death has something—"

But by then he'd smashed his stool across his locker and thrown the pieces into the middle of the room and left.

I just hope he's not mad.

The man who might be my dad keeps telling Mr. Stain that it's a very busy time for him and he'd love to come but he can't get away and I guess I can understand that because, growing up in a cave, I can understand how hole life can be very busy. But still, I'm starting to wonder if this man is really my dad because if I were so close to finding my lost-long son, I think I'd be on the first plane there, but what do I know, I guess?

MAR. 30, DENVER

We had a day off before the game here tomorrow against the Denvers, so I had my entourages rent me a bike and I rode up to Boulder although I admit I grabbed on to the back of my entourages' rental car now and then. And so I went by and saw my old high school, Most Virgin Lady, and I was so pleased I just couldn't believe it! It looked like an entire new school!

There was a new grotto, and the nuns got a new convent, and the school got a new "creationism" lab and the church got a whole new face on it and the priests got a new rectum, although I guess it's not big enough for Father DeMeret as he stays in a suite down at the Boulderado.

"Why the (f-word) a priest need a suite at the Boulderado?" Mr. Doggy $tyle asked.

"Well," I said.

"What, he take a vow of room service?"

I did not get to do too much, though, because Father DeMeret saw me and took me into his coaching office and told me, "Son, we're all so proud of you," and then I had to sign stuff for him for the next hour. Apparently, he is a very big fan of mine now.

After that, I rented a bike and biked up the canyon and people honked at me the whole way and asked if I wanted a ride, but I said no. I have to admit, I liked it better when I rode up that canyon by myself and not being followed by lots of cars and people screaming at me as I go by and my entourages waving their middle fingers at people all the whole time.

Anyway, I finally got there and saw the Spelunkarium, my childhood home, and I was also very amazed at it as they have made great, great improvements since I left. Apparently, they have decided that electronic things are not so bad after all as they have a home theater now and computers in each cubicle and some of the caves are actually just rooms now with thick carpeting and walls and ceilings and lights.

Also, the Elder and many others are driving new red Range Rovers, which was kind of a surprise to me, since I thought we Inner Doorians weren't allowed to own cars and that's why I still ride my Schwinn to practice each day, even though it means riding on the New Jersey Turn Pike, which is not exactly friendly.

But times change, I guess, and the Elder was *very, very, very* nice to me which was the biggest surprise of all, because when I lived there, she mostly referred to me as a "stalactite-scraping bonehead," and also "the carny," as in "We can all go. The carny can watch things." And she also had me sign many, many, many things for her, so I guess she's a very big fan, too.

And when I was done, I was rubbing my wrist and I asked her, very respectfully, if I could go on the Tuesday Spiritual Spelunking Sojourn and she said, "Aw, we don't do any more Tuesday spelunks. Or Thursday, either. It's mostly weekends now. Some of the Doorians decided we were spending too much time in sojourns and not enough time exploring our own inner dwellings in the peace and serenity of our rooms, especially those of us in the new town houses. Besides, we were missing *Frasier*."

And this seemed very strange to me, that my people, the people who helped raise me, no longer worshiped the inner God beneath us with their every breath like they used to, like I thought I was supposed to.

As I was leaving, the Elder talked me into buying one of their new Spelunkarium videotapes—*Get Down!*—and she showed me their Web site and I bought a T-shirt with my face on it for the day when I finally find my father, with the slogan printed underneath, which was, "He Can't Dunk, but He Sure Can

Spelunk!" And they also gave me a bumper sticker with my face on it and the Spelunkarium address and the slogan "We Do It Deeper."

And as I left, I thanked her although I'm not exactly sure why.

You wouldn't believe what happened to Death tonight. See, the NBA doesn't allow you to play with any jewelry on and they said that the gold caps were jewelry. Well, it took Bruce, our trainer, more than thirty minutes and a jar of solvent to get Death's teeth off and then they were really late and they tried too fast to get the eye chain out and he got his eyelash caught on one of his skulls and his eye wouldn't open, so Bruce tried to cut it—the eyelash—with a pair of scissors and accidentally stabbed Death in the eye and the cut got infected and now he's on the disabled list for two weeks and Bruce got a large stab wound in the thigh but he wouldn't exactly say how.

But it wasn't bad news for everybody. As I was leaving, I heard Mr. Lowery asking Bruce how much an eye chain might cost.

MAR. 31, DENVER

Things are going pretty well I have to say for me and Microchip. I had 53 points last night and we beat the well-intentioned Denvers, who aren't very good at all, and won our tenth straight, a record for all the New Jerseys through the years, although it seems like I spend all my time doing interviews and answering mail and signing autographs even though Mr. Woody said to-

174

night as he walked past me, laughing, "Whatchu gonna do, sign every time somebody asks?"

And I said, "Well, yes."

And that seemed to make him stop laughing.

I'm asked to do so many interviews and autographs after games now that it makes the bus late and I'm afraid it gets the team mad at me. Tonight, Mr. Barkley and Mr. Big County and Mr. Lowery actually came back and picked me up and took me off, right in the middle of a four-part interview I was doing for Casper, Wyoming, TV. Just picked me up and carried me off. I felt bad for the people who had been waiting and wouldn't get an autograph, too, so I yelled to them to write me at the Newark Airport Ramada Hotel and I'd send them an autograph.

And the bus driver said, under his breath, "Good one, Mo! Like an NBA star would have a room at a Ramada! And they *believed* you!"

The fellas are really bothered about my eating habits and say they have made it their goal to try and get me to eat McDonald's.

"McDonald's *is* America!" Mr. Big County says.

"Slo, don't you know that by not eating at McDonald's," Mr. Barkley said, "you're turning your back on American history. McDonald's is as much a part of this country's fabric as Pearl Harbor."

"Mo," said Microchip, "you realize that on any given day, 7 percent of Americans will eat at McDonald's? Seven percent! That's more than will go to church! That's more than will screw! People in this country like McDonald's more than sex! That means McDonald's is better than sex!"

"What do you think of that, hoss?" asked Mr. Big County.

And I said, "I can't really say because I've never tried either."

And they all seemed very impressed with my discipline because they all just stared at me the rest of the way to the airport.

APR. 1, NEWARK

Mr. Stain came to me today with some bad news about the man he calls Jake, the last man who has a chance to be my dad.

"He's kind of tied up right now," said Mr. Stain.

"So he's not in hole life?" I mumbled.

"Sort of," Mr. Stain said. "He's in the hole for life. He's in Marion. Federal prison. Felony fraud, felony mail fraud, intent to deceive, gross misrepresentation, and, oh, yeah, murder one. Worked a Ponzi scheme on senior homes around the country, got nailed, and ran for it, but not very well, ended up givin' a detective the big dirt nap. Was also married to three women at once. I'm sorry."

"Why?"

"Well, uh, because he's not the guy."

"But he could still be my dad, right?"

"No, he was the mayor of Dry Rock, New Mexico, the month you were conceived, big guy. They're still trying to buy back their city hall."

I felt like somebody'd just hit me across the head with a stop sign.

"Well. Uh. That isn't so great," I said, because if I said any more I think I would've started bawling.

"It is for me," said Mr. Stain. "I can write this baby in the next forty minutes and have my nose inside a margarita by noon."

I've decided maybe I should stop worrying about my dad, Genghis Korn, and start thinking about my own life and my own family and that's why I've been thinking I'd like to see Lisa Stankowski of the Spinning Stankowskis again.

I want to go take her on a picnic in the New Jersey Meadowlands, not far from where we play our games, as my teammates have been encouraging me to do.

"It's gorgeous there," says Mr. Barkley. "Birds, wildflowers, gently babbling streams."

"Yeah, nothing makes a filly hop on pop more than a picnic in the Meadowlands," says Mr. Big County.

"She'll never forget you for it," said Mr. Lowery.

I can't wait.

And so I asked Microchip, my best friend, what he thought I should do about Lisa and he said, "You mean the little whirligig girl?"

And I said yes that was her and he said, "Ask her out, take her to dinner, bring her back, and maybe you two could do some crushin'."

I didn't get it.

Microchip put down his Dick Vitale basketball magazine and began pronouncing everything very slowly and clearly. "Arrange to meet her some night— just the two of you. Go to dinner—*with* her—at an expensive restaurant. Pay the check. Go home—again, *with* her. Then, if she's willing, enjoy sex with *her*— many times with great enthusiasm."

"I don't know," I said.

He looked at me awhile and then he said, "You still ain't gotten busy, have you?"

I nodded yes, because I *was* a little behind on the herpetology course I was taking for him.

Microchip's face fell flat. He seemed very disappointed in me. Then he jumped up and made a phone call and I didn't catch much of it except him saying, "The big, slow one needs you right away. Uh-huh. Right. Soon as you can. Right. Later." And then he hung up and he said to me, "Hang on, big'n, Dr. Ruth is comin'."

The doctor never came but you'll never guess who did thirty minutes later! Jinx! And just then Microchip said to me, "Stump, just tell her what you just told me" and then he closed and locked the door between our rooms, and Jinx was looking very pretty and smelling even prettier and looking at me funny.

"Whassup, sugar?" she said, stepping up close to me.

"Uh, me, I guess," I said, trying to be funny.

"What'd you wanna tell me?"

And I explained, "Well, there's this girl I really, really like . . ."

"Yeahhhhh," she said, like syrup.

". . . and I'd like to do what other men do with women but I have no idea what that is or how to get her to *know* that I want to do that with her and I asked Microchip and he said she and I should come back to the hotel and do some kind of acrobatic tricks, but I don't think she'd like that as she has to do that for a living with her family, and he said he was going to call this Dr. Ruth but she hasn't come yet but you're here instead."

"Ohhh," she said. "Well, see, Maurice, you have to

178

give her little signals of what you want. For instance, you might get the room like this." And she pulled a little portable stereo out of her purse with these little tiny speakers and put on some real nice music and started turning off the lights and lighting these candles and making everything smell nice and seem nice. And then she got on my desk chair and put her arms around my neck real close and it was very nice. And then she said, "Then you might dance real, real slow with her, like this," and she was dancing very, very slow, mostly against my body, which is a dance I'd like to learn *very* much. "And then you could maybe gently nibble at her ear, like this," and she did it to mine, and I started feeling very, very good at my One Point or at least very *near* my One Point, "and then just lightly brush your lips across her cheek, her chin, and then her lips, like this," and she did that. "Then you should close your eyes and kiss her slowly and deeply, like this," and then she kissed me for such a long wonderful time that when she stopped, I don't think I knew it for thirty seconds.

And finally, when I opened my eyes, she was looking at me with a gorgeous smile and saying in my ear, "You didn't have to tell Microchip you needed me, sugar. You could've called me yourself."

And I said helpfully, "Well, I just didn't know you even *knew* Lisa."

And she jerked her head back a little and said, "Who?"

"Lisa Stankowski of the Spinning Stankowskis. I can't *wait* to try this with her!"

And she and Lisa must not get along *at all* because she jumped down off the chair and kicked me very hard right in the shin and called me a jerk and packed her stuff up and stormed out.

And when I opened the door to Microchip's room, he was right in front of me, on his knees, with a glass in one hand and his other hand on his forehead.

"You the only guy in America can block his own cock," he said sadly.

APR. 2, NEWARK

I am the happiest man in the world! Mr. O'Connor signed me to go to the opening of the new, giant Super Jiffy Lube in Trenton this afternoon but that's not why I'm the happiest man in the world! In fact, I really didn't want to go because I've decided that people steal a little bit of your soul with every autograph. It just seems the more I sign the more people stare at the piece of paper and the less they talk to me. I know if I wanted to meet someone, I'd shake their hand and talk to them, but instead, they just keep their head down and ask and I sign and they walk away. That's it? That's why they wanted to meet me, was to see what my handwriting was like? It's like, they all must have friends who don't believe a word they say or else they'd just tell them, "Guess who I met?" Like an autograph is proof that they're not lying. And besides, if they would just talk to me, then maybe I could make some friends, but instead, I just have to keep scribbling my name over and over. It bothers me.

But I went anyway because Mr. O'Connor said I could go to jail for ventilating the contract. I couldn't believe how many people are big Super Jiffy Lube fans] because the place was absolutely packed with people—maybe a thousand—a lot of whom had cameras and videotape machines to capture the ribbon-cutting.

When I came, they turned the cameras on me, but I had a surprise for them! I turned my video camera on them, the one I was given by Mr. Mad Man and the Coach. And I was looking through the video camera and who did I see but the loveliest face in the whole world—Lisa Stankowski's!

And I zoomed in on her and saw her beautiful face and so I made up my mind to speak to her but as soon as I got over there, they started their act on a stage that they'd set up in front of the Jiffy Lube. She was being spun around crazily by her heels, held by her brother who was being spun around by his father who was faceup on a merry-go-round contraption being spun around by her mother.

She waved at me as she went by and I decided, "Well, now or never," and so I ran up to her and as she went by I said, "Would?"

She came by again. "You?"

Again. "Like?"

"To?"

"Go?"

"Out?"

"With?"

"Me?"

"Tomorrow?"

"Night?"

And the next time through, she said, "Why?"

And I was just crushed but then the next time through she added, "Not?"

And then Mr. T-Bone and my other entourages pulled me away from her because I had to start signing the free air filters the owners of the Jiffy Lube were giving away.

She said yes!

I knew I would have a great game against the Houstons being so happy in my One Point and knowing I was going on a date with Lisa and that is exactly what I told Mr. Dalton, our well-dressed p.r. man, who never fails to ask me exactly how I'm feeling ten minutes before tip-off. And I asked him why he always wants to know so badly and he said he just cares about me and also he has many, many friends who call on the phone asking about me who also care a lot about me and he likes to keep them updated at all times.

But I never dreamed I'd have a night like this, which is to say that I could hardly miss. I made twenty-one out of twenty-two hooks and nine out of nine free hooks, which works out to 72 points, which they say is the third highest in NBA history and, as Microchip said, "You is so crazy phat you just straight-up stupid," and I'm sure he didn't mean I was crazy, fat, and stupid, because he was hugging me the whole time he said it. He was probably just kidding around. And anyways, we beat the Chicagos easily, 144–120, in front of our first sellout of the year.

At one time, I was doing so well that Ron Harper and Mark Bryant of the Chicagos got right up in my face and yelled at me, "You ain't this good, you pencil-neck geek!" Microchip heard that and got in between them and said, "Hey, fellas, how's it feel to be one of the Pips with no Gladys, huh?"

And Mr. Harper took a swing at him and missed and skimmed the bald spot on the top of the head of referee Dick Bavetta and got thrown out and I got to shoot a free hook besides.

As Mr. Barkley said afterward, "That little Micro-chip's got more lip on him than Mick Jagger."

APR. 3, NEWARK

I'm just in Cave Nine, as we say at the Spelunk-arium, because I had my first date with Lisa, or, come to think of it, my first date with anyone of the female persuasion, and I'm sure I'm in love.

I was very excited about my date, so I tried to look my best and I wanted to wear a cool suit like the guys on my team wear, but I didn't think Jinx would want to get a suit for me as mad as she was at me, so I went to Montgomery Ward and got a really nice wool three-piece suit even though it was expensive ($199!). The legs were too short but the salesman, Nick, said that was how everybody was wearing it and the arms were too short and he went in the back and took them out himself and resewed it and I wasn't sure if they looked okay, but all the other salespeople said "I had it goin' on" so I guess it was fine. And it was nice to meet Nick, who took me aside to the corner and explained to me about tipping clothes salesmen, which I didn't know about and now won't have to be embarrassed next time.

Lisa and I were supposed to meet at one of my favorite restaurants in town, Sorghum City. Usually, I just go through the drive-thru there—well, bike-thru for me—but as I say, I wanted a table, so I got there an hour early, just to make sure we could get my favorite booth, right near the tofu dicer.

It was lucky I got there when I did because five

minutes after I got there, it went from completely empty to completely packed. The people were all so very friendly, as Newark people are so well known to be, and they all stopped by the table for a picture and an autograph from me. And it was so nice to know that so many people like Sorghum City like I do, because I asked them what their favorite thing on the menu was and each person would laugh and say, "How da (f-word) should I know?" which is how I feel because everything is so delicious.

Lisa looked so beautiful when she arrived even though she said she nearly forgot about our date and so didn't have time to shower after her jog, but I thought she looked very pretty even though maybe she didn't smell as pretty as she usually smells. I was so nervous but she didn't seem hardly nervous at all, almost like it wasn't a date for her, which I now realize she did just to make me feel less nervous.

She had the San Fransproutsco and I had what I usually have, which is the double Okrahoma City, and, for a special treat afterward, I bought us two rice milk shakes, which I know she liked because she said, very big, "Gee, Maurice, you'll spoil a girl!" Although she must've been too full because she hardly touched it and, actually, *didn't* touch it at all.

She was so easy to talk to, and mostly what she talked about was how she hated being a Spinning Stankowski but what could she do as she was the fifth generation of Spinning Stankowskis, and how much she hated being home-schooled by her mother and how much she wanted to be just a normal teenager and how much she hated her father and what a terrible man he was and how she very much hoped he would be involved in an I-95 pileup very soon.

And I usually wouldn't say something like this, but I did this time because it bothered me so much and what I said was, without sounding too bossy, "Maybe you shouldn't say stuff like that."

"Why?" she said. "It's true!"

And I told her that maybe she should be glad she even *has* a father, no matter how mean he is, because there are some of us who don't even have one and I told her about my father, Genghis Korn, and how I've never even met him and he may not even know I exist even though I do and that we could even be together but we're not.

And she listened for a long time and looked at me with those beautiful eyes and said, "Trade ya."

All in all, though, it was a wonderful date, even though we couldn't do the dancing that Jinx had taught me which hopefully would've been followed by the kiss that Jinx had taught me and that's because Lisa had another important meeting down the street because she said she "just had to get to Melrose Place" and I told her I was sorry but I didn't have directions there. And as she left, she reached up and gave me a little slug on my arm, and said, "Later, ya big lug."

It was just about the most romantic thing that's ever happened to me.

APR. 4, BOSTON

We always ride a bus to Boston because, as Mr. Barkley says, our owner, Mr. Trump, "is tighter than Brandy's ass." It was a very eventful bus ride, especially when a few of the guys in the back pitched in $100 for the longtime traditional NBA bus-ride bet, which was very embarrassing but I'm supposed to put stuff like this in, which was to see which one of them could maintain an erection all the way to Boston.

Once again, as is the tradition in the NBA, rookies are required to judge this kind of thing and, although I wasn't looking forward to it, I agreed, although Mr. Bruce said he was perfectly willing to pitch in if I absolutely didn't want to do it, but the fellas said there were no substitutions.

I wouldn't have judged if I'd known it would make Mr. Woody so mad, especially when I disqualified him near Providence.

"You got to DQ him, Slo!" Mr. Big County yelled. "Look at him! All the anger's done gone clean out of it!"

So I did DQ him, as provided for in the rules, which state that a man can be eliminated from the contest when his "hammer lacks anger," making Mr. Big County the winner. They said he'll go on to play Robert Dole in the semifinals but I'm not sure when we play them.

"Guarantee you what, hoss, I had it goin' today," Mr. Big County said in accepting the money. "Cold blue steel. You coulda blunted threepenny nails on it. I coulda made New Hampshire easy."

I don't know where I'd be without Mr. T-Bone and my other entourages, but I don't think I'm going to find out.

Today, for instance, Mr. T-Bone came to my room to escort me and my Schwinn to the airport, but before he did that, he said, "Gimme your wallet."

186

And so I handed him my wallet, the one I made myself on my lanyard at the Spelunkarium.

And he took my only twenty dollars out and took his Cuban cigar and lit it on fire and said, "You might as well just do this right here to it."

I was very shocked to see him do that and I tried to put it out but he wouldn't let me. "You do this every day with yo money, Mo!"

"I do?"

"You need somebody to take on your investments," he said.

"But I don't—"

"—have any investments, I know," he said, "which is the exact goddamn problem. You just throwin' yo money away, Mo!" he explained to me. "Anybody in the stock markets, bonds, futures, commodities, they makin' 30 to 40 percent and you got all your money stuck in a dumb-ass checking account, makin' 3 percent!"

And I said, "Well, Mr. O'Connor called me last night from Acapulco and said he's decided we need to meet and discuss some things and he'll be here tomorrow. Maybe you could talk to him then about that." And that made Mr. T-Bone much happier as he has much experience in handling his cousin Detrius' unemployment investments and agreed to handle my investments from now on. They'll be in a separate account, known as a powerful attorney, and he said I shouldn't worry because "I'm fixin' to really take care a you."

And that's a very good feeling.

The Bostons are a very tricky team and they tried something very tricky this afternoon in our game even though it didn't work and we won anyway. They fouled Microchip every time he got the ball, even if it was in the backcourt, which it usually was, which meant he got two shots, which he usually made. They also fouled Woody most times he got the ball and I'm afraid Woody wasn't so good.

Three times the ref called him for taking too much time to shoot the free throw. He dribbles, touches his lips, dribbles, holds up his right arm at the rim, closes one eye and aims, dribbles some more, mumbles something, dribbles some more, picks up the ball, spins it until the lines are just perfect and finally . . . finally . . . the ref either blows the whistle or he finally shoots. He missed all eight of his free throws today, plus the three violations, which means he was 0–11.

"I *got* to unload," he said on the bench, holding his head in his hand. "Got to, got to, got to."

But Mr. Barkley and the others told him to hang in there and eventually good things will come.

Mr. Lowery got into the game tonight but refused to shoot unless he had a wide-open short jumper and he missed half of those, so he is still above his percentages for his big bonus, but just barely.

He didn't take the team flight home with us because he said he was going out into Boston tonight in hopes of finding a bowl of bad clam chowder.

APR. 5, NEWARK

Mr. Woody walked into the locker room today with his arms over his head, like a champion prizefighter. Then he took his two thumbs and pointed them to his chest and then his two index fingers and pointed them to his you-know-what.

"I have broken the friction barrier!" he yelped. "I am through the looking glass, people! I'm the Neil Armstrong of sex!"

We all gathered around.

"See, I been doin' this gorgeous little gymnast type," he said, "with a little body that can stop on a dime and get into positions that would make a chiropractor weep. Best athlete available, no question.

"But that's not what makes it pefect. What makes it perfect is that even though she was so hot and practically slidin' off the bed and wanted to jump on ol' Trigger in the worst way, she's still a virgin! Can you believe that! It's a Rare Virgin Sighting!"

I looked at my shoes.

"And she won't ride the pony with nobody who's not married to her, even me, if you can believe that."

"How is that perfect, hoss?" Mr. Big County asked. "That sounds about three dirt roads and an interstate from perfect."

"That's why you are a mere citizen and I am a science pioneer, 'neck!" he said. "This li'l ho wants to ride it so bad it hurts. She'll get naked all you want. She'll pretend and dry hump and come about as close as humanly possible without touching it. She talks like pages 3, 4, and 5 of the *Penthouse Letters!* But she *will not* have sex with me and I know it!"

"Congratulations!" Mr. Barkley said. "Cold showers for everybody!"

"All the other hos, I knew they'd let me mount up as soon as I said the word. I knew I could have them so I was always holding something back. But with this girl,

I knew it wasn't going to happen. It just kept building, night after night, and I'd never spank Cheetah to relieve the pressure, and then, last night, she did this balance beam thing in her parents' basement and I just blew! Mt. St. Woody!"

"No touching?" said Mr. Barkley.

"Nope."

"No spitting?" said Mr. Big County.

"Nope."

"No dripping of orificial juices?" said Mr. Lowery.

"Nope."

"No Life Savers?"

"Nope."

They all looked at him, sitting there, beaming.

"Somebody find Clinton," said Mr. Barkley. "He's gonna want details."

After the game tonight—we beat the most-athletic Miamis, which means we haven't lost in almost three weeks—Mr. Soals brought the president of his company in with him, but I can't remember his name because ahead of him Mr. Y. Leonard O'Connor had the president of Reebok and the CEO of McDonald's and somebody with Pepsi. And I told all of them the same thing, that I was sorry, but no, thank you. I could never tell kids to use their products if I didn't use them myself and I didn't use any of them myself.

Then Mr. Y. Leonard O'Connor got real serious and took off his sell phone headset and pulled me aside and whispered, "Maurice! This isn't Hu Lin's House of Ginseng! This is McDonald's and Pepsi and Reebok! Hello? Hello? You gotta hit seventy home runs for this stuff! You gotta go to the moon! And you're turning it down? No, no, you are *not* turning it down! For the love of Jesus, please don't turn this stuff down!"

But I did.

I really thought I was going to see tears, but somehow, Mr. Soals held it together.

APR. 6, NEWARK

I had to go in for my daily massage today and Bruce seemed very nervous about something. He kept doing the same spots over and over.

"Maurice," he finally said, "do you know what that name, Maurice, signifies?"

"Signifies?" I asked.

"Yes. It's the name of the most androgynous character in literature. E. M. Forster's Maurice. It's a character I love more than any other."

"Well, I don't see many science fiction movies."

"No, no, no. Look, what I'm saying is, well, look, I've been trying to tell you now for two and a half months. I'll just come right out and say it. Okay? Here goes: Maurice, I love you."

"I love you, too, Mr. Bruce."

"You do?"

"Sure, you're a real nice man. All these massages you give me for free. I'll pay you back someday, somehow. But you're real nice about it."

"No, no. Look, when I say I love you, I mean, as man with man. I want to be *inside* you."

But I told him I wasn't really ready for any new kinds of massages on account of I'm already on the table for more than an hour a day as it is.

Mr. Lowery was placed on the one-week disabled list today with facial lacerations, a swollen eye, and a severely bruised foot. Police said Mr. Lowery mistakenly wandered into a Dorchester, Massachusetts, Harley-Davidson bar known as Fat Bobs wearing a Suzuki motorcycle T-shirt when he accidentally began throwing darts at a tacked-up American flag. Apparently, harsh words were said. Then, after Mr. Lowery drop-kicked a Harley motorcycle parked inside the establishment, fisticuffs broke out. Doctors said he was lucky not to break any bones.

APR. 7, WASHINGTON

This afternoon, the guys hijacked the bus on the way to shootaround and made the kind-faced man known as Bussie take us through the drive-thru at McDonald's and they said they weren't going to let us go anywhere until I ate a McDonald's hamburger.

I looked at Coach Jackson and he looked at me and then his watch and said, "We've really got to get to shootaround, Slo-Mo," he said.

Mr. Black leaned through the bus driver's window and ordered one hamburger and a McDonald's employee I couldn't see went, "Just one?"

"Yeah, just one."

"Anything to drink with that?"

And Mr. Black said, "What? You get a commission?"

And then he got it and they made Mr. Bussie pay

for it since none of them carry any money and a couple fellas had my hands held behind my back and I guess it was kinda funny if I didn't think about it too much.

"This is what we surface dwellers eat," said Mr. Barkley as he held one of these sandwiches in front of my face. "Partake of this, my son, and be saved."

I really had no choice. No offense to the fine people at McDonald's, but it looked gross. It was mostly bun, so I asked them to at least let me look inside the top bun and see what was in there. It looked like somebody had pounded it out with a sledgehammer. A tiny wafer of hamburger. Exactly five pieces of chopped onions. Two pickle slices that looked like they'd been sitting there for maybe a week. A squirt of not-quite-red ketchup and a squirt of mustard next to each other. I know blind cave eels that wouldn't touch this.

I refused until Mr. Woody held my nose, which eventually forced my mouth open, which is when Mr. Barkley shoved it into my mouth, all of it, whole. Then Mr. Big County moved my jaw up and down to force me to chew.

It was . . .

It was . . .

Terrific!

I was expecting something horrible, but it was delicious! There was a sweetness to it I liked! I loved the ketchup! I loved the pickles! It was so rich with flavor, the most flavorful thing I'd ever tasted! Ten times more flavorful even than carrot-juice-sweetened bulghar cookies with the guava-creme filling! One hundred times more flavorful than wheat-germ-laced rice cakes! Ten times more wonderful than my favorite breakfast cereal: Hummus with Pumice! So juicy and good!

They all looked at me for an answer.

I paused for a long time while I chewed and then, at last, I said, "I like it!"

Everybody went kinda nuts on the bus and started chanting—"Mo meat! Mo meat!"—and they started rocking the bus back and forth and Mr. Bussie was honking the horn crazily and the people at the drive-thru window were all leaning out trying to figure out what was wrong.

And when the noise finally died down, Microchip said: "Next up . . . furburgers!"

We beat the always-stubborn Washingtons easy to-night, and Microchip had fifteen assists and 17 points and I had 38 in only three quarters, but it wasn't a wonderful night, because Mr. Limpet got up and read quotes from other players in the league about me:

"Danny Ainge, coach, Phoenix Suns: 'I can't be-lieve this dope is seven-eight and won't dunk. What's next? Vegetarian wolves?'

"Shaquille O'Neal, Los Angeles Lakers: 'I think the guy spent too much time underground, man.'

"Charles Barkley, teammate, New Jersey Nets: 'He's either got the worst vertical leap in history or he's the biggest pussy this side of Socks.' "

I looked over at Mr. Barkley after this one. He just smiled and shrugged. He said later it was taken out of context but I told him I didn't care what paper it came from, I didn't like it one bit.

Microchip and I went to McDonald's after practice today and I had another hamburger. Well, actually,
I had three Quarter Pounders and I might've had more
except so many people kept bothering me for autographs and I finally told them to leave me alone so I
guess there's a first for everything.

Then Microchip said I should try one with a piece
of cheese melted on top of it and I just couldn't believe
how good those were and had four more of those and
then he said I should have a Big Mac and so I had three
more of those and then he said I should try the french
fries, which were just about the best thing I've ever
eaten, and I had six bags of those along with thirty-
seven of those little packages of ketchup and also four
milk shakes and then I said, "What are the fish sandwiches like?"

And Microchip suddenly stopped.

He grabbed my arm very sternly and looked me
right in the eye and said, "Mo, that's *not* what this is
about."

Microchip is very serious about his McDonald's.

I feel like maybe I'm starting to get used to this league.
I feel different. Stronger, maybe. More aggressive. I feel
like I'm really having fun now, like I belong with these
guys, finally.

Today, for instance, outside practice, a guy came up
to me and said, "Hey, stretch, how's the weather up
there?" and started laughing. So I spit right on the top
of his head and said, "Rainy."

All the fellas just fell on the pavement laughing. I had to admit, I was laughing, too. The guy wiped his head off with his wife's Kleenex and grumbled something at me and walked away mad and, for a moment, I felt bad about it, but then I thought, I've heard that line thousands of times. How many times do I have to hear it?

APR. 9, NEWARK

Me and Mr. T-Bone seem to be getting real close. He gave me $2,000 today!

See, he said he's got some friends in town who really wanted to see the game tonight and they have lots of money but the game was a sellout since we've been playing so good so he said, "Can I buy your tickets?"

And I said, "I'd be glad to, but I don't have any tickets, either."

"Oh, you already gave your four away?"

"What four?"

"You get four free tickets to every game! Every player does, man! You didn't know that?"

"I do? Well, sure, I'm not using them."

But he wasn't about to hear of that and, in fact, was almost mad about me insisting that he take them for nothing. "Look, these guys really want to pay for them. They can write them off anyway. They're suits, you know what I'm sayin'?"

Well, I'm not the kind of person who beats a dead gift horse in the mouth, so I sold him my tickets and he gave me a check for $2,000, so I guess it will go in my checking account, but still, it was nice of him. And not only that, I didn't have to do anything. He said he'd go and sign them on the sheet and the ticket manager would give them to him. And I didn't have to do anything!

T-Bone also asked me why I ride my Schwinn to shootaround every day to and from games and I said, "Well, I don't have a car for one thing and for another, it's the way of the Inner Doorians."

"(F-word) that," he always answered. "You should ride with me."

So, today, I was all set to get on my bike for the long and often dangerous trip to the Meadowlands on my bike—along the New Jersey Turn Pike to the scenic exit 16W—and I just said to myself, "Why am I doing this when the leaders of my very own Spelunkarium are driving nice Rovers and don't seem to be worried about spending eternity up in hell?" So I said, "Forget it!"

So I went with Mr. T-Bone in his new Ford Excursion, which was really very, very huge and which I, come to think of it, lease *for* him, and which has a stereo that was so loud, my McDonald's orange drink in the cup holder bounced around like a 7.1 earthquake, which is the one thing Doorians fear most.

Microchip was late to shootaround, which means a $500 fine, and he glared at me the whole time he was getting chewed out by our assistant coach, Coach Summers. I knew why, too. I completely forgot about him. Usually, he waits for me and tails behind me in his rental car, but I went with Mr. T-Bone and I completely forgot to knock on Microchip's door and he waited and waited for us and even went to Hu Lin's House of Ginseng thinking maybe I'd forgot and by the time he made it to shootaround he was late.

I told him I was sorry and he said, "It's cool," but he still looked a little mad.

I've been doing some thinking, well, actually, Mr. T-Bone and Mr. Li'l T-Bone and Mr. Doggy $tyle have been doing a little thinking and they've decided maybe I'm letting the team down by staying so far outside. After all, I'm 7-8! I ought to be able to get inside a little. True, we've won fourteen in a row and I'm shooting well and averaging 21.7 points a game and a lot more than that over the last month. But anyway, that's what I decided, too, because I feel stronger, I decided to take it inside a little more tonight in our game with the underranked Torontos.

"What the (f-word) you mean?" Microchip said. "You take it inside and I'll Bruce Lee your groin!"

But I just wanted to try it a few times, so I'd give the ball up to Microchip on the inbounds and then go down and set up underneath. Greg Ostertag, the Torontos' center, seemed very surprised at first and, in fact, wasn't watching, thinking I'd set up high, like usual, and I ran by him and I was wide open for an easy layup but Microchip was still trying to get the ball upcourt and didn't have his head up to see me.

"Microchip," I said at the next time-out. "I don't want to be rude, but I was wide open!"

"Blow me, Mo," he snapped. "The only reason you were wide open is because you didn't help me get the ball up. You can be open as a Dunkin' Donuts, but I can't get you the ball if I got Damon Stoudamaire on me like the mumps."

"Well," I said, sort of meanly, "how do other point guards in the league get it up the court without picks?"

Microchip looked up at me with a real hurt look. I shouldn't have said it, I guess.

Anyway, we lost. I told the press, "We've only got one person to blame and that's each other," but I really don't think it was my fault.

I don't care what Microchip says. I think I've learned enough about the NBA after three months that I can try some new things. Harley the Stain says we've practically got the play-offs made anyway. Why not try a few new things?

APR. 10, NEWARK

The guys on the team have been calling me "Tommy Lee" and I think it's because I'm always taking home movies with my home movie camera and that is a compliment because they say this Tommy Lee is such a famous big movie maker, but I can't help it because I like doing it and it takes my mind off Lisa and my father, neither of which I can find lately.

Lisa and the Spinning Stankowskis have been nowhere around lately and I don't know what to do about it because if two people are dating it doesn't seem right that they can't even find each other.

I did call her once because I have her phone number now and I asked her if she'd like to go to a picnic with me in the Meadowlands but she just laughed and laughed about that until she realized I was serious.

"It'd be fun," I said. "We could spread out a blanket and throw the Frisbee and maybe find a stream. Want to?"

"Yeah, right. Let's go to the Meadowlands for a picnic. After that, we can go to the Bronx and see the bucking horses! I can't wait!" And I guess she got so excited she hung up and broke the phone somehow because I kept calling her back but the phone wouldn't answer.

You'd think everybody would be excited with the way we're playing lately, but Mr. Big County says he's not all that interested in us making the play-offs. He says if we did well in the play-offs, it might wreck the trade his agent has set up for him with Dallas. He said he's already got a ranch picked out in Plain Old, just outside Dallas, where he's going to play power forward for the Mavericks "and get me some scary chicken-fried steak, biscuits and red-eye gravy, and beer that's just colder 'n the smile on the graveyard-shift waitress at Shoney's. Livin' in this town for a year, my bloodstream's just about a quart low on good red-eye gravy."

"How you gonna get traded?" asked Mr. Barkley. "They love you here. The fans love you. You go demanding to be traded, the press'll fry you and you'll lose endorsements."

"I got a plan, hoss."

APR. 11, NEWARK

I've been spending more time with Mr. T-Bone and Li'l T-Bone and Doggy $tyle and Doc Star lately and not as much with Microchip. It's not that I don't like Microchip. I do like him, but my entourages say that asking him to go along with us to some of the clubs we go to wouldn't be fair because "he's only making the minimum," as they say, and could no way afford it and would be highly embarrassed about it so they say it's better if we just leave him behind.

Only problem is, it makes it difficult when I get ready to leave our connected rooms at the Newark Airport Ramada Hotel. Like tonight, I tried to sneak out to meet my entourages in the lobby and he poked his head in at the last second and said, "Whassup, Tiny?" which is what he calls me sometimes when he's just horsing along.

I felt kinda bad but I didn't know what to do so I said, "I'm going to the, uh, club."

"What club? A *dance* club?" he asked.

"No, no, no! Not a dance club!" I said. "No, like, uh, like a club for, well, big guys. The Big Guys Club."

"Yeah?"

"Yeah. I wish you could come, but, you know, it's just for big guys, which is why they call it, you know."

"Uh-huh. Whadda they do at the Big Guys Club? Discuss ceiling patterns?"

"Uh . . ."

"What? Bowl with midgets? What?"

"Yes! Yes, exactly! Well, not exactly like that, but kinda like that, yeah! That's what we do! How'd you know? We do things big guys do, you know, there's a lot of big chairs and you know, big *things* to just be *big* with."

"Just supersize everything, right?"

"Yeah! Exactly!"

"Where you goin', Slo?"

"To the Big Guys Club!" I was pretty rattled.

"Yeah, right."

"Good."

I started to go. As I was going out the door, though, he said, "Yo, Slo."

"Yeah," I said.

"One thing, man. Just because you're a big man, doesn't make you a big man, y'know what I'm sayin'?"

It bothered me for a while until I told T-Bone about it and he said, "Ahh, little man's just jealous of big guys, man. This is the best thing for him, I'm tellin' you. You'll be buyin' drinks for everybody all night and he won't be able to buy hardly one and how would that make him feel?"

"Smaller 'n the shrimp already is," T-Bone said.

"Exactly!" Mr. Doggy $tyle said.

And I felt better after that.

Guess who we saw at the club? Jinx!

Li'l T-Bone tried to keep her away from me because I think she was a little drunk and he knows I don't drink alcoholic beverages, although T-Bone keeps ordering yummy-looking drinks for me that are very colorful, but so far I've resisted since it's strictly against Inner Doorian beliefs, although it's been a long time since I attended Undermass. But I like Jinx very much as she's been so much help to me and she wasn't even there with any of her group of bitches and so I was glad when she asked me to dance, especially since it was a slow one and maybe she might give me some more tips.

But she didn't want to give me tips, she only wanted to talk.

"Slo-Mo, I have something to tell you," she said as she was pulling up a chair to stand on again. She put one arm around my neck and another around my, well, butt, and looked right into my eyes like it was very, very important. "I've been trying to tell you this for the longest time but I haven't had the courage."

"Oh," I said.

"Well, there's something you have that no one else I've ever met has had."

"Ohh!" I said. I backed a little bit away and reached in my pocket and pulled out the plastic carrying case that Gwendolyn, my Brazilian mouse snake, travels in. "It's just Gwendolyn."

She gasped for a second and then asked me to put it in my back pocket for a second and then she shook her head a few times and then said, "No, it's not Gwendolyn. It's *you*. It's what's *inside* you. I admit, when I first met you, all I was trying to do is get you to sleep with me."

"Oh, don't worry about *that*," I said.

"Why not?" said Jinx.

"Because I sleep fine by myself."

She sighed.

"No, no, what I meant is, at first, my intentions for you weren't honest. I just wanted to trick you into something. But that's not how I feel now. The way you are, the sweetness you have, the things you've said to me, the way you *listen* to me, and the way you *care* about me, as a person, not just as a cumstop, well, no man has *ever* treated me that way before."

She was just inches from my face now. "At first I didn't know how to react, what to think, but now I know. You may not know it, Slo-Mo, but you've changed my life, how I think about myself, what I *want*. I know you like Lisa, but maybe someday, you'll see that AYEEEEEEAAHHHHH!"

The scream was so loud that everybody in the place came running over and I guess what happened is that when I put Gwendolyn back the case must've popped open and she crawled right down my leg and up the stool behind Jinx and then up her back and rubbed up against her nose, just playing, of course. Gwendolyn is kind of a trickster.

But it scared Jinx so bad she jumped back and forgot she was on the chair, I guess, and fell off it backward and hit her head on the bar rail, which completely knocked her out. I was trying to catch Gwendolyn as she was starting to crawl up Jinx's skirt and in all the craziness, the bouncers thought I'd done something ungentlemanly to Jinx, and so they yanked me away and called the police. And even though I didn't really want to go, the police took me to jail even though Mr. T-Bone tried to tell them it was nothing. Luckily, he got me to sign the check first.

Jail wasn't so bad except I spent the whole night signing autographs for the guards and the night-court judge and the other prisoners and I couldn't sleep because the beds were too short, but at least I got to become friends with a former NBA superstar, Roy Tarpley, who was in there, too, because, as he kept saying, "The cops *dissed* me in front of my homies, bra! Can't *broach* no disrespect, bra!"

Roy is out of the league now, but he says it turns out me and him got a lot in common. We're both just misunderstood.

Microchip heard about me being in jail and came and bailed me out this morning, which was very nice of him, although he hardly said anything to me at all, except, "Man, you better take a look at your beanpole self."

And when I got back to my room, Mr. T-Bone was waiting there, all angry because the check I signed at the end of the night was for more than $2,000 but my Visa didn't have enough money in it and Mr. T-Bone had to promise I would come in today and pay it and he had to leave all his ice there but I thought, *Doesn't everybody?*, and he said that meant he had to get in his limo "lookin' all lame and shit" and he said it was gonna cost me some serious overtime.

See, all my bills for my hotel room and anything I eat there goes straight to Mr. Y. Leonard O'Connor and anything else that comes up—like clothes, restaurants, bike repair, basketball shoes, newspapers, anything—I'm supposed to pay for out of my Visa card, but I guess now there's no more money in my Visa card and it made Mr. T-Bone very angry and so he made me call Mr. Y. Leonard O'Connor right then and there and tell him he wanted to set up a meeting.

"Y.B.O.N.T.," he said and they all laughed, so I did, too, because it is always a good idea to laugh when Mr. T-Bone laughs.

At shootaround, a bunch of reporters were there and the story was in the papers and it made it look like I'd done something terrible to Jinx when I hadn't and in reality, only something terrible had happened to me, which was that I lost Gwendolyn forever even though I went back to the club this morning and looked. And the headline on the back page of the New York Post said, "Slo-Mo Finally Slam(mer)s One!"

Mr. Lupica in the Daily News wrote: "And so, out of the city's darkness comes the beginning of the end, the poison police report that breaks kids' hearts. Turns out the lovable, peaceful giant teddy bear is just another scumbag with a good cover. Fooled again."

Then our announcer, Ahmad Rashad, pulled me out of practice, turned the camera on, and said, "Kind of a wild night," and put the microphone in front of me.

"You had?" I said.

"No, you had," he said.

"Oh, right," I said. "I had."

He started at me.

"Something you wouldn't repeat," he said.

"Not if you don't want me to," I said.

And he turned to the camera and said, "That's the story from here!"

I wonder if Jinx is awake yet.

I was suspended by Coach Jackson for one game, so I sat the bench the whole time next to Mr. Lowery, who has to start playing again tomorrow, and we lost to the deep-seated New Yorks and afterward I drowned my sorrows in twelve Large Macs.

APR. 13, NEWARK

T-Bone and Mr. Y. Leonard O'Connor met for breakfast at the Newark Airport Ramada Hotel coffee shop this morning and T-Bone looked at Mr. O'Connor fussing with his new wristwatch personal organizer and then Mr. Y. Leonard O'Connor looked up at T-Bone in his giant Hummer-hood-ornament gold chain and his huge three-finger diamond rings and his Brooklyn Dodgers jersey and his sagging jeans and huge black belt and big army boots and *his* headset sell phone and wristwatch organizer and then they both said at the same time, glaring at each other, "Slo-Mo, can you eat at another table?"

And so I moved to another table across the restaurant, where I couldn't hear what they were saying, but I could see them. At first it seemed like Mr. Y. Leonard O'Connor was doing all the talking and gesturing, but then Mr. T-Bone seemed to take over and started doing a lot of gesturing and Mr. Y. Leonard O'Connor got real quiet and looked kind of sick. And then they both came over to me and handed me the check and Mr. Y. Leonard O'Connor said, sort of quietly, "Maurice, we've worked it all out. I'll arrange for you to have a $25,000-ceiling Visa card, plus I'm increasing your weekly spending allowance to $10,000, cash, to be delivered each week to you by Mr. Sylvester."

"Who?" I asked.

"Me," said T-Bone.

"I hope this meets your satisfaction," he said. "Call me if I can help in any other way."

And he looked at T-Bone and sorta sniffed and left, holding his new wristwatch organizer up to his ear.

Coach Jackson has this new punishment for us that some of the guys don't like very much. If you miss the winning shot or the winning free throw or blow the winning rebound, you have to stand and watch while the rest of the team run "karma" gassers. It's not very nice at all and makes the guy who's not running the gassers feel very bad.

Guys have been grumbling about it but Coach Jackson just says, "Knowing truly means suffering truly." And somebody mumbled, out of breath, "I wish Coachie-san would get fired truly."

In fact, there was a bad story in the paper today about how nobody likes Coach Jackson and how fellas don't even like playing for the heralded New Jerseys at all if not that much.

There were a bunch of quotes in the story but nobody was named. One quote from a player was really bad. The writer said the player asked not to be identified, but his quote was, "I tell you what, hoss, the Zen master is crazier 'n a room full a Iraqis. Only guy I like is that little owner. That man must have more cute nieces 'n Elvis." The player went on to say this, which was, "I don't want anybody to figger we ain't behind Coach Jackson. We are. We're behind Coach Jackson 30 percent."

All I can say is good thing he kept his name out of it.

APR. 14, CHARLOTTE

Well, since nobody pressed charges, I don't have to go back to court and the team didn't fine me or make me run laps like Father DeMeret, but the sports-writers are still readin' me the right act about it, saying they thought I was so different but it turns out I'm just like all the rest. On one hand, that makes me so mad because I didn't do anything at all—it was just Gwendolyn's fault—but I can't tell anybody that because it's illegal to have a Brazilian mouse snake in New Jersey without a license.

On the other hand, I kinda like people saying I'm like the other players on the team and in the league, because most of them are very cool, even though, I have to admit, I didn't think so at first with the way they carry on with different women every night in every city, sometimes two and three girls, and prostitutes, and say yes to drugs and sit there all night long and play Nintendo in their rooms or take the backs of the TV off and mess around with the TV until they can get free Spectravision movies, which are almost all dirty. But now something new inside me tells me it's not so bad. In fact, I think some of that sounds kinda fun, although I hope the Elder doesn't read this.

T-Bone told me what to tell the sportswriters who keep asking about Jinx and even though I didn't quite understand it, he said it was a pretty nice thing to say and made me look like a gentleman, so tonight, when they asked me again, after the game, I told them what he told me to tell them, which was, "I wasn't trying to have sex with her. I didn't have enough penicillin with me."

And they all laughed and wrote it down so I guess everything will come out all right.

———

Tonight we lost to the Charlottes and Mr. Lowery had to come out of the game twice tonight with a bloody mouth, because of the league rule about him catching the HIV virus.

"Man, those must hurt," I told him on the bench.

"Not as much as swallowing the little capsule afterward," he said.

We were at McDonald's, me and T-Bone and everybody, and this guy came up to me and said, "Do you play basketball?"

And I said something I heard Mr. Death say once at the mall that day, which was, "No, I clean giraffe ears."

And we all broke up laughing and the guy called me a jerk, but, hey, it's like T-Bone is always saying, screw them if they take your joke.

APR. 15, NEWARK

Today, T-Bone was telling me how stupid it is I have to pay for shoes when I could be getting lots of money and free shoes besides, just for signing with somebody like Mr. Soals.

"Look," he said, "you think Bill Gates does his own ironing? You a fool, Slo, not cashin' in on the shoes! Half the money my homeboys made in college came from shoes! You missed college so you missed all them snaps! It ain't fair!"

The more he talked, the more it made sense. If I sign with Mr. Soals, they'll have me do ads, which is even more chance that my father will see me and he's going to see right away that I'm his son because I'm sure we'll look so much alike. Plus, if he hasn't seen me by now and tried to contact me, then he probably doesn't watch the NBA and never will and I'll have to find him by some other way and I'm just about out of ways. And then he said something else.

"With the shoe money, you could get you a private I," T-Bone said, explaining that the "I" is for investigator.

And he explained that he has a cousin who dabbles in private I'ing and I could hire him for cheap, maybe $5,000 a day, plus expenses, and he'd come back with my dad "probably within a week."

And I got so excited with this new idea about a private I that I told him to go ahead and do it and I decided to call Mr. Soals up on the phone right then and there. Well, I didn't. T-Bone did.

"I got somebody right here that I know you got a wooden dick for," T-Bone said to Mr. Soals on the phone. "I might be able to swing a little deal for the right finder's fee. Who? Li'l white skinny-ass drink a water named Maurice Finsternick, chief."

There was a big whoop on the other end, but T-Bone kept telling him to "chill" and "cool down," that "this was gonna involve a negotiation that was going to be more complicated than Father's Day at Shawn Kemp's house."

And they talked on the phone for the next two hours while I just sat there. And while it made me a little sad when I looked at my dad's shoes to know that I would have to take them off, I also knew that it was T-Bone who was going to help bring me to him.

After practice today, Jinx was waiting outside the locker room, looking angrier than you can possibly look and perhaps more so. I came out with Mr. Barkley and he said, "Uh-oh," and disappeared and she grabbed me by the belt and dragged me into the corner and whisper-screamed, "You are the biggest asshole I've ever met in my life! Even if you were five-foot-two you would be the biggest asshole I've ever met in my life! I never, ever, never want to see you again as long as I live or as long as you live, which, if there is a God, won't be more than another ten minutes!"

And she jumped up and slapped me hard across the face. And I tried to ask her what I did wrong but by then she was running full speed down the hall like a scolded dog.

Poor Mr. Lowery doesn't know what to do next. He's too chicken to really hurt himself but he's lost all confidence in his jumper to keep playing.

Mr. Big County said he ought to try choking Coach Jackson. "They'd have to suspend you the rest of the year for sure," he said.

"No good," said Mr. Lowery. "Morals clause in my contract. I'd lose everything."

I suggested he go get a flu shot.

"You don't *get* the flu when you get a flu shot, Slo," he said. "You keep from getting the flu. Big difference."

"String of horrid untimely deaths in the family?" Mr. Barkley said.

"Sportswriters would check up on it," he said.

We all sat there, thinking and thinking, and then suddenly Mr. Lowery bolted upright, yelped, "Got it!" and ran out.

APR. 16, NEWARK

I'm sad about Jinx and I hope there's a way for us to be friends again, but as Microchip says, "Slick, you've changed," and I thanked him for that.

Sometimes I'm amazed at what a dork I used to be. I mean, I actually used to *like* Whey to Go and Sorghum City and health-food crapola places like that. And all the time, I could've been "dinin' Chez Ronald," as T-Bone likes to say, having my usual order: four No. 3 meal deals, supersized, three shakes, two apple pies, and an ice cream Sunday.

Bruce, our trainer, says it's added some "love handles" to me, which was nice of him to say, I think, but that might be because I'm trying to lift weights now with T-Bone and Li'l T-Bone and Mr. Lowery, who is only cleaning and jerking because he's hoping to pull something. True, it's affected my shooting a little—I was three for twelve tonight and we lost, but I did get two rebounds and blocked a shot and fouled out, which I hear is something the coaches like to see, a fella working hard on defense—but I want to learn to play inside anyway, "where the sick (f-word)s are" as Death likes to say. I hope someday my dad sees me and knows I'm bangin' in there with the sick (f-word)s.

I also realized today how stupid it's been to stay in the Newark Airport Ramada Hotel all this time, which is really kind of a dump when you really look at it, and no reason I have to stay there since, as Doggy $tyle says, "Just 'cause you come from white trash doesn't mean you gotta sleep with it."

So my entourages and I have decided to go look at some houses tonight, or, as they're known to say, "sweet cribs," for me to live in and also them, since that'd be a lot of fun for all of us to enjoy a sweet crib together.

Mr. Lowery will be out for a while, maybe more, with jury duty. The team tried to get it postponed, but he was already seated for a trial.

"Bribed the assistant to the county clerk," Mr. Lowery said. "First guy in history to pay money to get *on* jury duty."

I asked him how long he thought it would be before he's done with the jury duty.

"A long-ass time," he said. "Pliers murder deal. I just have a feeling deliberations will be very, very lengthy, don't you?"

I said I didn't know because, of course, I didn't know as much about the trial as he did.

Microchip is really bothering me lately. He's been sweatin' me about T-Bone and my entourages, saying they're no good for me and they're changing me, but I think he's just jealous and, besides, he wouldn't even *be* in the NBA without me, 'cause I was the one who sent for him. He really makes me mad sometimes, dissing my homies like that.

I didn't even open my half of the dividing door today, that's how mad I am, even though Juan is in there right now and I know he gets depressed if I don't come in and rub his forehead when I'm home.

A large black man walked into the locker room after the game tonight and none of us recognized him for a minute and the security officers were starting to kick him out when it suddenly hit me.

"That's Death!" I said.

We hadn't seen him in almost three weeks, and he looked completely different. I mean, *really* different. His nose was smaller, his eyes had a kind of Chinese look to them, his chin was much more like a woman's, and his ears were smaller and pointier.

"What'd you do?" Mr. Big County asked, staring at him. "Lose you a fight with a Cuisinart?"

"It's art, you (f-word)in' 'neck," Mr. Death explained.

"Art," he said.

"Yeah, fool. I'm the first person to use his face as an artistic canvas."

All of us were just sort of shocked.

"Shoot, big'un," said Mr. Big County. "If you needed canvas money, I coulda lent it to you."

"Yeah," said Mr. Barkley. "You didn't have to become Rae Dawn Chong."

The problem was none of the Mousses or the sportswriters recognized him at first, so I let them know who it was and they all gathered around and asked him a lot of questions and I think it made him very happy. In fact, one guy gave him his card and a contract to fill out and said he wanted to have him on *American Journal*, a TV show, and pay him besides. And after, Death asked me to read him the contract because he forgot his reading glasses again.

APR. 17, NEWARK

I'm very angry at Harley the Stain because I thought we were friends but I guess we're enemies now because he wrote in the paper that we're a terrible team now with me in the middle and not outside and that I'm "the worst thing on defense since the Yugoslavian Air Force" and that I'm "slower than a DMV employee" getting to the defensive switches and even if we do make the play-offs, we might as well be "polishing the brass on the *Titanic*" because we got no chance and will be swept in the first series if I don't "get my increasingly widening butt outside the three-point line where God meant it to be."

The coaches are saying the same thing to me, too, so I set up outside to shoot in the games but then I just want to get inside and do some bangin' with the "sick (f-word)s" inside, which is my game now that I'm stronger and older, and that makes them mad so they take me out. That's their problem, to me, because, as Mr. Doggy $tyle says, I'm real mad about my skills.

Guess what? I bought a "sweet mother crib" in East Rutherford, New Jersey, which means I bought a big, huge house! This house doesn't look so much like a house as much as it looks like a castle with even a moat and it has a whole entire rec room that I'm going to put all my snakes in. And T-Bone's bedroom is even bigger than the rec room.

He said he would've let me have that bedroom but "I knowed you wanted to be down in the cellar buggin' out wich your snakes and shit," so he took it and I guess he's right as usual.

It's got a cool swimming pool that I can use when they're not having their family parties and a big huge yard and a huge room that looks just like one of the Odoplexes and a big, big workout room and a seven-car garage, even though I don't own a car, but T-Bone says they're going to have a special place for my Schwinn with its own automatic door!

It doesn't come with any furniture, but T-Bone says all we need is something to watch TV on and king-sized water beds with sable bedspreads "like Tyson have," says Li'l T-Bone. And I stupidly asked won't that look a little weird with all those rooms (forty-one) and no furniture in them and he said, "You ever been to Kevin Garnett's house? He got fifty-two rooms and only two with anything in it. All you care about is that it looks mother(f-word)in' *big* on the outside and you got somewhere inside to catch you some video and some *SportsCenter* and a place to hide you some hot and cold runnin' pussy, you know what I'm sayin'?"

Mr. Y. Leonard O'Connor laughed at that, which surprised me a little. See, he's been showing up more often lately and he came along to talk to the Realtor although he was actually mostly out in the hall talking on his headset sell phone now that it's got triple call waiting. I thought he would be angry about me spending so much money ($3.1 million) but he actually thought it would be pretty smart because he said they were going to work a little "tax magic through the church" with it. And I wondered how a Roto-Rooter man knows so much about taxes but then he introduced me to this little Pakistani guy he had along with him who had a slide rule on his belt and a calculator that he kept punching and saying, "This'll crunch!"

The only bad thing happened when I got home and told Microchip I bought a house and he said, "Yo, boy! Now you makin' sense! We're leavin' this sorry-ass, cheesecloth-towel, shrunken toxic-waste dump! This is the smartest move you've made in a month! Where is it?"

He was bouncing around from bed to bed again. I couldn't hardly tell him the bad news.

"Well, uh, that's the thing. It's in East Rutherford, but, see . . ."

Microchip looked at me like I'd just shot his cat. "What?"

He stopped bouncing.

"Well, see, all the bedrooms are already taken. You know, T-Bone, Li'l T-Bone, Doggy $tyle, Dirt, Dirt's main boy, Master C."

He just stared at me.

"But you could sleep on the couch!"

He slammed the door between us so hard that Simone fell off the dresser.

". . . if T-Bone lets me get one!"

APR. 18, NEWARK

Barter Soals of the Nikey shoe company found me at my favorite McDonald's today and when he rushed in, he looked like he'd just been Christmas shopping. He was carrying about ten boxes of shoes in a stack so high they went over his head. He flopped them down and said, "All right, pally, you don't even *shower* without a pair of these on."

Apparently, Mr. T-Bone had made a deal already and I was supposed to start wearing the shoes "as a good-faith gesture" even though "there's still a few t's to cross," Soals said. In fact, I was supposed to start wearing these new shoes on the court and off the court, starting right now. "You're a walking Nikey logo now," Barter Soals said to me.

"But did Mr. T-Bone say his cousin was going to help me?" I asked.

"Say again?"

"His cousin, the private I, he's going to help me, right?"

"Oh? Oh! Right, right," said Barter Soals.

"Good," I said.

Soals started opening up the boxes. He had to ask Mr. and Mrs. Kawulok, an older couple sitting next to us, if they'd please move, since we had business to do, which was too bad, since I'd been talking to them and they seemed pretty nice.

He spread the boxes out and started pulling out the Nikey shoes. They were all exactly the same, size 22, black and blue—"teal and midnight" Mr. Soals corrected me—with this horrible cartoon picture of a bomb on the side. Black and round with a fuse? And down the tongue it said, "The Bomb."

I really didn't like it.

I looked at my shoes. They were starting to fray at the toe and the rubber was almost gone underneath and I had to replace the shoelaces a bunch of times and also the little eyelets three or four times, but I loved them.

I just couldn't bring myself to put the Bombs on. They were so, so, so not pretty. I've seen petrified cave guava lumps that were prettier than these shoes. But Soals was smiling like crazy. "You can't escape Barter Soals, pally," he said. "Barter Soals will get you sooner or later. That's why Barter Soals is the king!"

I put one of them down on the ground to start lacing it up and the weirdest thing happened. They began to tick, like a bomb. *Tick-tick-tick*. It scared the bejesus out of me. I jumped up on the seat, but since it was a swivel seat, I couldn't keep my balance and fell backward over the planter right onto the table of Mr. and Mrs. Kawulok, my back landing right square in their fish sandwich, which squirted tartar sauce right on Mrs. Kawulok and ketchup on Mr. Kawulok.

I think they wanted to yell at me but we all three kept looking at the ticking shoe, which Soals now had as he came sprinting around the table.

"Are these dope or what?" he said. "Tell me kids won't be jackin' each other for these sweet kicks, pally!

"Well, gotta roll, big boy!" Soals said. "Don't let me catch you, day or night, without a pair of these babies on! If you die, I wanna see these shoes on you in the morgue drawer, you dig? Two-grand fine every time, pally! It's in the contract! Ciao!"

And we all three watched him go. And the shoe was going *tick-tick-tick*. And I was thinking how in the world I ever got into this mess when—

"Do you *mind?*" said Mr. Kawulok, trying to get his fries out from under my butt.

At least there was some good news around here today and that good news is that Mr. Woody is engaged!

When he told us, Mr. Barkley spit out his Dr. Pepper. Bruce, our trainer, cut a guy taking off his tape. And three guys ran screaming out of the shower.

It was true. Mr. Woody said he realized it was the only way he was ever going to have real sex with his gymnast girl, and he seems very, very anxious to do that.

"Woody's marrying a virgin," said Mr. Barkley. "And Slo-Mo's gonna ride the winner at the Kentucky Derby."

Why am I always the last to hear things?

APR. 19, NEWARK

This was a very bad day.

This was the kind of very bad day that very bad days have when they're having very bad days.

I called Mr. T-Bone to see what his cousin, the private I, had found out so far and he kinda grumbled, "Who the (f-word) is this?"

"It's me, Mo," I said.

"Whatchu callin' me at six-thirty in the morning for, bitch?"

"Well, I'm wearing the new shoes you arranged for and I was just seeing if your cousin had gotten anywhere finding my—"

"Come over here right now, bitch, and I'll teach your ass who's your daddy."

"Really?"

But he went on to say in very loud tones that he didn't mean *at all* what I thought he meant and then he hung up.

I guess maybe it *was* a little early but I'm so excited about his cousin finding my dad I could hardly sleep.

So, since I was up, I decided to ride my bike over to my new house in East Rutherford and once I was inside I was very surprised to see that T-Bone and Li'l T-Bone and the rest had already started moving boxes in, even though the closing wasn't until 3 P.M. tomorrow.

And so I was walking around my new sweet crib and feeling really good and happy and I went up to T-Bone's room because it's just so big and beautiful, just to have a look at it. And I was looking at it and laying in the spot where T-Bone said the revolving water bed would go, because I figured I might never have that chance again and I moved a couple boxes out of the way and one tipped over and what do you think came out of that box?

Two brightly colored hockey masks!

I knew I'd seen them somewhere before and I stared at them for the longest time until it hit me where I'd seen them before and it was when I was robbed on the New Jersey State Turn Pike by the two men in a red and black Range Rover, who took all my money plus my WheyStation bonus card.

And I said to myself, "Holy crow!" but not out loud.

And so I rode my bike back to the hotel and I knocked on Microchip's door and he opened it but he didn't look very excited to see me.

"Well, if it isn't the world's largest living bag of smegma," he said.

"Can I come in?"

"No."

"Can I ask you a question?"

"Only if it's 'How's it feel being screwed by a pre-historic cave boy who treats poisonous cave eels better than a friend who practically dragged him to his millions?' "

I said no, that wasn't it.

"Then that's the end of our game!" he said. "Don Pardo, tell 'em what he's won! Extra-long stainless-steel steak knives, perfect for sticking in the backs of your best friends! Goo'night, everybody!"

And he slammed the door and locked it.

"It's about that time I got robbed!" I yelled through the door.

"Yeah, that was a shame," he said. "They shoulda killed you, too."

I told him it was about the house I'd just bought.

Silence.

"Well, I went over there today and you wouldn't believe what I found at my new house, up in T-Bone's new room. In a box."

"A conscience?"

"No, two hockey masks painted bright colors! Exactly like the ones the guys were wearing who robbed me!"

There was silence, then the door opened.

"Holy shit!" he said.

"Are you thinking what I'm thinking?" I said.

"Word," said Microchip.

"The guys who robbed me . . ."

"Were . . ."

"The guys who owned the house before I bought it! All I gotta do is bring the police to the closing and we got 'em, hook, line, and sneaker!"

Microchip stared at me in disbelief.

"No, you eight-foot Jell-O mold! Not the guys who used to *own* the house. The guys you're letting move in the house *with* you!"

"Micro, I'm not letting the old owner move in with me! I'm calling the police on him!"

"Brainless!" Microchip said. "You said T-Bone and his Crips had moved in a bunch of stuff to your house already, right?"

"So?"

"Boxes and stuff, right?"

"So?"

"So that box with the hockey masks in it was T-Bone's or one of his boys'!"

"Oh," I said flatly.

"Oh," said Microchip.

"Ohhh?" I asked.

"Oh!" said Microchip, warming.

"OHHHH!" I said.

"OHHHHHHHH!" said Microchip.

"T-Bone robbed me? T-Bone robbed me! Why would T-Bone rob me?"

"Man, what's the first thing you did after those guys rolled you?"

"Hitchhiked to practice."

"After."

"Practiced."

"Then, the very next day, you hired T-Bone, right?"

Silence.

"Oh, Mary Mother of Jesus! Had you ever had any trouble before T-Bone started asking to become your backside boy?"

"Uh, well, no."

"So you told him no at first, right?"

"Right."

And then, *the next day*, you get mugged, making you think you better get security, so who do you hire?"

"T-Bone!"

"Ding-ding-ding-ding-ding!"

"T-Bone robbed me so I'd hire him!"

"And he's been playin' your sorry ass like a PlayStation ever since!"

"He has?"

"Hell, yeah! You pay him, what, $50,000?"

"No," I said, "$100,000."

"Damn! You pay his posse, what, $50,000 each?"

"Yeah."

"Damn! You been buyin' 'em cars and pickin' up every check and paying 'em overtime for stuff they don't even have to do and rentin' limos and buyin' 'em ice and now you movin' 'em into your house, totally free, right?"

"Yes, so?"

"So they just usin' you! You don't need no security! Everybody loves your ass 'cept me! You don't need no scheduler! You got one damn sock deal and one damn ginseng-ginkgo-jerkoff deal! What you gonna schedule, what time the phone's not gonna ring?"

"I guess not."

"They robbed you so you'd hire them and you hired them and now they goin' through your money like an ATM!"

"But they're my friends!"

"Long as you're flush. How they when you tapped out?"

I didn't get it.

"Where do you think they'll be when you run out of money?" he said.

"Gone?" I said.

"Ding-ding-ding-ding-ding!!!"

I was shocked and stunned and almost mad at them, too. I wanted to go find them and do something crazy, like tell them that they couldn't stay in my house anymore. In fact, I didn't even *want* that house.

"So don't buy it!" Microchip said.

I hadn't thought of that. "Would I have to go to jail for backing out?"

"No!"

"I'm *not* gonna buy it!"

"You're finally makin' some sense," Microchip said.

"I gotta call Death and tell him what's going on!"

Microchip walked over and disconnected the telephone from the wall.

He asked me if I noticed that it was Death who introduced me to T-Bone and the rest of my entourages in the first place. He asked if I noticed that Death seemed to want very bad things to happen to me because every minute I was on the floor was one *less* minute he was on the floor. Had I noticed that since I'd come to the team, Death's minutes had gone from twenty-five a game to three or four? He asked if I'd noticed the way Death ripped me in the papers and glared at me and would probably do anything to make stuff go bad for me and, from what Microchip could see, it was. Had I noticed that I was putting on too much weight, wasn't shooting near as good as I used to, was trying to go underneath, "where you some weak-ass Kool-Aid shit, Stump," and the team was losing? He asked if I'd noticed that my minutes were going down and Death's were coming back. He also asked if I noticed that the fans were riding me lately and the team had lost five in a row. And did I maybe notice that he was mad at me and Jinx couldn't stand me anymore and Mr. Barkley wasn't hanging around as much?

I said no I hadn't.

There was a long silence. Microchip just stared at me.

"You ain't exactly Columbo, are you?"

"Well," I said bitingly. "You aren't exactly Lewis and Clark."

He stared at me.

"And another thing," I said. "I don't appreciate you saying bad things about me and my friends like that."

And he said, "Lemme tell you somethin', Slo. We got enough dicks in this game. We don't need another."

And I said, "Says you!" and slammed the door on him for once.

And then we went out and lost to the arduous Orlandos again.

APR. 20, NEWARK

Each day just seems to get worse.

For months, Mr. Y. Leonard O'Connor has been after me to do a paid autograph appearance, where all I do is show up and sign people's cards and photos and basketballs and they only want you to take seven seconds with each person, and I wasn't ever going to do that because I didn't think anyone should have to pay just for you to be nice to them.

But lately, I've heard some of the guys talking about autograph seekers and how they felt "used" by them.

"A lot of these people don't give a damn whether you live or die after they get the graph," said Mr. Barkley, who signs more than any of us. "In fact, they'd rather you died to make it more valuable."

"Half the time," Mr. Big County said, "some slimy fella comes up to you while you're trying to dig into a mess of vittles somewhere—"

"—and says, 'I don't mean to interrupt your dinner,' " said Mr. Barkley. "Yeah, you do. That's *exactly* what you mean to do, interrupt my dinner, or else why would you have come over to my table and interrupted my dinner? You saw me eatin', right? I mean, you weren't bringin' me ketchup, right?"

"—and so you sign on a napkin," said Mr. Big County, "and the guy thanks you like you just saved his family from a burnin' farmhouse or somethin'. And then, as you're leaving, you see the napkin rolled up on the plate, bein' carried out by a busboy."

"You know Lee Trevino, the golfer?" Mr. Barkley said. "Well, he told me once that he was in this bar one time and this woman came up to him and said she was like his biggest fan on the planet Earth and if he would sign something for her she'd treasure it forever and always. And Trevino says, 'Sure, but I don't have any paper or anything.' And the woman says no problem and she pulls out a five-dollar bill and has him sign it. And when he does, she practically melts right then and there and thanks him twenty-five times and says she'll have it framed and put above her bed. So she leaves and later, Trevino buys a beer with a twenty-dollar bill and the bartender gives him the five with his autograph back in change."

"Sick."

So that's why I decided that why shouldn't I do one of those paid autograph sessions because we're being "victimized by the false idol worship of the fans" as Mr. Mockmood often says, and so why not?

So I've been doing these now and again and today was probably my fifth one and I really didn't want to do it with all my other problems going on but usually it goes all right although I'm not doing them anymore if I don't at least get a limo with it but this one was different.

Mr. Y. Leonard O'Connor and I went to the signing in his Ford Excursion, which was actually too big to get through the hotel drive-up and too big to park in the lot but that's okay, as Mr. O'Connor says it's fun to pick Hondas out of your tread, and so we had to park four blocks away and walk.

This one was done in the clubhouse of the Trenton Country Club, which is a very nice place to play golf, I guess. Only it was so crowded that they had to move it out to the big open area where people practice their golf shots. There must've been two thousand people there and we only signed to do two hours of autographs, so at the end of the two hours, Mr. Y. Leonard O'Connor said it was time to leave or else "you water down your value," so we started to leave, but people didn't like that.

They were yelling, "Hey, what about me?" and "You can't leave!" and "Goddamn selfish jocks!"

I was trying to sign as many as I could as I was walking away, but I got stuck in this little grove of thick evergreen trees and I had nowhere to go. The people started closing in on me and one guy stuck me with a pen that actually drew blood and I got a little scared and so I ducked and tried to go through the trees and the most horrible thing happened.

All of a sudden Mr. Y. Leonard O'Connor said, "Oh, no!" and pointed down to the bottom of my right Bomb, and there, plastered to the patented Belgian waffle sole of the Bomb was the most gorgeous little green and yellow garden snake, probably about two weeks old, just starting his life in the gorgeous spring.

Mr. Y. Leonard O'Connor looked at me with wide eyes and I felt such an iciness in my stomach. And then the fans started in on me. "Real nice, you big ape!" and "Poor defenseless little thing" and "Why don't you go back to your cave?"

And as I stared at that poor thing as the fans stuck their pens and papers and cards in my face and Mr. Y. Leonard O'Connor was saying, "Okay, twenty-five an autograph. Cash only. We'll do five hundred more and that's it!" I started to feel like I was going to cry.

I ran for the Excursion, fast as I could, with Mr. Y. Leonard O'Connor and the entire group of fans running after me and that poor garden snake on my new, ugly shoes and the ticking going off. Only the door was locked and the people were coming, so I kept running. I ran across the street and through a neighborhood and past a strip mall and into a real mall, where I finally stopped at this weird playground where kids were playing. It looked like either the kids had shrunk or everything in it had been blown up huge. It had a marshmallow that must've been four feet high and a ten-foot-long spoon and a donut that was eight feet around. I laid down on a six-foot-long ant and started to cry.

These two little kids came up from underneath the ant and one of them, a little redheaded freckled kid said, "See, I tole you! It's the giant who lives here!"

And the other kid said, "Aww, he's not real. It's a

dummy!" And, to prove it, he took this giant four-foot toothpick and stuck me in the eye with it.

I ended up at my favorite place in the world, the Newark Herpetology Society, and just sat on the bench near their really good widemouthed exhibit. I don't know why, but that's always a good place to go when something's eating you.

I just thought about what had happened to me and all the people I knew and I was ashamed and embarrassed when I really looked at it.

Jinx hated me now. I had been fooled by T-Bone and his friends. Not just out of my money, but out of my friendship. That's what really hurt. I had treated Microchip so bad, not wanting him around, trying to leave him behind, when he was my only real, true friend. I'd let myself get talked into playing down under the basket where I really and truly hated it but went just because I wanted to act like a big man. But I'm not a big man. I'm a big man but I really want to be a little man, like Microchip. I like to shoot from my One Point, but I gave that up to try and be a big man and my shooting has gone to hell and, in fact, I couldn't hit a broad in a barn lately. Plus, I've let my teammates down because we've lost our last five games in a row. No wonder Mr. Barkley and Mr. Big County don't talk to me much anymore. I feel like boa meat.

And I was thinking about Death and was it true he'd arranged for T-Bone to steal from me and then it suddenly hit me that I was supposed to be at the real-estate closing with Mr. Y. Leonard O'Connor at 3 P.M. It was already 3:10! And so I went running out the exit without even stopping at the shedded-skin exhibit and out onto the street and signaled for a cab to stop for the first time in my life. And I got in and told him where I wanted to go and I also explained that we'd have to borrow some money from my friends when I got there because I didn't have any money on me. And next thing I knew I was back out on the street and he was squealing off.

So I ran. I ran the whole way. It was probably eight miles, though I grabbed onto the bumpers of a few FedEx trucks and dairy trucks and furniture trucks like I used to on my bike up the Boulder Canyon but this time I didn't have a bike.

And I rushed into the closing office at 4:55 and I said, "I'm really sorry," but they were all smiling!

It was T-Bone and Li'l Bone and Doc and Dirt and Mr. Y. Leonard O'Connor and Death.

And I said, "I have something to say. You're not gonna like it very much. I've decided I'm *not* going to buy this sweet mutha crib."

And Mr. Y. Leonard O'Connor said, "Too late!" and everybody laughed.

And I asked what he meant.

"Well, you gave T-Bone powerful attorney and that means he can sign your name to any deal. He signed *for* you. The house is yours!"

"Well," said the little Pakistani guy, "not really *yours* yours because we've worked it through the church as a charitable nonprofit, which allows us to depreciate it over five years, which is kind of a trick(f-word) of the IRS."

"Mr. O'Connor?" I said.

"Oh, relax, Slo," he said, lighting up a cigarette. "You're in the big time now. Act like it."

232

And I thought to myself, *If this is the big time, I want back in the small time,* but by then everybody was congratulating each other and hugging and high-fiving.

"I'll try to get you a key sometime soon," said T-Bone, and Dirt had a big laugh about that. "Until then, just come by and knock."

And I tried to get Mr. Y. Leonard O'Connor's attention to tell him all about T-Bone, which I'd been trying to do all morning, too, but he said, "I'll call you, Maurice!" And I tried to get Death's attention to ask him if what Microchip said was true or not, but he didn't realize I was behind him and he was talking to T-Bone with his arm around him and saying, "Don't never say I didn't hook you up, bra!"

And unless he was talking about ladies' undergarments, I think I've been *really, really* gypped.

And so I just couldn't take any more and so I went up to Mr. T-Bone and said, "Mr. T-Bone, I've had a *very* bad day, but if you'd just give me your cousin's number so he can start asking me questions so he can start finding my dad, I'll be so much happier."

And he said, "What you talkin' about?"

And I said, "Your cousin. The private I. Who's going to help me."

"Aw, bitch, I was just kiddin', man! I don't got a cousin who's no private I! I got a friend who's a private lingerie model, though. You want me to hook you up?"

I could hardly even speak. Then I got about as close to downright mad as I've ever been in my life.

"Well, then I'm not signing your shoe deal," I yelled.

"Too late, bra! We already signed it. Barter said it was the first shoe deal they'd ever done with three different commissions: Mr. Y. 10 percent, Barter's 15, and my standard 30. Still, you'll make out all right, after taxes! Peace!"

And he left laughing.

I remember once, when I was only five, all the Spelunkarium children got taken into the coldest cave in the "known" world. It was really cold and damp and dark in there and they made us stay for *two hours* praying and chanting and meditating. They said it was to help us overcome our fear of the dark. It was so cold and lifeless in there I thought my whole body had frozen from the inside out. But it was nothing compared to how I felt then, when Mr. T-Bone told me he was lying about helping me find my father.

I went home, took a bath, and sat in it for, I don't know, two or three hours, my feet clear up by the little metal thing with the retractable clothesline Juan likes to play on. I kept hoping Microchip would come home so I could apologize to him, but every time I hollered for him, there was nothing.

Finally, I knocked on the door between us, knocked and knocked until finally, it swung open wildly and there was a fat unshaven guy standing there in his boxer shorts and knobby knees, going "What?!?"

And I looked in the room and all of Microchip's Magic posters were off the wall and all his stuff was gone.

APR. 21, NEWARK

I woke up at 4:30, couldn't sleep, because I knew what I had to do. I rode my bike through the Holland Tunnel into New York City to the office of Barter Soals of the Nikey company.

I waited outside his office until he showed up at 7:30.

"Slo-Mo!" he said. "Look, you're in violation of your contract already! That's two grand! Every day, every hour, you need to be in the Bombs, okay, pally?"

I was trying to tell him something, but I couldn't get a word in hedgewise.

He kept talking and handing me papers and schedules and all kinds of junk to read.

"Marketing's going planet with this sucker, Slo-Mo! Research says your worldwide Q rating is higher than Scottie Pippen's, man! People see you as a fresh, innocent face in the quote-unquote sports landscape, a naive giant Boy Scout having kid fun in a man's game! Saatchi and Saatchi says we're going after quote-unquote juveniles, seven to thirteen, pricing it around $140 to $150. Nothin' better, pally. Do you know how fast those kids grow out of shoes?"

"Mr. Soals, I—"

"We're going with the whole twenty-first-century approach. See, you're in this video game and you're pursuing all these diaperhead Muslim terrorists and midgets and bad-guy babes with big tits and all you've got is your bomb and you've got to get rid of your bomb before it goes off! And suddenly, you see the diaperheads' suicide car heading straight for the embassy and so you heave the bomb at the window, only now we see the bomb turn into a basketball and the window into a hoop and now we're in real film and you swish it! And the place is going nuts and all the Muslims turn into your opponents and all the bad-guy babes become the cheerleaders and you end up in the sack with all of them. Like them apples, pally?"

And by now we were in his office and I closed the

door and pushed him down in his chair. He looked sorta surprised. And I said, "Hold on! I got somethin' to say! I don't mean to be mean, but I'm not gonna wear your shoes!"

He just stared at me.

"Hey, a sense of humor! I like it!"

"I'm not funny."

"Sure you are!"

"No, I mean, I'm not being funny. I won't wear your stupid shoes."

He stared at me. "Fine. We'll begin litigation against you immediately. You'll lose everything. You'll go to jail. You'll understand jail. Very small spaces, many of them underground, wet, clammy, lots of insects, people who've never been in the sun."

I swallowed hard. "I don't care. I'll give you back any money you've already paid me. But I'm not wearing anything but my dad's shoes and that's final."

Mr. Soals looked right at me for the longest time. I never stopped staring him right back in the eyes.

"Well," he said. "If that's how it's going to be, then—"

"That's how it's going to be," I said.

"Then you might be interested in this."

He took a piece of paper out of his bottom drawer and handed it to me. It was a copy of the check T-Bone wrote to me for $2,000 for the tickets a few weeks ago.

"Recognize that?" he said.

"Yeah, so?"

"You admit cashing this check from a Tyrone 'T-Bone' Demetrius Sylvester?"

"Yeah, so?"

"This check with the note in the corner which reads quote-unquote, 'Nets-Raptors Consult'?"

"What's that mean?"

"I don't know. But it appears you did some consulting work for Mr. T-Bone in regard to your game with the Toronto Raptors that night, a game the Nets lost, by the way, and a game in which you played conspicuously poorly, shooting six of eighteen after a stretch in which you hadn't shot worse than 60 percent in weeks."

"Well, is that the game where I started to go inside more?"

"I can't recall."

"Well, so?"

"Well, so, Mr. Tyrone 'T-Bone' Demetrius Sylvester is willing to testify in a court of law that you agreed to play very poorly that night in order that your team would lose."

I didn't get it.

He kept going. "Mr. Demetrius bet a quote-unquote sizable sum that your team would, indeed, lose, and therefore made quite a tidy sum thanks to you, pally."

"That's not true."

"Perhaps not, but it wouldn't look too good to the papers or to the league office or the police owing to the fact that young Mr. Sylvester has already been on scholarship twice at New Jersey State Penitentiary for gambling, fraud, and extortion. This is not the kind of man you do $2,000 worth of consulting for the night of a game."

"No! That money was what he paid me for my four tickets to that game! Call him up and he'll tell you!"

"Okay!" he said, all singsongy. "Let's do! Let's call up Mr. Sylvester!"

He punched up T-Bone on the speakerphone. We

all said hello, although I wasn't very friendly, and then Mr. Soals asked him why he wrote me a check for $2,000 on April 9.

"Whaddya think for? He was shavin'! Did a nice job, too. Takin' it inside like that when he hadn't missed with that goofy hook since, like, what, February!"

"How much did you make?"

"Twenty large."

"Twenty dollars?" I said. "Well, that proves—"

"Twenty *thousand* dollars, pally," said Soals.

"I've got the receipt from my bookie in Vegas if you want it."

"You're lying!" I screamed.

Soals looked hard at me and grumbled, "Got any proof he's lying?"

I sat there and thought about it. Then it hit me like a lightbulb.

"Call the ticket office! There's a sheet you have to sign when you give away your tickets! It'll prove I gave them to T-Bone because he was going to sign for them!"

"Okay! Let's do!" he said, all singsongy again. And he punched off T-Bone and called the ticket office. But the lady said that the players' ticket list for that night showed that I didn't use my tickets at all, as usual. Nobody had signed for them. "They were turned back into the general ticket sales pool at six forty-five P.M., as per league policy," she said.

So not only was T-Bone lying, he forgot to sign for the tickets, too! Or even take them!

My stomach felt like a ball of bees.

I loosened my grip and fell back into the chair in front of his desk. Barter Soals came around from behind his desk and came toward me. He put his hand on my shoulder and said, "I know it's hard, son."

I stared at my dad's shoes on my feet.

"I'm *still* not wearing your shoes," I said.

"Fine," said Soals, punching his phone again. "Greta! Get me Peter Vescey over at the *New York Post*. Tell him I've got a helluva story for him." He punched it off again. "Pete's gonna love this little story. I can see the headline: 'Young Innocent Superstar Was a Fraud All Along.' Except that would be much too long for the seventy-two-point type they'll use. How 'bout just: 'No Mo' Slo-Mo!'

"And when your poor father reads that, wherever he is, he'll realize it's you and collapse in shame."

I wanted to slug him. But I couldn't bring myself to. I was so weak all of a sudden.

"Okay," I sighed. "What do I have to do?"

"First, you fire that silly agent of yours. I become your sole agent. We split everything 50 percent. I redo your ridiculous deal Mr. Y. Leonard O'Connor signed you to and get you something worth signing."

I shook my head but I wouldn't look up.

"Try to quit or run or squeal and your part-time consulting job is page one, *USA Today*, dig, pally?"

I shook my head yes.

"I'll start the new paperwork today."

He dialed a number and handed me the phone. "Tell him he's fired."

My stomach felt like it was a ball of knives. I'd never done anything this mean.

"Uh, it's me, Maurice," I said.

"Maurice, I can't talk right now. I'm very busy. We're meeting the lap-pool installers at your house in five minutes."

"Oh, uh."

Soals looked at me and pretended to slit his throat with his pen.

"Well, uh, Mr. O'Connor, I don't wanna do this, but . . . well . . . I've got to. You can't be my agent anymore. I have to fire you."

"What?!?" he said.

"I know—"

"I'll call the archdiocese! I'll call the archbishop! You'll wish you never—"

Soals grabbed the phone right out of my hand. "It's over, plumber!" And he hung up.

I sank back in my chair. He threw me a shoe box.

"I'm in *such* a good mood," he said, whistling. "Now, put these shoes on *right now*. And I don't ever wanna see you in those old pieces of shit again."

Slowly, I took off my dad's shoes and started to put on the Bombs and while I was tying the bows on each of them and feeling an ulcer start to form in my stomach, Soals snatched my dad's shoes and put them behind his back.

"Give those back!" I yelled.

"Soon as the paperwork is done, pally!" he said.

I got up, grabbed the stapler off his desk, and came at him. I'd never purposely tried to hurt someone, but I was going to this time.

"You better think of your father before you do anything stupid, pally!" he said, backed into the corner. "If he finds out you cheated your own teammates and your fans, he'll never want to claim you. You'll be the world's tallest orphan forever."

I looked at him and decided I was tired of being the nice guy. I let him have it.

"I don't *like* you," I snapped. "At *all*."

And I spun on my new stupid shoes and stomped out of his office and through the hall toward the elevator, ticking as I went. At every desk I passed, secretaries looked at me funny.

I guess they could tell I was just about to explode.

APR. 22, NEWARK

I made a big decision today. As nice a place as it is, and as nice as the people are, there's nothing left for me in Newark, so I called the Spelunkarium and asked if I could come back.

"What?!" the Elder said. "Are you nuts?"

I thought that maybe I was starting to be, possibly, yes.

"You've *got* to play basketball, Maurice," she said. "We need you to, to, to spread the word of the Doorian faith. You're our seven-eight ambassador, a huge shining beacon, symbolizing the caves that light our lives!"

I told her I didn't wanna be a beacon. I told her I just wanted to come home and get back to the caves and people I knew even if they didn't know me so well and I promised I wouldn't break off any more million-year-old stalactites or cause any passages to collapse as I did that one time with my forehead. I just wanted to get my own cave and live there the rest of my life with my snakes.

"No, Maurice, you'd hate it back here! We don't hardly go underground anymore. I guess we're all just so busy with other things."

"I thought the caves lit your lives," I asked.

Silence. Then: "They do, Maurice," she said. "The glow reaches us clear up here in the new convention center/hotel/casino complex we're building."

Worse news.

Microchip's parents came to practice today and took Microchip.

They had a fancy-dressed lawyer with them and an East Rutherford police officer. Turns out the extra-credit reports on snakes I'd handed in from my Web site classes won an award from YAASS, the Young African American Scientists Society, and when they went to give it to Microchip, they found no Microchip. One thing led to another and they tracked him down to our team.

He didn't want to go but the lawyer said if he didn't come, he'd be charged with fraud, mail fraud, and financial malfeasance, so he went. Coach Jackson didn't seem to put up much of a fight maybe because since I've been so stupid to play inside, Microchip hasn't played much at all. And I couldn't hardly go up to his parents and say it wasn't his work that caused the problems, it was mine, because then he'd be in *serious* trouble.

Poor little guy. I totally abandon him and then he gets taken home by his parents. I'm the number one worst friend in the world.

And as his ear was being pinched by his dad as they left, Mr. Barkley said, "Only starting point guard in the league to get grounded."

———

Coach Jackson called a special meeting after practice and he was really mad at us. He said if we don't start winning some games, "there's gonna be some people in this room who won't be on this team tomorrow."

APR. 23, NEWARK

Well, Coach Jackson was right. He got fired this morning.

I felt bad for him as he packed his stuff and left today, but I don't think any of the other guys did.

As he was leaving, Mr. Barkley said, "Here's one for you: If a coach in the middle of the forest gets the axe and nobody cares, does he make a sound?"

I'm so down about everything now. We only have two more games to go and we only need to win one to get our record to forty wins and make the play-offs and even though I told the sportswriter gentlemen that it's not over until the fat lady is hung, I honestly don't really care. I mean, I understand it's a big deal to some of the other players. As Mr. Barkley says, "Making the play-offs in the NBA is like making the white pages," but I just don't share his enthusiasm right now.

So far, I've spent most of the day just sitting in the room, looking through my video camera lens at the old videos I've taken and feeling lower than a sightless cave eel.

I'm trying not to think about my father even

though I do all the time. I'm trying not to think that maybe somewhere out there he will see me on a television set or on a highlight show and look at my new shoes and not recognize them, of course, and not recognize me and change the channel and my one chance will be gone. I'm trying not to think how ugly and horrible these new shoes are, but I can't help think about them because the fellas keep bringing them up because they're always ticking.

"Hey, Slo-Mo," Mr. Barkley said today at shoot-around. "You know who else wears those? The Unabomber."

"Really?" I asked, and then he dove at me and covered my mouth with his hand and said, "No, just no. Whatever you were going to say, just, no."

Security stopped me three times today just coming into the gym and one janitor who only speaks Spanish dropped his broom and ran when he heard it.

"You'd make a lousy jewel thief," Coach Summers said.

Actually, he's right. Today, every time I tried to do my little patented defensive move, where I come downcourt behind everybody else, sneak up behind a guy who's dribbling, and reach under with my long arms and flick the ball away, the guy would hear me coming and dribble away. I'm not sure the Nikey company understands the game of basketball.

One good thing. I figured out how you can make them stop ticking, but only for a little while. If you lift your heel off the ground for two seconds, they stop. Problem is, you have to stand there on your toes and you look pretty stupid.

"You look like the world's butt-ugliest ballerina," said Death.

After an hour of it, my calves hurt like crazy and my toes had blisters from standing on them and my ears hurt from hearing them tick all the time. All the sportswriter gentlemen wanted to know about them. "Tell us you're getting paid at least," Mr. Stain said.

"Yeah, I'm getting paid."

"How much?"

"I don't know. I just know I get the usual 45 percent of whatever it is."

"Forty-five percent?"

"Yeah, after the agent's fees."

"What kinda agent takes 55 percent?" they asked. "Who's your agent, Sweden?"

And I said no, who do they have?

I got fined $10,000 by the league for criticizing the officials, which is completely unfair and "straight-up whacked," as Mr. T-Bone said, because I *didn't* criticize the officials. In fact, I told the sportswriter gentlemen I wouldn't. I said, "I'm not allowed to comment on crummy officiating." And look what happens!

We lost again tonight, to the hard-charging Seattles, our sixth straight, by 24 points, and I didn't make a single shot. I went back out top tonight like I like it, but every time I'd go to shoot I'd be thinking about the ticking instead of my One Point. Also, my feet hurt so much I had to come out in the third quarter and Coach Summers told me to go get my old shoes on, but I told them I don't know where they are, which is true.

So now we have to win against the Detroits Sunday in our last game of the season or we can forget about the play-offs.

You'd think we'd be all excited about the game, but afterward I didn't want to just go home and sulk so I went out with some of the fellas to Step Away from the Car and I was shocked to hear guys talking about next year already.

"My agent's already worked out my next two moves," said Mr. Barkley. "We sign with the Lakers next year for one year, $3 million plus play-off bonuses up the wazoo, try to finally win me a title, hook up with Shaq, let some starlets rub their titties on my bald, black head. Then I close the career out with Philadelphia at $3.5 for one last farewell tour, not playing much, just accepting gifts in every city, have a little guy with me to carry it all, you know?"

"Cool," said Mr. Woody. "Reebok's already swung a deal with me to the Celtics, where the shoe plant is, in exchange for Tim Hardaway, who wants to come to New Jersey because it's closer to NBC's offices. They want him to be the third man on the number two game the year after that with Marv and Rodman. I'm down with Boston. Lotta clam in that town, baby."

Mr. Woody said it was kind of a complicated deal, though. He said if we make the play-offs, it screws the deal, because then our management would have to give up a first-round pick instead of two second-round picks because the deal was contagious on how we did when we got Mr. Woody from the Charlottes in the first place and if that happened, then they'd need him because the high school kid they wanted in next year's draft wouldn't be around by the second round.

"Oh," I said.

Mr. Mockmood said he personally hoped we didn't make the play-offs and that he was going to refuse to play with us New Jerseys next year because of our blatant trivialization of his religion and force a trade to Miami, a multinational city "far more spiritual and worthy than any other American city."

"Hell, Miami ain't in America anyhow," said Mr. Big County. "Any damn place where you need a damned United Nations interpreter to order you a Dairy Queen chili cheese footlong ain't no America I ever heard of, you know what I mean, Chris?"

Mr. Big County said the bosses have already told him he's got his trade to Dallas on account of both the owner and the coach want him out. Turns out they've heard he's saying not such nice things about them.

"Wonder how they got that idea?" Mr. Barkley said.

"Goddamn press," Mr. Lowery said.

Mr. Lowery said he hopes to be playing in Greece next season but that won't be so bad, he said, especially if he doesn't miss a shot in our last game. "I'm shooting exactly 45 percent. One more miss and I go to 44.995 percent. And there goes a cool million. You know how many drachmas that is?"

Mr. Reggie said that first the Lord told him he ought to sign with the Chicagos because "they're going to have some serious room" under the celery cap, but then he said the next night the Lord told him to make a run at the Sacramentos "because their G.M., Larry Reynolds, runs a more free-form style that will set up better for me."

I had no idea the Lord knew so much about the NBA.

Some of the others said they hoped to get to the West Coast and Mr. Barkley said I had some very big plans, too. "Mo just signed a deal to be the right-field foul pole at Yankee Stadium," but that's not really true.

But the thing I noticed was that almost nobody said anything about staying with our own team, trying to keep it together and win a title.

"Don't you feel any loyalty to our fans?" I asked quietly, staring at my ugly new shoes.

Everybody got real quiet and looked at me and then all of a sudden they started laughing like crazy.

"You funny," said Death, pulling off leg hairs. "I always knew underneath there you was funny. (F-word)in' weird as shit, but funny."

Afterward I went to the bar with Mr. Barkley and I was very depressed about the team and the way my whole life was going.

"Why was I even born?" I said. "Why did I come here in the first place? I'm no use to you guys. But I wasn't any use to anybody back at the Spelunkarium, either. I'm no use to anybody."

And Mr. Barkley said that wasn't at all true. "It could be that your whole purpose in life is to serve as a warning to others."

But even that didn't make me feel that much better, so Mr. Barkley decided I was ready to have my first alcoholic drink, a rum and Coke.

I drank the whole thing in one gulp. And four more after that.

The fifth I threw up on his leather pants.

APR. 24, NEWARK

This morning when I woke up in my room at the Newark Airport Ramada Hotel, I felt very terrible and maybe worse.

I slept so long I was late for practice and Coach Summers started screaming at me and told me to get the F out, and that made me even more sick, so I went home and turned off all the lights and laid in bed and stared into my viewfinder.

Really, my viewfinder was the only happy place I still had left. In there, everything was still happy. Me and Microchip were still friends and me and Jinx were still friends. In there, we were still a team that wanted to do good and stick together and I still loved basketball and I still had my shoes. And I just stared at my homemade videos for I don't know how long, wondering what I was going to do now because I couldn't go back to the Spelunkarium and I couldn't find my dad and I didn't want to play in the NBA anymore and I couldn't find Lisa and I was thinking about all that when I saw something that made me stand straight up in bed and hit my head on the ceiling!

It was just Mr. Barkley goofing around funnily in the locker room, as professional athletes are so well known to do, pretending to interview Microchip with his penis, as though his penis was the microphone.

"Well, Mr. Chip, do you have a few words for our viewers at home?"

And Microchip responded, like he was actually talking into a microphone, "Yes, I think all the home viewers are a bunch of dicks."

And then Mr. Woody hollered from the front door, trying to let the people in the hall see in, "Hey, Chuck, do those things come in men's sizes?"

And that's when I saw it. As Mr. Woody was holding the door open, talking and laughing and trying to let the people in the hall see in, I could see something strange in the background. I saw Mr. Soals, his face to the camera, talking to a woman whose back was to us. The woman had a manila folder in her hand and she had it open and paper-clipped inside it was a picture of my dad!

I just knew it was my dad even though the view-finder was so small and Mr. Soals was even smaller in the background, which means that the photo was even smaller, but I was totally sure and then some and the reason was because the man in the picture had on a giant crown made of corncobs, like my dad always wore in his traveling and entertaining duties as Genghis Korn!

In the video, Mr. Soals is talking and the woman with her back to us is nodding and jotting down something in the folder, but not so we can see it. Then she nods big one more time and puts the folder back in her briefcase. Then the door closes behind Woody and I pan back to Microchip, who goes into his impression of our announcer, Ahmad Rashad, speaking into the "mike" and saying, "Please fill thirty seconds of airtime so I can go play golf."

I rewound it and rewound it and thought and thought about it and I decided that if that's my dad in the picture, either the woman or Mr. Barter Soals might know where he is. Otherwise, why would they be carrying around a picture of him and jotting things on it if they didn't? Plus, whatever they've known, they've known it since whenever this was filmed, which had to be a month ago, although I never learned how to set the date thingy, and haven't told me. Why?

But that's where I got stuck. I knew there was a lot more to do but my brain seemed like it was staring at one of those cartoons in the Sunday paper that's supposed to be 3-D but always just looks 2-D to me.

Only then something popped into my mind. It was what Jinx told me one night, which was, "If you like home movies, Slo-Mo, I've got a *lot* of equipment at home we could try out." And so I got dressed as fast as I could and I even forgot to feed the guys before I left and pedaled over to her house so incredibly fast I surprised myself.

My heart was in my throat when I rang the doorbell, although that's just a figure of speech, and I was covered in sweat, too, so as soon as she answered, I just blurted it out, all at once, the way I'd practiced it, like one of those dolls who you pull their string and they just talk in a steady stream until the string runs out.

She opened the door a crack.

"Jinx, I'm a big jerk and I never meant to hurt your feelings and I'm so sorry and I never wanted to say what I said to those sportswriters but T-Bone told me to say it and I didn't even know what it meant and I miss you so much because you're such a good friend and my entourages robbed me and they're still robbing me and Microchip got taken by his own parents and I can't get ahold of him and he probably wouldn't return my calls anyway because he hates me too and I'm in really big trouble and I might be able to find someone who really does know where my dad is and isn't just trying to gyp me and you're the only one who can help!"

And then I inhaled.

She looked at me for a while and then looked away and I didn't say anything more. And then she said, "You're right. You are a big jerk." And she started to slam the door and my head sank to my shoes practically.

But then I heard her say, "But I guess you're a sweet jerk. Get in here."

I told her my problem and she took the tape out of the video camera and got her video player out from next to the bed and had me unhook it from the set in the ceiling and then we hooked it up to her big-screen TV and all of a sudden instead of having to look through that tiny viewfinder you could see everything very big and clearly and so we looked at it.

We went over that video like a find tooth comb until she got to the part where you could see the photo, she froze it and then hit a button that zoomed the picture closer. And there was my dad.

I'd never seen his face that close-up. The picture I had when I was a kid was a full body shot to show how tall he was, standing outside his Corvair. What we were looking at now was a much newer picture and just of his face. He looked older now, but friendly. He had green eyes, like me, and a crinkly forehead and a nice nose and curly black hair, like me, and thick, black glasses like I have!

And, I don't know, something came over me right then, *that instant,* and I just got mad. I got as mad as I've ever been in my life. And I decided right then and there I was going to stop all this.

I turned to Jinx and I took her by the shoulders and I said, "Jinx, I really need to do something kinda wrong and nasty and immortal. Are you up to doing it with me?"

"God, what took you?" she said, and she did what she does when she wants to really help somebody, I guess, which is she took off her sweater.

I thought it was a pretty good plan I dreamed up, my first ever actually, but pretty good for a guy who'd never tried anything nearly like this. It was just about two in the morning when we were finally ready to spring it.

Jinx and I were dressed completely in black, with black paint on our faces, and we were standing in Barter Soals' backyard in Fort Lee, New Jersey. Jinx got the address over the Internet somehow. I had the tool belt and the cage. Jinx climbed up on my back, then on my shoulders, and braced herself against the ivy-covered wall.

Now, *she* would be a very good jewel thief. She was like a cat, practically walking up the wall and perching herself on the ledge. She got a rope out of her backpack and tied it to a tree limb and then I climbed up that and sat on the window ledge with her. I started unscrewing the window very quietly and I was having a hard time with it until Jinx just pushed the window open because it was already open to begin with, which I didn't know but maybe should've checked.

We opened it all the way and crept in, Jinx first with the flashlight, me right behind. It was easy for me to see even without the flashlight, maybe because I spent half my life in very dark caves. It was a really fancy bedroom, fanciest I'd ever seen, full of art on the wall and three televisions.

There were two people laying in the bed and they still hadn't woken up. They must've been very sleepy when they went to bed because they didn't even put their clothes away, which were laying all over the floor, which the Elder would give you a weekend in the Fluid Room for. There were men's underwear and a lot of women's underthings, some of which were even going to get stains on them from a bottle of wine that was laying on its side but I wasn't about to help Soals now.

I opened the cage and let Lassie, my Latvian widemouthed copper, crawl out on my arm. It was kinda cold so Lassie was moving pretty slow, but she still looks kinda mean, so, if you didn't know what a big teddy bear she was, you might be a little scared of her. Jinx did not like this part at all and stepped back to the other side of the bed. I could tell Lassie liked being in a new, dark, quiet place like this. She started to get some spring in her tail, you know what I mean?

I nodded my head to Jinx, who eased their really nice soft and fancy blanket and sheets down from around their shoulders, down past their waists, past their feet, all the way off the bed. I was sort of embarrassed because neither of them even took the time to put on their pajamas but of course you never know when company is coming. Mr. Soals, laying on his back, was fumbling for the covers in his sleep, but the body next to him started to wake up.

I put Lassie on Mr. Soals' foot.

The other person turned toward us and Jinx put the flashlight up just in time to see . . .

Mr. Bruce?

"Mr. Bruce!" I yelled out.

And all that woke up Soals, who sat up in bed and said, "What the *hell* is going on?"

I said I'd tell him all about it but first I told him it'd be better if he didn't move even a half an inch because it might upset Lassie, who was now slithering up his shin toward his knee.

The look Mr. Soals got on his face made me actually break out laughing. His eyes got big as Frisbees and his jaw dropped so far it looked like somebody had disconnected it at the hinges. Mr. Bruce was trying to cover his body and spring out of the bed at the same time. He ran for the fancy purple curtains and covered himself in those, and at the same time, kept an eye on Lassie and on me and on Jinx all at once.

"Mr. Bruce, why are you sleeping here?" I asked.

Jinx sighed heavily and Mr. Soals was still sweating and Mr. Bruce started to stammer. "Uh, well, Maurice, this is, uh, this is, a, you found us in the middle of some deep-tissue therapy which—"

And Jinx just burst out laughing so hard that Mr. Bruce had to stop, so I guess Jinx did not think it was a very important therapy at all.

"Maurice, they're sleeping together," she said, "because they *sleep* together."

"Yeah?"

"They (f-word). Okay?"

"Yeah?"

"Yeah."

"Why?"

This is when Mr. Soals screamed, "G-g-g-et that th-th-th-thing off meeeee!"

He was talking about Lassie.

"Sure," I said as Lassie made her way over Mr. Soals' knee and was starting up his thigh. "It's a good idea, too. Because what you're looking at is one of the world's only meat-eating Latvians, and, well, sorry, but I haven't fed her in three days and she's *very* hungry."

"Sllllo-Mo, you fffff(f-word)," he yelled in a very loud whisper. "Get it off me! I'll sssssue you to your last d-d-d-dime!"

"Well, Mr. Soals is finally getting a case of his own medicine, huh, Jinx?"

"Guess so," she said.

"Do you think Mr. Soals cares what I feed Lassie, Jinx?" I asked.

She thought about it. "You know, he might."

Lassie was on Mr. Soals' upper thigh and heading for his you-know-what now.

"I feed her a Vienna sausage every day," I said. "Lassie *loves* Vienna sausages. The problem is, she has *very* poor night vision."

"Oh, Holy Christ!" said Mr. Soals, dripping sweat in his eyes now. "What do you want? *What?* I'll do anything! *Anything!*"

"I want to know where my dad is," I said calmly. Jinx was standing by with a notepad and pen. "*Exactly* where. I want a city, an address, a phone number. I want exactly where my dad is and I'd give it to me right now or even sooner if I know Lassie."

Lassie had just discovered Mr. Soals' you-know-what and was almost there. Mr. Bruce covered his head with the curtain and screamed.

"He's in Florida!" Mr. Soals screamed. "Last I heard, he's working in the Florida State University Veterinary Hospital. He's a, he's a, he's a doctor for, uh—"

"A vet?" Jinx said.

"A vet! He's a vet in the holding pen, where the sick animals go after surgeries but before they, uh, before they go back into the—"

"Wild?"

"Yes! Back into *wiiiaaahhhhhh!!!*"

Right then, Lassie took a big bite of Mr. Soals' penis.

Mr. Soals screamed bloody murder and Mr. Bruce fainted and Jinx hid her face in her hands. And Mr. Soals had his eyes clenched shut and finally stopped screaming and then looked at me and said, "How come nothing's happening?"

And I replied, "I never *said* she was poisonous, did I, pally?"

We put Lassie back and hurried out of there, same way we came in, before Mr. Soals decided to call the cops on us, but as we were driving home Jinx said I shouldn't worry.

"First of all, with Brucie Boy there, Soals isn't going to want any part of the cops and police reports and publicity. Second of all, let's say you're a cop. You show up at this fancy house at three in the morning, you see lots of clothes and wine bottles around and *nothing stolen* and some of that, uh, gymnastic equipment in the corner, and then the guy shows you this big bite on his cock and nobody else in the house, and what's the first thing you're gonna think?"

I stared at her blankly.

" 'Where's the gerbil?' " she said. "Am I right?"

I knew what I had to do next and Jinx helped me make the reservations at her house. I was going to be on the 7:15 to Atlanta, then to Tallahassee, which Jinx told me is the home of Florida State University. It was five in the morning. I gave her a big hug and told her how much she meant to me. I told her I couldn't have come this far without her. I said when Lisa and I ever got married, I hoped she'd be my best man.

I know it meant something to her because as I said goodbye she had a tear in her eye.

APR. 25, TALLAHASSEE

Even though I hadn't slept all night, I still couldn't sleep on the plane, I was so excited. I told all the stewardesses my story and they were so excited they let me sit in the jump seats in the back instead of in my seat, which was 23D, because my knees were up in my face and, besides, they couldn't get the little tray of toy food to the kinda fat man next to me and he *really* wanted that food.

It took my new friend, Hazzam, my cabdriver, a long time to find the Florida State Veterinary Hospital and then even longer to find the holding pen and so I really didn't get there until two in the afternoon, but suddenly, there I was. I took a big gulp. After seventeen years, here was my moment of proof.

When I walked in the door, I was trembling and I took a big gulp and I said to the secretary, "I'm here to see my father, who used to be Mr. Genghis Korn, of the Krispy Korn imitation frozen food products company," and she looked up and saw how tall I was and she said, "Oh, my God!"

So I thought, *I guess that proves how much my father and I look alike because this secretary knows I'm his son just by looking at my face.*

I said I was sorry I didn't call ahead of time but I wanted it to be a surprise.

And she just couldn't speak and she started to cry and hold a Kleenex to her nose and she motioned for me to follow her.

So my hands were shaking and my heart was thumping as the secretary took me back, through a hallway, through a room full of cages of birds and falcons and hawks, through a room with raccoons and coyotes and even a moose, outside past a big tank full of alligators and out to a yard, where a very tall man on the other side of the fence had his back to us, reaching up under the eaves of the building, trying to catch something in a little Tupperware bowl.

I froze.

"Stumpy?" the secretary said.

They call my dad "Stumpy"? I thought. *That's what Microchip calls me!*

The man didn't turn around. "Guilty," he said.

"There's a young man here," she said, quietly weeping. "Looking for his dad."

"If he looks rich, he's mine," Stumpy said without turning around.

She started crying worse and ran away.

Stumpy turned around. He had a friendly fat face, a smile that was a little lopsided, his crazy curly hair a little gray, crow's-feet and a nice tan from working outside, I guess. He saw me and his face fell and he said, "Oh," kinda sad.

And then, just like that, he got about three feet shorter, right in front of my eyes. I guess he'd been standing on a bucket or a stepladder or something, because his head disappeared behind the fence and next thing I knew this little sawed-off man was walking through the gate in jeans and a T-shirt that said, "We

Don't Care How They Do It in Miami," and big muddy work boots.

My head was spinning.

"Sit down here, son," he said, and he pulled up a bucket.

I knew this wasn't good.

He didn't look anything like the picture.

"You aren't my dad, are you?" I said.

"No, son. I'm not."

I really didn't want to hear that so I guess I just kept on talking nervously so it wouldn't really lock into my brain. I said, "My mom, she died in a shopping accident, but she gave me this picture of my dad. They said he worked here." And I showed him the picture of my dad and the Corvair.

"Right," he said. "What's your name?"

"Maurice Finsternick," I said.

"Maurice, I got real bad news. Real bad news. Your father did work here. But he died six weeks ago."

I couldn't speak. I tried to, but nothing was coming out.

"Stomach cancer. His wife's got a lawsuit goin' on it. Turns out he was forced to eat these fake corn sticks the FDA banned a long time ago. Poor bastard had to eat dozens of 'em every day. Hundreds of 'em. She probably won't win it. They're owned by some monster megalith company owned by Donald Trump. Might get a settlement, though."

He was just staring at me, standing there in his muddy boots, and he dropped his shovel, and he said, "I'm awfully sorry. He was just one helluva good guy. Everybody loved him."

I was too sad to even cry.

"What was his name?"

"Jim. Jim Campbell. We called him 'Tiny.' He had to be seven foot if he was an inch."

"Can I see her?" I asked.

"Who?" he said.

"His wife."

So we got in his Jeep and I just couldn't say anything and we drove awhile until we were in the city. We pulled up in front of a Wild Oats market, which is one of my favorite places to eat when I'm on the road, and we walked into the store and back to the deli counter. And he asked for Mrs. Campbell, and a young woman with a nose ring said she was in the back, on the wheat-grass juicer.

And so we went back there and Stumpy went up to a woman working on the juicer and said, "Lela?"

And you will not believe who turned around!

Phyllis!

My mother!

I just about ate a cow! There she was, looking older, short as ever, with a little butterfly tattoo on the side of her neck and her strawberry hair pulled back in a ponytail and her green eyes I remember. My knees got all buckly and my head was all tingly and nothing would come out of my mouth.

And Phyllis, my Life-Giver, my supposed-to-be-dead Life-Giver, screamed so loud it made a baby cry in the store. She started shaking and crying crazily and hitting us both with the long stalks of wheat grass and then she screamed again and ran for it. I sprinted after her, except as I came around a corner I must've hit something full-on with my forehead and everything went blacker than Cave No. 314B, the back one.

———

Next thing I knew I was laying in some kind of paradise. I knew I was in bed, but it wasn't like any bed I'd ever been in, because, for the first time in my life, I fit in it. My feet weren't hanging off the edge. In fact, I sat up on my elbows to look at them in amazement, except that made my head feel like ten thousand tiny toothpicks were being poked into it and I flopped back down on the pillow and grabbed it and found that it was covered in a big bandage.

When I opened my eyes again, I noticed three things right away. One, it was dark out. Two, Phyllis wasn't looking down at me. Three, Stumpy was, along with a little blond girl and a black man. I thought maybe I'd dreamed it but then I remembered hitting my head and I felt the bandages again. Did Phyllis really *not* die in a collapsed King Soopers grocery store? Is my mother alive? Do people really call her "Lela"!

"You're gonna be even taller with that bump, Maurice," Stumpy said, looking at me.

"Just chill," the black man said to me.

"How are you?" said the little girl.

"Where's Phyllis?" I said.

"Don't you have a game tomorrow?" said the black man.

"Who's Phyllis?" said Stumpy.

"Lela. Yes," I said, answering both men.

"Against the Celtics?" said the black man.

"The Detroits," I said.

"Phyllis is in Detroit?" asked Stumpy.

"No, Phyllis is in Lela," I said. "Who's that?" looking at the black man.

"So Lela is Phyllis and Phyllis is your mother?" said Stumpy.

"No, *him*," I said, holding my head, which was starting to throb.

"Oh, oh, sorry. This is Dr. Irving. He came over to take care of you. Friend of mine. Doctor, this is, apparently, Tiny's son."

And Dr. Irving said, "Stumpy, don't you know who this is?"

And Stumpy sorta shrugged.

"This particular person would be leading the NBA in field-goal percentage *and* three-point percentage if he had enough shot attempts, which he doesn't. Slo-Mo Finsternick of the New Jersey Nets. Mr. Automatic. Got the sweetest, craziest hook shot in the league. Only shoots it from three points and from the free-throw line. With either hand! Can't box out to save his mother's life"

I don't have to, I thought. *She's alive.*

I asked Stumpy where Lela was now.

"I wish I knew," he said. "People were screaming at all the blood and I was on my knees trying to wake you up and when I looked up, she was long gone."

"You've been here for almost twelve hours!" said the little girl.

"We brought you here because everything in this house is your size," Stumpy said, "and I've got a key anyway and she hasn't been around here once. The baby-sitter said she hadn't seen her, either."

And then I looked at the pretty little blond girl with a volleyball under her arm and I said, "Who are you?"

"This," said Stumpy, "is apparently your sister. We tried to put her to bed but with all the commotion and all—"

She looked at me wide-eyed.

"Hi," she said.

"Hi," I said.

"You're bigger than my daddy," she said.

Dr. Irving decided he better go, but he asked me to sign a gauze pad for him. "You play in, lessee, sixteen hours, in New Jersey, and you got to win to make the play-offs, and you got twenty-one stitches in your head and a freaking *All My Children* episode just broke out all over your life. I think I'm gonna call my bookie."

And Stumpy said he was going to lay down on the couch for a while, on account of it was three-fifteen in the morning and he had to be at work at seven and he had no idea what he was going to do. He wasn't sure Lela was ever coming back at all.

And so I was left with my new sister and no father and a missing mother and a throbbing head.

What do you say to a sister you never knew you had?

"What's your name?"

"Kaitlin," she said.

"Did we have the same dad?"

"Guess so," she said. "Do we have the same mom?"

"Guess so," I said. "Why are you up so late?"

"I'm scared," she said. And so I let her lay down on the bed next to me.

I had a lot of questions. Like, how come Phyllis was alive when the police told everybody she was dead? Like, how come she didn't come back for me? Like, how did she and my father get back together when she said they only had one date and that was the end of it? Like, why didn't she tell *him* about me?

And, of course, where could I find a bed this *big*?

APR. 26, NEWARK

Well, this is probably my last time writing to you, because as I lay here in bed, the season is over and my life is completely changed so here goes . . .

I dozed until maybe five and felt half sick, but I got dressed and Stumpy fixed breakfast for me and Kaitlin on countertops that were a good foot higher than most people's, and we sat on chairs that were much taller than most people's, and ate at a table that was a good foot higher than most people's out of big bowls and spoons that, for the first time in my life, weren't too small for my hand.

They wondered why I had to go back so quickly and come to think of it, so did I, but I told them about my game and sorta said to myself, "Gotta make the white pages." I wanted to stay, but I knew I had a game to play and, besides, the guys were counting on me, I think.

"You guys could watch me if you wanted," I offered. "It'll be on T and T at seven-thirty."

"Sure!" said Kaitlin. Then she looked at Stumpy. "Except we don't have cable."

"We'll go down to the Whiskey Dent," said Stumpy. "They'll have it on down there."

"You don't get cable?" I asked Kaitlin.

"Nah. We used to have a TV. Back when there was a lot more stuff on and a lot less channels."

And Stumpy folded me into the Jeep and Kaitlin came, too, because she said she'd never had a brother before and wanted to keep having one for a while in case I never came back. On the way, Stumpy asked me how life in the NBA was. Did I mind the travel? Are the fellas nice?

I mentioned that I have a pretty good shot but people yell at me because I won't dunk.

"Too predictable, eh?"

"Yeah," I said. "Exactly! If I dunk, they think that's all I'm good for!"

"Your dad told me he used to get that all the time. They'd say to him, 'Hey, I bet you played a lot of basketball, huh, treetops?' And Tiny'd say, 'No, why?' 'Well, you're so tall! You *had* to play basketball!' And he said he always wanted to say back, 'Well, you're fat, how come you don't sumo wrestle?' But, a course, he never would. He said he always *hated* basketball for that reason. Said he never played 'cause a that."

I think I would've liked my dad.

And we went on like that, me trying to hear as much about my dad as I could—he loved Lucky Charms, kept his Genghis Korn outfit around for Halloweens, hated cigars—and Kaitlin trying to get as much out of me as she could—my favorite color, did I have a girlfriend, did I have a dog. I gave Kaitlin piggybacks in the airport even though she kept holding on by my stitches, but it was worth it just to hear her giggle and scream at being so high, and to yell for her to watch out for the low-flying airplanes. And after I said goodbye, I felt worse because now I'd lost my dad not once but twice. And I kept thinking, why didn't I look at that video two months earlier and then maybe I could've met him.

And I felt lousy for myself that I didn't have what Phyllis and Kaitlin had, which was a home and family. At basketball games, coaches and fans and players are always yelling, "You gotta *want* it, Slo-Mo," and just now, right then, I knew that no, I *didn't* want it. I don't want any part of it. I didn't want to be within a toll call of it. But what could I do? I signed a three-year contract. I signed a shoe contract. In sports, you can't just go around asking them to redo your contract. I'm trapped.

I thought about the fact that Phyllis left me, and I tried to feel horrible about it but every time I did, I kept giggling to myself that she was alive—she was *alive!*—and I just couldn't get to feeling bad about it. Mr. Big County always says, "Hoss, most people are 'bout as happy as they wanna be," and so I decided to be happy about it and I fell right into a peaceful sleep, even with my knees up by the stewardess-call switch. Then I fell asleep in the Atlanta airport and missed my flight, and got home too late for shootaround.

When I walked into the locker room, everybody got quiet.

"What, your cobra was feeling a little under the weather?" Mr. Barkley said.

"Good for you," said Mr. Mockmood. "You, alone, refuse to be a slave to the white devil's schedule."

And I explained it all to them, about everything, my father dying and my mother living and Kaitlin and Stump and everything.

And Mr. Reggie said, "A woman like that ought to be stoned. Says so in Revelation. I'm callin' Americans for Family Values."

And Mr. Mockmood said, "The woman is a she-beast. She only fouls the man and causes him ruin. This Phyllis deserves to have her eyes plucked out. It says so in the Qur'an."

I went into Coach Summers' office, and he was watching videotapes of the Detroits and he said, "Fifty-thousand-dollar fine. You're sitting the bench tonight and if you say one word, I'm gonna cram this remote so far up your ass you'll have to switch channels with your spleen."

Then I saw Mr. Lowery, who said his jury duty thing was over.

"It was going great," he said. "It was a murder trial. I was ordering up transcripts of all the evidence and video and everything. We were going to be in there for another week. And then something terrible happened."

"What?"

"The guy confessed. Now you're not going to play so I'm gonna get a ton of minutes. I'm screwed royal. My only hope now is to get hit by a UPS truck."

I wished him luck and went home.

The whole day, I was in this trance. I wasn't even thinking about what I was doing. In warm-ups, I think I made every single shot I took, didn't matter what spot it was, and yet I didn't care. I think I could've scored 100 if I was playing, but I wasn't. The crowd was buzzing and reporters were looking at me sitting on the end of the bench and photographers were shooting me, but I didn't disagree with what Coach Summers did. I didn't practice. I shouldn't play.

We were behind by 22 at halftime and sitting around the locker room, everybody feeling bad, when our owner, Mr. Trump, burst in. He had a big cigar in his mouth and one of his nieces trailing behind him and a real grouchy look on his face, although not everybody noticed since most of the fellas were looking at the niece, who was full grown, if you know what I mean.

"First I get rid of Timothy Leary!" he screamed. "And now I get goddamn Wilford Brimley! Ol' do-the-right-thing, huh? Ol' Mr. Discipline! Now you listen to me and listen hard: If the big cave geek isn't in there for every minute of the second half, you and your Birkenstocks can just keep walkin', buddy, right out the exit because your granola butt is fired! Period!" And as he walked out, his niece lagging behind, and she gave Mr. Black a look and Mr. Black gave her a look and he whispered, "Tonight? One o'clock? The usual place?"

And she blushed and said yes.

And as the door closed, I whispered to him, "Mr. Black, you just made a terrible mistake. You already told us you have a date with one of the exotic dance girls for one o'clock tonight."

And he whispered back, "I like an audience."

When we went out for the second half, I was starting, and I knew one thing, I wasn't going to go into the middle.

I asked Mr. Big County if he would please pick my man so that I could get open for my first shot. It was the first time I'd ever asked for a pick from anybody and he seemed very surprised and he said, "Hail yes!"

And he did. He picked this little guard and I was wide open and Mr. Barkley fed it to me and I fired away. And I knew as soon as I let it go that I could make every shot all night if I wanted to. Maybe it was just finally knowing about my dad. Knowing what became of him and that maybe now he was down in heaven. Maybe that's what was giving my One Point such peace and harmony. It swished right through. I hit my next five in a row like that. Plus six free throws out of six. I had 24 points in seven minutes! It was crazy. The Detroits called time out and we were right back in the game, down by only 3 now and a mile of time to go. And Mr. Big County said, "Hoss, you keep that up and you gonna shoot me right out of Texas!"

I walked back to the bench and even then, even after I'd made everything, I could still hear a couple people yelling, "Why don't you ever dunk it, you big beanpole!"

Coach Summers just told us, "Don't let up! Step on their goddamn necks!" And then he told us to get a breather and I sat down and who should come up from behind me and tap me on the shoulder but Lisa!

It was the first time I'd seen her in weeks. Her face was glowing and her smile was about a mile wide and she hugged me around the neck and said, "Oh, Slo-Mo!" and gave me a monster hug. "How do you feel about weddings?" she whispered into my ear.

And I was about to turn and give her my answer, which was going to be "Yes!" only when I turned around she was showing me a big diamond ring on her left hand.

"You already bought the ring?" I asked.

"No, silly. I didn't!"

"No?" Because I knew I didn't and I didn't see how this was gonna work out if neither of us bought the ring unless maybe it was given to her by her great-grand-mother or something, who I hoped to meet someday.

"Aren't you even going to ask who did?"

And just then she moved down one player and grabbed Mr. Woody by the neck and said, "Woody, you big silly!" And they kissed right on the lips.

Lisa was the gymnast? Lisa was the one doing those things on a balance beam? Saying all that stuff? Lisa was the one who made science history?

"He is sooooo sweet," she said. "Do you know that for the longest time, on any of our dates, he didn't even *touch* me! What a gentleman! But we're going to touch soon, aren't we, lover?"

"You'll have to get me off you with a spatula," Mr. Woody said. And they kissed again.

The horn blared for us to go back in, but my knees could hardly hold me up. I went up to Coach and told him, "I feel sick, Coach. Don't put me in."

He laughed. "Hilarious!"

But I knew I couldn't have hit the backboard, much less a 3-pointer. I could hardly run. I was just so nau-seous. All the way home, I'd been thinking, *Wait till I take Lisa down to meet Stumpy and Lela and Kaitlin. Maybe we could move down there someday. Get our own little house next to theirs. Make our house smell like that.*

And now she was going to marry Mr. Woody, the man who once told me, "If I don't get laid by ten in the morning, I ain't worth a (s-word) the rest of the day."

I had a monstrous headache. I passed off every time I got the ball. I would've rather been trapped in a small closet with Mr. Limpet than be out on that court right then.

Luckily, Mr. Barkley took over and got hot. He kept us in the game. I did nothing. I did worse than nothing. Still, we were right in the game. Mr. Barkley made a fadeaway, and Mr. Woody made a terrific driving layup (though I did not give him a very enthusiastic high five afterward) and we were still within 5 with thirty-eight seconds left. That's when Mr. Mockmood stole the ball, went down the other way, didn't pass it to a wide-open Mr. Big County, and made an impossible one-handed off-balance shot. That got us within 3.

The Detroits came down and Grant Hill missed a twenty-footer, Mr. Barkley came down with it, and there were 5.6 seconds left. We called time out.

"Okay, men, we've *got* to have a three-pointer," Coach Summers told us on the bench. Then he turned to me. "Mo, they're gonna be doublin' Charles. We need one last three out of you. You haven't shot once this whole quarter. They won't be expectin' it. Big County's gonna backpick for you, you roll to the top and take the pass from Chris."

"Mockmood," snipped Mr. Mockmood.

"Oh, (f-word) off! Slo, you oughta be wide open. Bury it for us."

I didn't want to bury it. I had no idea how I was going to bury it. I didn't *feel* like burying it. Lisa was going to marry Mr. Woody and I was stuck playing a game I hated and all my friends on the team were either cut or only interested in money and shoes and other teams. And now, with everything falling apart, they wanted me to bury it.

I took my spot, waiting for the ref to hand the ball to Mr. Woody, who would inbound it. The fans were literally blowing the roof off the arena. There was some kind of problem with the guy guarding Mr. Woody too closely and so there was a delay and it seemed like the whole place was screaming at me. I saw them all, bloodthirsty, as if this was the single most important moment of their life—and they weren't even playing.

Along courtside, in the expensive seats, I saw Mr. Barter Soals, in his Italian suit, on his sell phone, making some poor guy unhappy and rich at the same time. He *purposely* tried to keep my father from me until it was too late. I don't know if I've ever hated anybody, but if I ever have, this was the man I hated. I saw Mr. Limpet under the basket, screaming something through a megaphone and holding the Inner Doorian Doo'an in his hand. He must've flown here from Washington just to humiliate me some more. Mr. Barkley had seen him, too, and told me, "The man's takin' *vacation* time just to sweat you, Mo!"

And behind our bench, I saw Lisa, looking down at her engagement ring, watching it sparkle, with a huge smile on her face.

And then I thought I heard somebody calling my name and I looked up higher, ten rows above her, in the aisle, and saw something that gave me chillbumps.

It was my mother.

Smiling. She was with Stumpy and they both still had their jackets on so they must've just gotten there. Must've flown all the way just to be here. The security guards were trying to get them to move back to their seats, probably way higher, but my mother was trying to get my attention. She stuck her chin out and patted underneath it. *Chin up,* she was saying. *I love you, and chin up. Everything will be fine.*

Next thing I knew, the whistle had blown, and Mr. Big County was setting a backpick for me and I was spinning off it to my spot and there was the ball floating toward my hands. It must've been a great pick because I had lots of room. But I just didn't feel like helping this team anymore. I didn't feel like helping the fellas or the fans or the owner or anybody. I passed off to Mr. Big County, who was standing outside the 3-point circle in the corner. I guess he didn't want to help, either, because of his trade to Dallas, so he fired it to his left to Mr. Mockmood, who didn't want it, either, because he doesn't respect our ownership politically or spiritually, so he flipped it outside the 3-point circle to Mr. Lowery, who *for sure* didn't want it and hot-potatoed it back to me at the same place I was three seconds ago, wide open again.

"Finally, some great ball movement!" Mr. Rashad told the viewers.

Faced with no other choice, I started to bring it up to shoot it. I knew that was my moment to swim or cut bait.

I started to go into my big, swinging left-hand hook and as I did, a couple of the Detroits leaped at me to try and block it and you should've seen their expressions when, for the first time all season, I put a reverse spin on them. They went flying over me, like guys flung from a catapult somebody set two settings too high. I started dribbling right-handed down the lane, barreling full speed. Nobody was near me. I exploded off my left foot from three feet inside the foul lane. It looked like two more Detroits were thinking about trying to get in front of me but nobody in the world could've stopped me anyway and, besides, why would they want to? I was palming the ball with one hand behind my neck, and my eyes were way above the rim and I finally got all-out, full-frontal *angry* and I slammed it through the rim with every ounce of mad and frustration and strength I had.

I dunked it. I slammed it. I jammed it. I flushed it. I crammed it. I rammed it. Two the easy way. Suck on that.

The first thing I felt is this wonderful feeling of release in my body, like all the darkness came blasting out of my insides and left me light as a feather. I remember the quiet of the crowd and the glass coming down on top of me like an ice storm and the ball bouncing off the floor to God knows where. Not only did I have the rim still in my hand when I landed, but I'd dunked it so hard that when the backboard sprung back, T and T's backboard camera went flinging fourteen rows into the stands.

The buzzer ending the game was blaring and there was a huge roar that vibrated you inside and then it turned into all these "Boos!" I looked up to see what I thought I'd see: Detroit 101, New Jersey 100, 00:00, Drive Safely.

The first thing I did after the dunk—or, as Harley the Stain called it, "the Fatal Flush"—was take off those stupid ticking shoes. I sat down in the middle of the floor, yanked them off, and threw both at Mr. Limpet. The first one hit him right in his megaphone. Mr. Barkley told me later it'll probably cost me $10,000 in court fees, but, like he says, "Sometimes, ten large is cheap," and I agree concurrently.

The next thing I did was go up to Mr. O'Connor back in the tunnel. He hadn't seen anything. He was on his headset sell phone. I tried to tell him but he wouldn't get off. He just kept holding his hand up, like, just one second. So I took a sell phone out of the hand of our p.r. guy, Mr. Dalton, walked right up to Mr. O'Connor, and called him. His triple call waiting rang through.

"Y. Leonard O'Connor," he said.

"You owe me a fucking dollar!" I said, and hung up.

Then I went straight to the locker room and sat

down in front of my cubicle and started to cry. I wasn't crying because I was sad, I was crying for relief. Then I started to give all the stuff in my locker to the club-house guys. Most of them were older than me, anyway. I always felt bad about them waiting on us hands over teakettle and never talking to us and having to come to the locker room way before we got there and not leaving until way after we left. It reminded me too much of the Fluid Room.

The first person through the locker room door was Mr. Soals, limping on both legs, I guess from the little "love bite" Lassie had given him, holding a sell phone in each hand.

"You blithering idiot!" he yelled at me. "You can't throw product on national television! Beaverton is going to go postal! They're going to cancel you for this! They're going to the morals clause and cancel the whole deal! Hell, they might have you killed! You just threw away millions, pally!"

"Do they have those for shoe guys?" I asked him.

"What?" he said.

"Morals clauses."

"Screw you, pally! Your life will never be the same!"

I said, "I sure hope so."

He limped out, swearing, as my teammates walked in, followed by Coach Summers, followed by Mr. Trump, followed by his niece. They all gathered around my cubicle.

"I owe all of you an apology," I said very seriously, the whole place going quiet. "Dunking *is* fun."

Mr. Barkley and Mr. Big County and Mr. Woody laughed. Coach Summers broke his clipboard in half. Everybody else just yelled at me.

I told them the same thing I would end up telling the sportswriter gentlemen. I said I knew I shouldn't have done it, but I didn't care what the TV ads said, I *don't* love this game. I loved my teammates and most of the fans and sorta my coach, but I didn't love basketball. And then I said, "I quit. I also retire. I'm hangin' up my shingle for good."

I got up before they could say a word and I thanked my teammates for everything, and everybody else, too, except Mr. Woody, who I just shook hands with and said, "Please be nice to Lisa."

As for Mr. Death, I gave him a little present that I didn't really mean to give. I was doing an interview with NBC's Ahmad Rashad at my locker and he said, "What an unbelievable night."

And I just stared at him, waiting for a question.

He looked kind of uncomfortable and said, "Some kind of feeling, I'll bet."

Again I stared at him. And I knew that no question was ever coming from this guy and so I took the microphone and shoved him out of the way and told everybody out there I was quitting and I went through and thanked all my teammates. And I said, "I'll miss Mr. Death, too, because I admire him so much. He's really working on learning to read and I'm sorry I won't be there to help him."

And I guess maybe I shouldn't have said it because I forgot there for a second that nobody else knew that and the look on Mr. Death's face was *I may just rip you in half right now* but then again, soon as the reporters and sportswriter gentlemen heard that, they zipped right over to his locker. And pretty soon, *SportsCenter* was on and Stuart Scott was saying how Mr. Death was a courageous young man to take on this big problem so publicly and that we should all support him and honor him for it and that who knows, maybe he could run for president someday.

And when I looked around, Death was surrounded three-deep by people and sportswriter gentlemen and camermen, asking him questions and patting him on the back and shaking his hand, and it seemed like Death was finally going to get what he wanted, which is to be liked by millions of people, none of whom knew him at all.

After I showered, I walked out into the hallway. Jinx was waiting for me and I saw Mr. O'Connor, the Roto-Rooter man, and ripped the headset off his head and they must've broke when I did that and anyway I told him I was done.

"You can't do that, Mo!" he yelled, trying to put his headset back together. "When the archdiocese finds out, they're gonna—" But he stopped.

I didn't get it.

"Why would the archdiocese care if he's out of basketball?" Jinx said.

"Aw, Christ, Maurice!" he said. "Why did you have to be so dumb? Anybody else would've seen what was going on the first week. You made it so easy! It wasn't me! It was the archdiocese! They always wanted the money! They *made* me turn you pro! I knew what I was doing when you signed the Wheyburger deal! I told them I wanted to let you finish your senior season, but they said no, the Lord was telling them He couldn't wait for the money. They needed it right away for the capital campaign."

I still didn't get it.

"Everything was run through the archdiocese," he said. "With an agreement through your bitch Elder, of course. It was a fifty-fifty split from the beginning. That's the reason the Elder let you go to Most Virgin Lady. Everybody knew you had a chance to make money in the pros."

"You mean there's been three cuts all along?" Jinx asked.

"Of course! All he ever got was 30 percent! Thirty percent of his signing bonus, 30 percent of his salary, 30 percent of his ads. The other 70 percent was divided in half by the archdiocese and the Spelunkarium! After my cut of 5 percent, of course!"

I still didn't get it.

Jinx turned to me and said, "This asshole tricked you. He lied to you. They've all been lying to you. He gave all your money to the church and the cave freaks and the rest he spent at Circuit City."

I was stunned.

Jinx asked him how much money I had left.

"Maybe $25,000, tops," he said, fingering the headset. "T-Bone and his buncha gang bangers took most of it. I had no choice. I had to let him in the deal. He threatened to expose me to you. Thanks to power of attorney, the archdiocese owns the house. The Spelunkarium owns the property. You might get maybe 10 percent of that. There'll be legal fees backing out of your contract. You'll be lucky just to come out of it broke."

Jinx gasped. I guess I didn't care. It didn't sound so horrible to me, but Jinx said, "Damn. Talk about white-collar crime."

And then I saw my mother and Stumpy coming toward me. My mother was walking up to me very slowly, her face all bright red and crying like at a funeral. I walked right up to her and hugged her tight and she started to say, "Maurice, I'm so sorry . . ." and she broke down sobbing real, real bad.

Stumpy said maybe it was better if they got a hotel and pulled themselves together and I said, "Fine. But meet me at the airport in the morning. Whatever the first flight is, I'm going back with you guys." And Stumpy smiled and Phyllis heard that and collapsed to her knees in sobs.

Jinx and I rode back to the Newark Airport Ramada Hotel without saying a word. I was thinking what it all meant, that I'd gone through all this and the whole time I was being tricked and that I was probably the last person to know it.

Jinx helped me pack all my stuff at the Newark Airport Ramada Hotel for my trip to Tallahassee, my new home. We were almost done when she pulled a big wrapped box out from I don't know where and handed to me.

It was my old shoes.

"I found them in Soals' closet," she said. "I snuck them into my backpack that night. Thought you might need them for gardening or something."

I was so grateful for that and then she told me she'd also found a whole shoe box full of stuff on Mr. T-Bone. "Guy's real name was Melchisadore Thomas, out of Fresno. He's got three parole violations he's wanted for. Soals must've known that and offered not to turn him in in exchange for the phony point-shaving thing."

"So maybe he wasn't trying to screw me," I said.

"No, he was definitely trying to screw you."

And that's when it hit me.

"You know, Jinx, you're the only person in this whole thing who wasn't trying to screw me."

"Well," she said, "sort of."

I picked her up so she could stand on the bed and I held her close. She smelled prettier than a block of flower shops.

I thanked her for what she'd done for me, which was almost everything, teaching me to dance, teaching me to kiss, helping me find my parents.

"No, Mo," she said. "I want to thank *you* for what you helped me find. Myself. I found out I wanted something more than stocks and jewels and houses and it feels good."

I could feel one of her tears against my chest. And I thought about how good she felt next to me.

"Any chance you could give me one more of those kissing lessons again?" I asked.

She looked up, her eyes wet.

"Why?" she said. "Lisa's gone, isn't she?"

"Just for practice," I said.

So we kissed. I mean, we really *kissed*. We kissed like they kiss on my Spectravision previews.

And she suddenly pulled back and looked in my eyes and then looked down and kind of gasped and noticed that in no way was I going to be disqualified for, as the rules state, "lack of anger."

And I asked her if that would be a signal for sex to her and she said no, it would be a signal for sex to the entire tristate region.

CHRISTMAS

Well, it's been almost three months since I sent something off to my coauthor on this book, who asked if I would add one last little chapter on to the end to tell how some of the people ended up.

Some people say I ruined an NBA career that day and I always say, "Thanks."

Only one thing I felt bad about was Microchip. So I tried and I finally got ahold of him, or, actually, he got ahold of me. See, *Sports Illustrious* did a little story about me after the dunk and told how I lived in Tallahassee now with my family—the man wrote that our story was so unlikely "even Disney wouldn't have green-lighted it"—and how I'd quit basketball for good and forever even though I could've stayed and made a lot of money and also because I didn't find it fun without Microchip anymore and the phone rang one day and there he was.

I told him how sorry and ashamed I was for the way I'd treated him, too, and that I would do anything so's we could be friends again and he said no problem, we never stopped being friends and, besides, he'd already got two travel alarm clocks and a toaster just going on radio shows telling stories about me.

He said he signed a contract to play next season with the Rock Springs, Wyomings of the IBL, which I hadn't heard of but sounds like a very nice league. In fact, he says it's the exact same as the NBA, "except instead of going to cities that are good for bush, you just go to bush cities." Which is nice, I guess, although I never knew Microchip to love the outdoors so much.

"I'm livin' up here with Shakinisha. You remember

Shakinisha, don't you? Six-three? Pink heels? Ramada maid? Wrote all my thermodynamics papers? These cowboys up here see her walkin' down the street and swallow their chaws. It's funny. I think we're the only two blacks in the state. They mean well, but you ought to hear them try to be nice to us. They go, 'Well, we just think it's *rail* nice to finally get us some nig, some nigero, some neeeeeegros up in these parts.' It's a word they kinda need a running start at it."

I asked Microchip how he and his parents were getting along.

"We ain't exactly in constant radio contact," he said. "I finally had it out with them. Had to. They were all Mike Wallacin' my ass about everything, you know, finding out Most Virgin Lady didn't really have a Slave Reparation Department, and there was no such thing as Eldridge Cleaver Hall, which meant there was no such thing as the Winnie Mandela Suite where I was supposedly livin'. They were just madder 'n the Million Man March.

"But I didn't care. I was sick of their attitude toward sports. I told 'em, 'Lemme axe you something. Who you think's done more for race relations in this country? Elijah Muhammad or Muhammad Ali?' I told 'em just be happy for any black person that's making a good living, not in jail, not on the streets, not pissed off enough to open somebody's head like a salt decanter all the time. I told 'em they was fightin' a race war that began and ended in their livin' room. I told 'em about the poll that *Time* or *Newsweek* or somebody ran the other day. The number one most respected person in the country is Michael Jordan, followed by Colin Powell, followed by Tiger Woods. I said I didn't know how old their glasses prescriptions were, but last I checked, all three of them were black folk. I said the number one shaper of opinions and lifestyle in this country is Oprah Winfrey. I said, hell, your average rich, white housewife in America doesn't read a recipe until Oprah says it's okay. I told 'em the only color I was worried about was the orange on a basketball. I told 'em the number one stereotype people have now of the black man is of the radical black professor still cryin' 'racism' and 'Spike Lee' and 'Attica' at everything Dan Rather says. I think it was somewhere in there they threw me out. But I don't care. They'll call back."

"How come?" I asked.

"I still got their car."

Mr. Barkley called saying that because I'd quit and turned my back on the money and the fame and the big corporations that I was more popular now in America than remote control and would I consider running with him as his lieutenant governor in the elections in Alabama in 2001? He's already signed with the Los Angeleses for next year, though. "I already got me my own radio show, a guarantee for an Oscar walk-on, and a three-picture deal. Plus, no more than twenty-one minutes a night. Sweet, eh?"

I asked Mr. Barkley about some of the other fellas.

"Woody signed with Reebok and is livin' in Boston. He and Lisa already broke up, though. He said she had a hard time with his definition of extramarital sex, which was that, to Woody, when it comes to sex, there was no such thing as *extra*."

He said the Spinning Stankowskis finally gave it up. They were at a church fund-raiser and Mr. Stankowski was laying on his back, spinning his son on his feet, with Lisa and Mrs. Stankowski hanging on to the son's hands and there was this terrible crunch and both of Mr. Stankowski's crucial ligaments ripped. And even though he was in terrible pain, Mr. Stankowski slid on his belly over to his son and took him by the throat and Mrs. Stankowski was knocked out cold because when the knees ripped, he let go of everybody and Mrs. Stankowski's head went smacking straight into the backup Lady of Guadalupe they stored down there.

He said Mr. Mockmood refused to be traded to the Houstons, because their team name, the Rockets, was a symbol of a space program that had not sent a single black man to the moon. He also refused to stay with the New Jerseys, because it was "the Deep North," he said, and refused to go to the Minnesota Timberwolves because of "blatant Euro-Nordic racism," pointing out how everything in Minnesota was white, from the snow to the huskies to the fish boils. He also refused to be released. He staged a four-day hunger strike in the New Jerseys' lobby, refusing everything but water and TV crews. He finally left when Converse said they could work him a deal playing for a league in Mecca.

Mr. Big County signed with the Dallases, like he said he would, and that I was invited down anytime for a "nice cold sebmup." Mr. Lowery got screwed out of his $1 million because Dalton, our p.r. guy, was kinda mad at him for not taking that wide-open 3 that would've covered a wager he'd made and so he went over the films and found a ball he'd tipped that didn't go in and that dropped his percentage below 45, although Mr. Barkley said that seemed surprising, since Mr. Lowery never went any nearer the rim than I did.

Coach Jackson was in Sedona, Arizona, for a while, doing "inspirational workshops" for a group of two thousand "Soulward Bound" adventurers to see if they couldn't lift a giant rock the size of a baseball field using only "group mindfulness" and their index fingers. But it didn't work and they ended up setting a new record for hernias instead.

Mr. Reggie signed with the Golden States because God told him he was most needed there to spread the word of the Lord on account of so many men had chosen homosexuality over the right way and also God gave him a heads-up on two Taco Bell franchises he could get for a song.

Pretty much the rest of the team was either released, traded, or retired and no new big talent was signed or expected to be signed. "This may seem drastic," said Mr. Trump, our owner, "but it sets the team up, celery-cap-wise, for a wonderful 2002 season." He was probably right, except not for New Jersey fans. A week later, the New Jerseys became the Raleigh-Durhams.

The only star left, Mr. Barkley said, was Mr. Death, who was all of a sudden the most loved guy in town. He was having a movie done about his life and now he was working on this idea he had of starting a chain of schools called Hooked on Ebonics that makes it easier for poor African American kids to read. He said the text they're going to use is *Dick and Jane Be Fly*.

He asked me how I was doing and I told him it's all worked out between my formerly expired mom and me.

She's asked me to call her "Lela" because "Phyllis died of shame" and she explained to me why she did what she did, which was leave me behind for five years. She told me the whole story on the flight home. We couldn't sit together but at least we were both on the aisle, one row apart, so she had to lean back and tell me. She was real nervous and she told me to close my

286

eyes as she talked so I could picture how terrible her life was at the time.

"I was so unhappy in the Spelunkarium," she said. "I cried every night. I didn't believe a word of what they were saying. I only went there in the first place to get out of a bad marriage. A bad life. I wanted to crawl in a hole and hide and that's exactly what the Spelunkarium was. But I figured out how unhappy I was there after about two months. I thought if I could have a baby, have someone to end my loneliness, I'd be happy. So I went out to get pregnant and I met your father. He was so friendly and so big and so sweet. You took one look at your father and you knew he was fertile. Believe me, honey, the man could've knocked up a tollbooth.

"At first, you brought so much joy to my life. But as you got older, they took you from me so much. They wouldn't let me be with you. It was always, 'It takes a village to raise a child.' And I kept saying, 'Yeah, but could the village maybe give him a weekend off once in a while?' The whole place was full of lesbians who hated men. Didn't you ever notice that there were no men around? The bigger you got the more they abused you. They made you do the lousy jobs, the heavy labor. They never thought you had anything to add to them spiritually, and you were so tall, so they kept you and I apart so much. I was so desperately unhappy.

"And then came this one cold, snowy, horrible day, at the King Soopers. It had snowed, like, eight feet in three days and all of a sudden there was this awful, huge groan and a loud crack and then the roof caved in. But I wasn't in the King Soopers. I was in the back, smoking. That's what I'd do. They wouldn't let us smoke anywhere in the caves because of the methane, so I'd smoke half a pack behind the King Soopers when I'd do the shopping. All of a sudden there's this huge roar and the roof had collapsed. I just panicked. I know this sounds horrible, but I saw my chance. I took the grocery money and put it in my pocket and threw my wallet and my bracelet and my shoes into the smoking rubble and ran for it. I did it so fast, I didn't even take time to think about it. I just ran. It was such chaos, nobody noticed me. It was horrible. I couldn't have helped anybody. Nobody lived through it, as you know.

"I knew it was awful but I knew I couldn't go back now. What would people think of me? So I took the bus to Denver and then bought a train ticket south to Albuquerque. I changed my name to Lela—I used that name with your father—and I faked a birth certificate at Kinko's and got a new driver's license and I set out to find your father. I just *knew* that he and I could be happy together. I thought once we were together, I'd tell him about you and that he'd help me go back and get you.

"But your father wasn't easy to find. He quit being Genghis Korn about a year after I'd known him. Turns out he just couldn't eat another of those awful Krispy Korn sticks. But he didn't quit soon enough. The end came when that bastard Krispy Korn company came out with a whole new line of imitation-potato dishes, fauxtatoes, made from imitation soy and processed imitation 'none-ions,' and they had a whole pile of faux fries he was supposed to eat and he just couldn't. He took off his crown of corncobs and threw his cape to a kid and got his stuff out of the Corvair with the front seat pulled out and walked out on the street and never came back. He always loved animals so he got a job cleaning up at the Tallahassee zoo and taking his night vet classes at Florida State.

"I finally found him down there. He told me that even though it'd been twelve years, he'd never stopped thinking about me, too, but his calls were never put through to me at the Spelunkarium and he was always turned away at the gate and so he just stopped trying. One month after I showed up again, we got married. We had Kaitlin exactly nine months later. I'm telling you, your father had seed that could swim the Ganges.

"He got the job he'd always wanted at the holding pen and we were happy. And I think it felt so good to finally be happy again, I didn't want to risk anything, so I kept putting off telling him. I thought he'd find out and hate me and end it. It was a horrible, horrible thing to do. And that's when you came back into my life."

She was really crying now and she said, "Maurice, do you think I'm horrible?"

And before I could answer, six different voices all around us, real angry, said, "Yeah" and "Damn straight" and "Of course you are!" and I opened my eyes and it was all the people in the rows around us, who had listened to the whole thing.

When you've gone your whole life without a family, you'll forgive a lot. I forgave her. Seems like a lot of people I've met on the surface are always looking for a way to be happy, you know? Always waiting until they get the right car or go with the right team or make the right kind of money, thinking *that's* when they'll finally be happy. But they never are. And I just decided I wouldn't look for a way to be happy. I figure being happy ought to *be* the way.

Anyway, that's about everything, I guess. I always wanted to get my high school diploma, so I'm taking classes at Tallahassee High School at night. I love it! I'm taking biology, chemistry, and zoology and nobody's putting the grade on my tests before I take them and I help out three days a week with the basketball team, trying to teach them my either-handed hook in the manner of feared NBA scoring machine Bob "Bobby Hoops" Houbregs.

I also tell them never to eat McDonald's because I think McDonald's makes you fat and slow and mean and if McDonald's really is the center of America then America's center is getting fat and slow and mean and I tell them if I ever drive by and see them in a McDonald's I won't teach them anymore although it's a threat that doesn't seem to scare them much because I see them in there a lot.

Some of them are wearing these new shoes called Bangers, which happens to be a company started by Mr. Soals and Mr. T-Bone, who went into business together. Mr. Barkley said this was the best combination of business minds since Bonnie and Clyde. The company seems to be very successful already, especially their Bobby Knight 187 line, which are better known as "B.K. 187s," although Mr. Barkley said some young inner-city youth are inadvertently mistaking those letters to mean "Blood Killer 187s," which, he said, in Los Angeles, means Los Angeles crime no. 187, which is murder, which most any Crip like T-Bone would like to do to most any Blood. So it's unfortunate that misunderstanding is happening but sales are way up just the same.

Mr. Y. Leonard O'Connor is now the hottest agent in sports. The players all think his headset sell phone is the coolest thing around and they go to lunch and talk to each other from across the room on their headsets and everybody's happy. I guess he's come a long way from raw sewage although Mr. Barkley says not as far as I might think.

He was right about one thing, though. Those Penney stocks. I showed the certificates to my mother, Lela, and she looked them up and they hit big, which was good because Lela lost the lawsuit against Krispy Korn imitation frozen food products owing to the fact that my dad once had a mole removed from his armpit which they said meant he probably would've died from massive stomach cancer anyway. Well, the stocks didn't all hit big, most of them were worthless, but one, a company that made funny buttons, hit it big, big enough to make me $27,622.31, which was enough for us to build an addition on to Lela's house that was big enough for me and Kaitlin's own little mini-snake zoo for all my guys. It's great that they're all together. I've never seen them happier and now when we play "YMCA" by the Village People, Juan can spell out all the letters.

I still have to work, though, but it's fun because I took a job with Orkin, the pest control people. I wear a bright orange and white uniform—well, actually two sewn together pretty much—and I wear my dad's shoes, which go perfect! Only don't let them know, but I don't use their methods to get rid of bugs. I'm a strict believer in trap and release.

Oh, and I bought one other thing. I spent $350 on an old Corvair and took the front seat out, just like my dad's. It's blue with white coves and it's a convertible. Jinx loves me to pick her up in it and I take her to her classes at Florida State—she's studying family therapy there—and to her receptionist job at Plant Parenthood.

It's funny. Once she got down here, Jinx started looking a lot different. Do you know she's only nineteen? She's been lying to people about her age all these years, "just to try and get over," she says. She looks a lot different without all that makeup and sparkly stuff on. She looks even more beautiful to me.

Plus, she's got a great little apartment my mom is helping her pay for until she finishes college. And Lela gave me the best present of all—that great big bed of theirs—and now my feet don't have to sit on Lassie's cage anymore although I think Lassie misses the smell.

I don't play basketball anymore except sometimes at night on a full moon I'll go out by myself to the playground of a school near our house and shoot my hook shot for hours and hours, either hand, and feel so good at my One Point and hardly miss at all and I always end it with a dunk, just to remind me that I never want to go back.

Anyway, I'm very happy now, happier than I've ever been, which isn't saying much, I guess, and I plan on keeping it that way, because I found out that being JAG is perfect for me.

And I knew that for sure the other day when I was chasing this really beautiful butter-bellied bull and it happened to wander out onto this baseball field. Turns out it was where the Florida State baseball team practices. The center fielder recognized me, which happens a lot, and said, "Slo-Mo! Whassup!"

And I gave him a line Mr. Barkley gave me which I always use now which is, "Just me, I guess!"

And he hollered to his coach and the coach came out and introduced himself. He said he was a big, big fan of mine and I said thanks. He asked if I wanted to "hit a few" and I said, "A few what?"

And next thing I knew I was standing at the plate, with a helmet on my head, getting ready to hit, just like I've seen them do on *SportsCenter*. And the pitcher threw me a baseball and I swung with the biggest bat they had and I guess I must've connected pretty good, because it cleared the center-field fence and the backstop of the field behind it and landed past second base on *that* field. And they all went nuts, yelling and hooting and screaming, and the coach looked up at me with that exact same look in his eyes that Mr. O'Connor, the Roto-Rooter man, had that first day back in the Spelunkarium, so I threw the bat down and sprinted for my Corvair.

I mean, done there, been that, am I right?